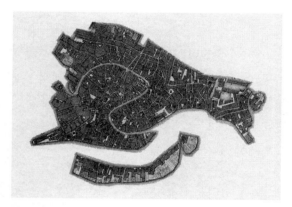

Map of Venice

ABOUT THE AUTHOR

Giulia Morosini, MA. currently splits her time between Copenhagen and Venice. She teaches art and languages, and has written numerous articles about art. The Venitian Secret, 1620, is the first in a series about the Morosini family.

MOROSINI PRESS

Published by Morosini Press in 2010

First published in DK in September 2010
www.morosinipress.dk

Printed and bound in DK by Norhaven A/S Viborg

ISBN 978-87-992990-0-3

Drawings: Tania Brassesco, Artist, Venice, IT
taniabrassesco@gmail.com

Language Consultant: Kevin McKechnie
www.lykill.dk

Graphics: Morosini Press Design

PRAISE FOR

The Venetian Secret
1620

"The writing is terrific. . . Giulia is a stunning new talent."
REBECCA SAUNDERS, LITTLEBROWN

"It's an ambitious, fascinating story, and I love the period detail
here. The portrait Morosini paints of the tough existence women
faced in 17th century Venice – Maritar o monacar? Marriage or
the convent? – is vivid and as brutal at times as it is beautiful."
GABE ROBINSON, HARPERCOLLINS U.S

"This is a very competent historical romance, with a wonderful,
willful heroine...The historical extremes depicted in the book
are very striking indeed."
ALEXANDRA PRINGLE, BLOOMSBURY PRESS

"It's a strong premise, and Venice always appeals... the narra-
tive is efficient and energetic."
WILL ATKINS, NEWWRITING MACMILLAN

The Venetian Secret
1620

Giulia Morosini

A Novel

MOROSINI PRESS

Contents

Contents

The Venetian Secret
1620

Prologue

"By the light of a candle you do not judge women or paintings."
Venetian proverb, Anon

"You have to make a nun of Marietta," Paulina Morosini told her brother in the parlatorio, where the nuns received visitors. "She practically grew up in this convent. She is familiar with life here, even if she has been at home for the past two years." Fabrizio Morosini had listened reluctantly to his ageing sister speaking through the grating, which separated the nuns from the rest of the world. He remembered with unease how Paulina had been forced into life as a nun, in spite of her furious protests. His parents had asked themselves the question that he was asking now: Maritar o Monacar? Was their daughter to marry, or was she to become a nun?

"You know very well," Paulina had said sharply, "that if her mother hadn't broken her leg, Marietta would have stayed here. Don't tell me that you seriously consider her for a bride! Think of her temper! She is pretty and bright, maybe, but she is unfit for marriage. Marietta has no respect for customs and conventions. She has too much spirit. If she married, she would do as she pleased, rather than listen to her husband. She would dishonour the Morosini *family. Mark my words, Fabrizio. She has too many ideas of her own! Just think of Rosalba and the scandal she caused! Even if it is a long time ago, it still casts a gloomy shadow on the Nani family... and on the painter's too, for that matter. Marietta reminds me too much of Rosalba! If you wait until Beatrice comes of age, you can keep the dowry at least another four years. Fourty-thousand ducats! You know very well that it is out of the question to squander money on two dowries. The family fortune must remain in as few hands as possible. Beatrice is the most sensible choice, Fabrizio. Marietta will just have to do as you say – the family's honour is at stake."*

Fabrizio had left the convent with a heavy heart. Marietta was his favourite daughter. He had come in the vain hope that Paulina would agree with him, even help him persuade his wife. Manuela was difficult. For him to go against her will was impossible due to the money her family bestowed on them to keep things running smoothly. Still, his sister was probably right. Any family member who remembered Rosalba said that Marietta took after her great-aunt, that she was too strong-willed and passionate. He prayed that his daughter would never learn of Rosalba's cunning and scandalize the Morosinis once again. There was nothing for it. As much as he lamented it, Marietta would have to take the veil.

Marietta had pleaded with her father and begged to stay with her family unmarried. Fabrizio had even hesitated for a few moments before saying, "But it will be safe for you, and you will be happy there. You'll be with aunt Paulina and many of your cousins too. They are pleased with their lives. You will still be with your

family. It is dangerous and shameful for a woman to live at home unmarried. You ares easy prey for a male servant, or any man."
But he had not been able to meet Marietta's eyes while he said it.

He would never forget the sight of Marietta heartbroken on the day she left home for San Zaccaria. Fabrizio had tried to cheer her up by sending an extra chest to the convent with little gifts and food.
But he knew her world had been crushed at only fifteen years of age. When he had visited Marietta in the convent shortly afterwards, she had whispered to him, "I feel cornered by a tide, father, as if insistent waves were pushing me up against a wall."

PROLOGUE
THE VENETIAN SECRET, 1620

1.

Money Is Our Second Blood

I put down my pen at the sound of footsteps in the campo. Now the organ begins to play. I get up from my seat on the chest, pull my footstool beneath the small window and, standing on tiptoe, catch a glimpse of the Patriarchal Visitation. The Patriarch Giovanni Tiepolo and his clerics are entering the church of San Zaccaria, bringing with them the chill of January. I imagine the Abbess Francesca Grimani hastening to the nuns' chapel in the garish light of morning. She will wring her hands and worry about the Visitation after Mass. I know we will be questioned by the Patriarch, one nun at a time, and thoroughly. How else can Giovanni Tiepolo hope to learn our secrets?

I place my densely written pages on the floor and open the chest. From its depths, I bring out the mirror hidden underneath my banned books and paintings. I haven't looked at myself for some time. Francesca Grimani always impresses on us that to possess a mirror is a mortal sin. But what the Abbess really means is that the convent intends to rob us of our personalities.

"I won't allow it to happen!" I whisper to my face in the mirror. "Within just a few phases of the moon, I will forget who I am if I don't look at myself from time to time. The reassurance that you exist is something only a mirror can give you. Without it, the convent building will wrench your life away as a corset chokes the body. I will find a way out of here," I solemnly promise my reflection in the mirror.

I have watched doors and windows being walled up, hidden behind bars or planks. For the nuns' safety, the Patriarch had explained. It has happened that nuns have escaped; I have heard about it from the gossips. That would be another reason for the Patriarch's meticulousness, because there is not a single opening he has not inspected. The gates towards the campo and the canal are kept locked at all times, each one with several keys. "Contact with the world will render your souls in serious jeopardy," I can hear the Abbess' feeble voice saying.

Francesca Grimani has become genderless, like all the elderly nuns with their pasty faces and sagging bodies. I am certain they have dissolved over time because they never gave themselves up to love and caresses. Sister Fiorina and Sister Archangela have completely withered away. They will have no more lascivious looks from the monks and young nobles in the parlatorio.

"The parlatorio," I say aloud to my melancholy image, "is our only salvation: one last crack to the outside world."
Every day in the convent, I mourn not being able to move about Venice. How to live with only the memories of a morning on the Riva degli Schiavoni, the broad and brilliant quay facing the lagoon, with its profusion of scents and colours? To remain

MONEY IS OUR SECOND BLOOD
THE VENETIAN SECRET, 1620

forever within the strict enclosure of the convent is impossible. I don't desire a life dedicated to the service of God. Will I never again enjoy the hush of the city, sailing in a gondola late at night? A heartbreaking thought. And love. What of that?

I am Sister Cynthia now. My childhood friend, Adriana Doná delle Rose, is Sister Cherubina. Adriana had tried not to laugh when old Sister Pax first pronounced her new name. The nun had looked at Adriana reproachfully through her thick lenses and quoted the Benedictine Rule: 'Laughter is unseemly.' How can they expect us to live without laughter.

Chiara is an exception. She says it gives her peace of mind being Sister Celestia. But then, Chiara is the most passionate and pious of us all.

I like the sound of my own name. Marietta Morosini. When I say it slowly, it sounds like an old Venetian tune.

I place the mirror up against the wall in my cell on one of my chests and examine my image. I am not quite as tall as my younger sister, Beatrice, but I have an abundance of soft natural blonde hair, the colour all Venetian women desire. My mother spent hours on the roof terrace of Ca'Morosini bleaching her hair in the sun. I can still hear her shouts tolling down the stairs from the terrace, "If you don't behave yourself Marietta, I'll make a nun of you!" I was humbled with fear.

It is four years since I took my vows. All this time, I have flouted convent rules and let my hair grow. I move close to the mirror and carefully study my features: my face looks pensive, intent. My eyebrows are arched, my eyes a clear blue, I have the aquiline nose so characteristic of the Venetian nobles, and a small heart-shaped mouth with full lips, fit for laughter rather than for prayer! My complexion is white, but still gently coloured. I like my face, think it pretty even. Then I realise that my face has already become slightly unfamiliar. Like when you gaze at a word on a page and it becomes just a constellation of letters, its meaning blurred. Does that happen because you look at it apart from its natural context, I wonder, like my face in the mirror? Is that how I appear to Tommaso, when he looks at my portrait in Constantinople? A meaningless stranger?

No, nothing can come between us. Like me, Tommaso doesn't want the life laid out for him. We want our own kind of life. We always did.

I return the mirror to the chest, and pick up my notes from the floor. I mostly write at night by candlelight, but this morning, due to the threatening visit, I have an urge to write. I dip my father's blue and white quill into the golden ink and write on a blank sheet of paper: To the Republic of Venice, which forces girls to enter convents; to the grand Senate, which hopes to make you last forever, Queen of the Adriatic, by locking up virgin girls to pray for you, unconquered like the city herself. Impossible vows they make us take. How can we live forever in poverty, chastity and obedience?

I hear footsteps in the cloister outside my cell, and quickly put my notes and writing material in the hollow beneath the loose marble slab under my bed. I open the chest, throw my lace blankets on top of my silk dresses and the little jewellery I have left. I grasp the pair of gilded angels, the chandelier, and cram everything into the chest.

I pray the clerics won't confiscate my few belongings. I would mourn the loss of the two small portraits by Tiziano Vecellio my father gave me, and my miniature painting of Tommaso. I lock the chest, the one with the wine and the food too, hoping the clerics will leave them untouched. I put the keys in with my notes. Should they ask for them, I'll say I lost them.

Is put on the high-necked white dress, and kick my platform shoes under the bed. I tie my boots, and cover my hair with the veil. It is fine but not transparent. So degrading, I think. A woman's hair is a sign of liberty and beauty, but when you enter a convent they cut it off.

I glance around my cell. No, I have forgotten nothing. Then I run down the cloisters to the chapel.

MONEY IS OUR SECOND BLOOD
THE VENETIAN SECRET, 1620

2.

Fear of Scandals

The Abbess slams the door to her apartment and hurries down the stairs to the nuns' chapel. She must be there on time. She is already a little late, and mass begins in a moment. The Patriarch will be furious if she isn't in the choir behind the grate. She knows only too well that Tiepolo likes to stage his Visitations and impress upon the nuns the solemnity of the occasion.

Flushed and out of breath, she drops into her seat in the choir by the grate, just in time to watch the grave procession enter San Zaccaria. Sitting in the choir, she regrets as always that their chapel is sealed off. Twenty years ago, everything was still theirs. The nuns' protests had been furious when the Patriarch ordered their relics removed from the crypt and placed in the public part of the church, relics given to the nuns by popes, emperors and doges; precious gifts they had watched over for nearly eight centuries. She had heard the former Patriarch Priuli whisper to a priest that "these valuables should not be in the hands of mere women." The Abbess peers through the iron grates at the Patriarch pacing the aisle. Tiepolo is strikingly tall and so terribly devout, she thinks. He looks majestic with his long grey beard, and the black robe trailing behind him like a peal of thunder. There is a sharpness about him that she fears. Nothing ever seems to escape him. She worries because she hasn't had time to see to the decoration of the tabernacles the way he demanded. She couldn't find the crimson velvet anywhere. And the oil flacons… hadn't he told her they must be embellished with silk embroidery?

The Patriarch glances up towards the grates in her direction. She bows her head at him as he passes, and feels drops of sweat trickle down her brow. If only the Patriarch wouldn't order her to have everything illegal removed. Last time she had such a hard time. She knows it won't be less difficult on this occasion with so many spoiled novices and young choir nuns, and she is not at all strong. They are so troublesome and disobedient.

She remembers how Tiepolo's predecessor, Lorenzo Priuli, instructed her to carry out unannounced inspections twice a year in all the private cells. Over the years, she has really tried to do her best to obey his orders. But the resistance she has met! She fears rebellion if the young choir nuns are forced to give up their pet dogs, the nightingales or their embroidered veils. The clerics' report will expose her weakness, and she is sure to be reprimanded by Giovanni Tiepolo. Francesca Grimani hopes that with forty-eight convents in Venice and the lagoon to supervise, the Patriarch and his prelates are far too busy to do all they should.

Francisca Grimani's only comfort today is the thought of their Confessor, Orsolo Lupi. She treasures the hours she spends in the confessional with Father Lupi. He is different from any confessor previously appointed to the convent. Nothing like the last one; he had only been popular among the nuns because he was deaf. All the same, she hopes that Father Lupi won't mention the basketful of little gifts she sent him the other day. How to explain to the

Patriarch that it was merely a sign of gratitude?

The Abbess prays that the nuns won't tell Tiepolo too much of the goings-on in the convent. If they do, the consequences will be never-ending. Francesca Grimani can't even begin to imagine the damage to herself and their small community.

* * *

The Patriarch sits on the Abbess' high-backed throne. From the dais, he has a commanding view of the room. His face bears a naked eagerness to correct any nun who has wandered from the dictates of church and state. But the convent is home to gossip and backbiting, and Tiepolo is aware too of the need to separate truth from fiction. He has ordered the inspection to cover every inch of the place, and he fears that the lists of disorders will be endless. He watches the choir nuns disapprovingly, how they lapse into whisperings among themselves, standing in small groups at the back of the large Chapter room, where all convent business is conducted.

He is impressed by the riches this prestigious convent has accumulated over the centuries. On the walls are large paintings of the Blessed Virgin and the Saints, all bought with the nuns' personal fortunes, and the high-backed chairs made of walnut, lining the sides of the room, have been commissioned from renowned craftsmen. This is the only room in the convent with a fireplace, and today a fire has been lit. Tiepolo still finds the room raw and wintry. He feels the seeping cold in spite of the sable lining. He had hoped to catch just a little warmth sitting so close to the flames.

He watches the two approaching clerics and takes the bundle of sheets they hand him. 'Orders' and 'Disorders' it says on top of the pages, and he browses through the endless listings of violations carefully written down in a neat hand, before turning his attention to the nuns.

He is proud to work for the Republic, but the visitations have become more and more strenuous.

Tiepolo cannot bring himself to inform the state magistracy of less serious breaches of the rules. He finds it hard to increase the misery of the nuns. Never to leave the convent is surely punishment enough for the majority who never had a vocation. Looking at the gathering standing before him, Giovanni Tiepolo pities the women. But we have no choice but to force a vocation on these women, he thinks. If the noblewomen stored away in our convents, as if in public warehouses, had been able to dispose of their lives differently, scandals would have erupted with terrible consequences for their families and the city!

* * *

I step into the chapter room, pushing past Chiara. I look at her. It seems she has fully recovered from her illness. She is not as pale as she was for weeks in the infirmary when I sat by her bedside. I walk up to Adriana, who stands by herself. "Has Tiepolo started yet?" I ask, a little out of breath.

"No, everyone is dying to tell him their secrets." There is a cheerful expression on her face, when she speaks. "Do you remember,"

6

Adriana continues in a low voice, "how the Patriarch Querini once grabbed a nun by her long hair and cut it off with his own hands? Everybody here has let her hair grow – perhaps except for Chiara."

"Yes," I say, "I remember. He even brought the pair of scissors himself. Let's hope Tiepolo hasn't brought any today."

"Sister Cherubina, come closer." One of the priest calls out. He makes a sign to Adriana to approach Giovanni Tiepolo. I watch my friend and count the paces that take her to the other end of the room. Thirty-two paces. The room seems immense, and Adriana so tiny standing in front of the Patriarch.

His eyes are kind even if he looks austere, thinks Adriana, as she bows to Tiepolo standing in front of the dais. Maybe he won't question me about my dog or the chickens in my cell. Will the clerics have torn my chests apart and found the new dresses?

"It has come to my knowledge that you don't attend mass every day, Sister Cherubina." The Patriarch's voice seems to reach her from afar.

"But I do," she replies, "and I say my prayers at the right hours too. Ask anybody here, Your Excellency."

"I already have," Tiepolo says observing the girl's unabashed smile.

"Then you have been the victim of most scandalous falsehoods, Your Excellency."

She doesn't care if she doesn't tell Tiepolo the truth, so little she cares for convent life. Conscience is like tickling, she thinks. There are those who feel it and those who don't.

FEAR OF SCANDALS
THE VENETIAN SECRET, 1620

Tiepolo eyes her severely. "The clerics who searched your cell found silk dresses and elaborate shirts in the fashion of secular women. Not at all in accordance with the clothes you must all wear.

They also report two paintings depicting women in unholy, even lascivious poses. Paintings must conform to pious decorum and sacred beauty. Chickens privately owned are forbidden, as you well know." Tiepolo looks into the young nun's frank, freckled face, which is far too mirthful for his liking. "Nor can you wear shoes of the Roman type."

Adriana blushes and looks down at her platform shoes. How could she forget to change them?

"Also, my clerics have found a letter to you from Marietta Morosini, Sister Cinthia, in which she talks of her forbidden love for young Tommaso Contarini. Have you anything to say concerning that letter?"

"No, Your Excellency." Adriana says simply, and bows her head staring at the tessellated floor. She had forgotten about the letter. This could have serious consequences for her friend. Tiepolo decides to leave it for now. He realizes that he will get nowhere with the girl.

"You will dispose of your sinful possessions and obey your vows of owning no property. You must live as a pure spouse of Christ. Sin openly practised without shame enrages God," the Patriarch says sternly, regretting the fact that Adriana's disobedience is far from the only one among the choir-nuns. Relieved that the Patriarch didn't mention her beloved dog, Adriana retreats from his sharp eyes.

FEAR OF SCANDALS
THE VENETIAN SECRET, 1620

At only 16, Chiara is still one of the most devout nuns at San Zaccaria. She is so small that she resembles a child. Chiara wants more discipline and finds it difficult to live with the spiritual indifference around her.

She has prepared herself to complain to the Patriarch.

"This convent is full of vice," Chiara whispers to Tiepolo, "The Abbess fails to keep discipline. Not even the servant nuns obey her. She reads the Rule in Latin too quickly for anyone to grasp, just to get it over with." Chiara stops to catch her breath.

"I have seen her kiss Father Lupi. It is common knowledge that she entertains him in her apartment," Chiara flushes and pauses once again, not daring to look at the Patriarch.

She hesitates a moment. "Sometimes the youngest choir-nuns feast and drink wine in the laundry.

They don't care how they behave," Now Chiara can't stop. Her unhappiness presses her on. "When the boarding girls arrive, the choir-nuns tell them that here you can laugh and chat as much as you like. They are not taught the importance of silence. They are allowed to sing worldly songs and organise balls. Life in this convent is corrupted."

She speaks in such hushed tones that the Patriarch finds it difficult to hear all that she is saying. He leans forward a little to understand what Sister Celestia is confiding in him. But from the words that he does understand, the Patriarch realises how much religious life at San Zaccaria suffers. The Patriarch promises that he will consider everything she has said. He has heard rumours of Sister Celestia's visions and swoons, but, all the same, what she says is probably true. Chiara slips a small piece of paper into the Patriarch's hand. Tiepolo looks at the note, opens his mouth

FEAR OF SCANDALS
THE VENETIAN SECRET, 1620

as if to say something, but then decides against it and puts the note in the deep pocket of his cloak. Will he make any changes, Chiara wonders as she turns her back on him? She will continue with her plans. She has no choice. The vision yesterday in the chapel has made up her mind.

"Marietta," Adriana whispers to me, "Take care – the rumour is that someone told Tiepolo of your writings. And the clerics found your letter to me of Tommaso."

The Patriarch beckons to me. I am apprehensive when I stand in front of him. He speaks at once.

"I've heard rumours that you write critically about convent life. Are you aware that anyone doing so also criticises Christ?" The Patriarch studies my face intensely.

"Your Excellency knows very well that tales will flourish in a convent." I stare at Giovanni Tiepolo, and feel my cheeks burning.

"If necessary, I will have no choice but to report you to the State magistracy," he continues in the same tone. "I might also have to report a letter written by you concerning the nobleman Tommaso Contarini, which is in my possession." I start at the mentioning of Tommaso's name, but I am determined to say nothing, come what may. "For your salvation, you must meditate on the painting by Giovanni Bellini of the Virgin Mary. It is painted with great devotion, and transmits gifts and favours of divine generosity to those who contemplate it devoutly," the Patriarch orders me, sounding a little, I think, as if he is losing faith in his ability to change anything.

FEAR OF SCANDALS
THE VENETIAN SECRET, 1620

I am dispirited when I walk back to the other end of the chapter room. I had feared that someone would betray me and denounce me to the Patriarch. Writing is necessary to liberate my thoughts and challenge male authority, which governs every aspect of a woman's life in Venice. And the letter? Would Giovanni Tiepolo really turn it over to the magistracy?

* * *

The Patriarch is concerned by the number of complaints he hears today. The nuns criticise the garments from the convent's clothes store. The cloth is too rough on the skin and too heavy, they say. They want to have their clothes sewn from their own materials. Some object to the chickens, which are to be found in every corner of the convent; the canaries; dogs in the cells and numerous other laments. Disobedience is on a large scale. The Patriarch is not surprised.

He addresses the choir nuns and his voice reverberates in the large room.

"Humble life in this convent is the all-important issue," the Patriarch states, "and the discovery of all the worldly goods in your private cells tells me that humility is set aside. If you wish, you can be truly queens: for under Christ's standard you hold off the devil. Then you will be at peace and know that this life in exile is angelic."

Giovanni Tiepolo gets ready to leave, but before he does, he calls the Abbess to face him.

"One should never refuse to bear Christ's cross," he says. "An

Abbess must regard authority as a cross. Remember that." He instructs her to correct everything that the clerics have found within the next few days. Tiepolo severely stresses that it would be most prudent not to take too much of their father confessor's time. Orsolo Lupi has a lot to see too.

The Patriarch has tried not to be too hard on the Abbess. We are walking a tightrope, he thinks. The fathers, brothers and uncles of these women hold the most important offices in the city. And isn't Francesca Grimani related to the Head of the Council of Ten? And Marietta Morosini, she comes from a long line of Doges. There is hardly a more prominent family than the Morosinis. Her father, Fabrizio Morosini, is a powerful procurator of San Marco. It would be unwise to give her family the impression that we make Marietta's life more miserable than necessary.

Lost in thought, the Patriarch leaves the convent followed by the clerics. He hardly notices the extreme cold of January or the thin white blanket of snow on the ground. He feels the piece of paper in his pocket that Sister Celestia slipped into his hand. A most serious charge to make against anyone, he thinks.

FEAR OF SCANDALS
THE VENETIAN SECRET, 1620

3.

A Forgotten Painting

I wake up to the biting frost in my cell. This year February is colder than any Venetian remembers.

The lagoon is frozen over. You can walk to the main land and the Lido. All the houses are coated with ice and shine like mirrors, Maria has told me. As always, the Venetians turn an occasion into a festivity: she described how the lagoon is swarming with people skating on the ice and playing games. Across the high wall, I can hear the loud cries mingle with laughter when someone slips and falls.

I look at Giulia, still asleep beside me in the bed. A fragile child for her seven years, Tommaso's beloved sister, left in the convent a few months ago. I can't get out of my mind that morning when the Contarinis dragged her through the gate, how she cried, and pulled at her mother's sleeve, begging not to be left alone in the convent. Poor Giulia, she does not have a single close relative here.

The first sunrays saunter through the small window in my cell and illuminate the frosty flowers on the circular windowpane. I study their intricate pattern, which looks like a lace collar in one of Tiziano's paintings. Like the collar Tommaso wears in the portrait. The last time I had a glimpse of his face was on the day of my clothing ceremony. But it won't be long now. I know from

Tommaso's letters that he will return soon. I often wonder how it must feel to be on the deck, far from land, with only the wind and the foaming waves for company. I close my eyes and imagine the freedom of it.

How happy I was when my father asked me to come home, even if it meant taking care of my mother. It is six years ago now. I was thirteen and Tommaso nineteen. We always found a way to be together, and I was lucky enough to stay at Ca'Morosini even after my mother's leg had mended.

We met secretly most nights. By accident, I discovered a door leading to Campo San Stefano. Everybody had forgotten about it, apart from an old servant. A large painting, which showed my great-aunt Rosalba in her bridal dress, hid the door from the inside. It had been deposited here when my mother expressed a dislike for it. From the campo, no one could see that there was, in fact, a door. The usual bronze doorknockers and handle were missing, and the keyhole was covered by a piece of the iron lining, forming part of the gritted pattern. Only if you knew where to lift a small section of the lining could you find the hidden keyhole. The old servant had left the key behind the Morosini coat of arms on the wall. I would hasten through the secret passage, from room to room, thus avoiding the great hall, run down the narrow staircase from the piano nobile the first floor, through the storerooms, move the painting a little to one side, and I was out of the door.

I am suddenly wide-awake. There is something about that painting: a story I have not understood.

As a little girl, I loved 'The Chessplayers' as my father called the painting of Rosalba stored away in the portego. It was then in my father's study, where he kept his collection of art and strange objects. In the brief spells when I was back from the convent, I enjoyed being there with him, looking at the paintings and collection of curiosities, while listening to his stories. His study was not accessible to many; it was quintessentially my father's room. It had furnishings for storing household documents, and shelves and cupboards covered with intarsia, displaying my father's rare items. I remember the ornately decorated rare books, the scientific instruments, the vases of alabaster mounted on gold and silver, and the small bronze figures inspired by classical antiquity. The painting captivated me because of its usage of gold and red, black and white. The magnificent red, my father told me, was made from the essence of resin called dragon's blood. When my father taught me to play chess, he showed me, written in minute letter son the back of the canvas, the name 'Rosalba'. He said that it depicted my great-aunt, famed for her beauty.

The picture showed a luxurious room furnished with gilded chests, its walls covered with paintings and objects of art, paintings drawn with such splendid detail that you could recognize their subjects. In the foreground a middle-aged man, dressed in the black and white of the Venetian nobles, and a young girl were playing chess. The girl wore an elegant red brocade dress, no doubt her bridal costume, and her hair was plaited with golden threads. But there was no joy in the painting. I remember the girl's mournful expression and the man's stern face. I always wondered what made the girl so sad, and if it had something to do with the game of chess.

"Don't you see that her opponent has her in checkmate? The black bishop and the king have finished her," my father explained.

A FORGOTTEN PAINTING
THE VENETIAN SECRET, 1620

"When contemplating paintings you must notice every little detail. They all hold separate important meanings. Look closely, and you will gain an insight you didn't bargain for. Is the girl in red, in fact, checkmated? Maybe only on the board."

I adored my father and loved being with him. I listened carefully to his words, while turning the ivory chess pieces in my hands, feeling their smoothness. The white pawns in the painting seemed to wear the habit and veil of the nuns of San Zaccaria. The black pawns wore clothes just like my father.

"And the satyr and the satyress?" I wanted to know why the painter had placed the bronze sculpture on the white mantelpiece right behind Rosalba.

"I am not certain," my father's answer had been evasive. "Satyrs are enslaved by their passions; they are wild and savage creatures."

One day, when I came to the studio, the painting had gone. In its place was a large painting, which my father told me was by a Florentine called Alessandro Botticelli. "This is how I imagine the birth of Venice: the birth of a beautiful virgin who rises like a miracle from the sea."

My old aunt Fantina's words about the painting of Rosalba come back to me. She paid frequent visits to Ca' Morosini and was a favourite of mine, though she was a little crazy. Nobody paid much attention to anything she said because she talked as much to herself as to everybody else. Fantina had the weird habit of winking an eye at me, as if we were up to something together, when the others were talking at the dinner table. But if you cared to listen you soon realised it was not always nonsense.

Sometimes Aunt Fantina and I went to sit in my father's studio.

When she noticed that the painting of the Chess players was gone, she moved closer to me on the couch and whispered, "If it is ever your destiny to become a nun, child, remember the painting of Rosalba!" On that occasion Fantina winked a lot more than usual, and I was not sure what to make of this. Did Fantina think that this time we had really joined forces? I never got the opportunity to ask because the next I heard of her she had passed away.

The day it was decided that I was to go back to the convent for the rest of my life, I went to look at the painting in the portego. I had been before, hoping to find its secret. But I found nothing. Then I forgot all about it, until I remembered the Patriarch's words about contemplating paintings. Is there something I have missed? Some message?
I pull the blankets tighter round me, taking care not to wake the twins and Giulia. They have to get up soon for breakfast and their lessons. I won't join them in the refectory, but go straight to the library. I can't stand listening to the reading from the Rule of St. Benedict in the droning voice of an ancient nun.

Sometimes I was breathless running from my house to the nearby Rio di Santissimo, where Tommaso would wait in his gondola. I leapt into the boat, and hurried inside the cabin. Leaning back in the soft cushions, I admired Tommaso's tall silhouette as he rowed us down the Canal Grande. I loved the soft sounds of the water against the prow, as the boat glided towards our hiding place: a small house, which belonged to the Contarinis, once used for storing wine and cloth from the Levant. Some nights myriads of stars were out, and the windows of the palaces were illuminated by huge glass chandeliers, which reflected in the water. We spent most summer nights there huddled up on the floor in the soft silks and serge blankets left behind.

"One day we won't be apart," Tommaso had whispered in my ear. "I have no desire to sail the seas doing my father's business," he had paused and smiled at me. "Even if we could marry, I can't imagine living at Ca'Contarini with my elderly brothers, trading and going to the Great Council. I would feel chained like a galley slave to his bench. What a cruel torment it would be to make visits and give balls. I suffer in the company of many people. No, I shall leave Venice with you. I'll do anything for you, Marietta." He had kissed my neck and shoulders, burying his face in my hair.

"I can't stand my peers," he had added. "Most of them are like your brother, vain and violent. I hate their preferred pastimes of breaking up betrothal parties or ravishing girls in the churches."

I remember every syllable of his words on that night. They are branded into my memory.

"Where shall we go, Tommaso?" I asked him, looking into his strangely coloured eyes, one brown and one green. It was always a gripping sensation, as if I looked into the eyes of two different people at the same time.

"We will inhabit one of the blank spaces on the maps in the schoolroom where no one will ever find us." He had laughed as he said it.

"You are such a dreamer, Tommaso!" I told him.

"I know," he had looked at me seriously. "I have had to be. Even as a small boy, I was torn between my father's demands and visions of a life I could choose for myself. I thought I had been marked by destiny, having one blue and one brown eye. Split in two. It made me feel restless. I always admired your determination, Marietta. Are you afraid to go away?"

"No," I had answered him sincerely. "I am not. I was never afraid when with you. Nor am I afraid to run away."

I look at Giulia who hugs the two small china figures in her sleep: figures of Christ, but the only thing coming close to a doll. Most of the young nuns carry the figures around as if they are real babies. It makes me sad to watch them. The nuns in charge of the orphans are more fortunate. At least they have real babies to embrace. Giulia loves her dolls, even if they are hard and cold to the touch.

I miss having Beatrice beside me in the bed. It is a year since my sister left. I can't imagine her as the wife of Andrea Dandolo. How will she manage, knowing so little of the world?

"Four years younger than Marietta, and a lot more compliant. Beatrice is the ideal choice," I had heard my mother say one evening in Ca' Morosini. "Beatrice is the most robust, and by far the prettiest," she had added. "The twins are surely unfit for marriage, Fabrizio, they are far too delicate." Absurdly my parents had agreed that convent life is fit for fragile little girls. How could they not consider the cold, or the many rules? How could they pretend to be ignorant of the fact that you had to be strong to survive the convent, particularly if you felt out of place. A few even commit the one unpardonable sin of taking their own lives; Carlotta did, by refusing to eat.

A FORGOTTEN PAINTING
THE VENETIAN SECRET, 1620

Reluctantly, I leave my warm bed. The stone floor is freezing, and I dress as quickly as I can. I put on the hose and my white woollen tunic. The rough and heavy fabric makes me itch through my soft undergarments. I use the tunic this winter because it is the only piece of clothing that keeps the cold at bay. I tie up the long laces of my boots. It takes an eternity because my fingers are frozen. I cover my head with the hood and wrap the fur coat round me. Tomorrow I will go to the laundry for a hot bath. I don't care that it is strictly forbidden. The laundry is warm and soothing and, on these occasions, we enjoy ourselves. The laughter, the gentle touch of a hand when we scrub each other's backs, is consoling. What a relief to our neglected bodies that are never touched lovingly otherwise.

"Wake up! Lessons begin in no time." I haul the thick blanket off the bed and the girls are wide-awake with the cold at once. I pull the thick carpet in front of the bed for them to stand on. The twins dress sulking and complaining. Giulia looks a little dazed, slowly picking up her habit from the chest, as if still slumbering. At last, they are ready. We step into the corridor, and walk quickly down the cloister to the refectory. The reading has begun, and I quickly push the girls through the door, closing it quietly behind them.

On my way to the library, I go into the chapel to look for the twins' prayer books. They always forget them. The chapel appears empty. I walk to where the twins usually sit. Someone is sobbing, and I see Chiara kneeling in front of the wooden sculpture of Santa Marina with her hands folded. How odd that

Chiara should pray to Santa Marina, the saint who dressed like a man, living among pious monks all her life. I am reminded how Chiara in her fever mistook me for Santa Marina when I tended her in the infirmary. It was curious the way we became friends. Not close friends, but still.

Chiara's face is streaked with tears, and her small figure trembles. Chiara's sadness touches me, though I find her piety excessive. Chiara's visions of Christ, the Virgin Mary and other saints are frequent. She can seemingly get lost in these apparitions. She even has a tiny chair in her cell dressed in crimson velvet, where the Madonna sits almost daily to talk to her, Chiara once confided to me. I often worry about the consequences for Chiara, should the Inquisition hear of her visions. When she was ill, Chiara whispered to me that she prayed in heaven with several of the most notable saints. Chiara risks serious accusations of pretence of holiness and aspirations of becoming a living saint.

I sit down beside her and put my arms around her. "I told the Patriarch how wretched I am," Chiara sobs. "There is no godliness in San Zaccaria. I became a nun to serve Christ. I never doubted my vocation, not even as a girl." It is distressing for Chiara to speak of her passions. I feel sorry for her.

"I can trust you, Marietta. I will never forget how you nursed me last winter. I know how much you detest the convent too. We're conspirators, because we share an aversion to this place. I have decided to leave," Chiara continues, eyeing me. "I am willing to risk anything, even my life, to escape to a convent where the rules are respected."

"Have you thought about the punishment if you are caught?" I am concerned. "You risk imprisonment for years in a cell."

"No punishment can be worse than being a nun here." Chiara sounds determined, more determined than I have ever heard her. "I have plans, Marietta. But it is better that I tell you nothing more."

"I'll help you if I can," I say. I find it difficult, though, to imagine that Chiara will really run away. Can't Chiara see all the obstacles there are to an escape, let alone unlocking gates and getting past the gatekeepers. And if she succeeds, what then? How will she manage outside? "Do you know where you will go?"

"I can't ask for your help, and I can't tell you, Marietta. It is too dangerous for you. You might be questioned if they suspected that you were my accomplice. I know that you also want to escape. You can't live without your liberty. You have a strong will, and you are clever. Nothing can hold you back once you have decided you want to live."

Strange, I think, that Chiara comforts me. Where does she find the courage to plan an escape? I won't be afraid either. How tempting it is to go with Chiara! But I know I can only leave Venice with Tommaso. I study Chiara's face: secretive with an expression of spirituality; pained, not pretty; her brow too high; eyes too wide apart; head far too big for her small and gaunt body; meditative and withdrawn and yet always seemingly serene.

I kiss her on the cheeks and get up from the bench. The twins' prayer books are nowhere in sight. They will have to look for them later. As I walk towards the door, I turn my head. Chiara is gazing at Santa Marina again. Why I wonder. Why?

The library is freezing. Maria stands by the large desk reading a letter. We have been friends for years, in spite of our different situations, since Maria came to our house as my servant when we were both thirteen. Maria hadn't minded going to the convent, on the contrary, she was relieved to get rid of my brother. Domenico, with his threatening behaviour and menacing dogs, is someone I don't miss either.

"Morning, Maria," I say, as she gives me one of her bright smiles.

What a contrast to Chiara, I think, looking at her: chubby and soft with a round sweet face and lively eyes. Maria folds the letter and puts it in the pocket of her habit. "Morning, Marietta." Maria hugs me tightly and kisses me. "I have received a letter from Aunt Lucretia. She asks me to come for a visit as soon as it thaws."

"Will your brothers be there too, do you think?"

"They will, Marietta, and they'll have news of Tommaso and the Contarina by then."

I watch Maria as she walks through the marble doorway and down the long corridor. I can hear she whistles a tune softly under her breath. She whistles when she feels happy, she once told me. As a child, her father taught her old Venetian melodies when they were mending sails in the shipyards at the Arsenal.

I take the lists of the books from the shelf. The clerics have condemned more or less half of the books as unfit reading for us and ordered them removed from the shelves. I think about Chiara as I look down the library hall with its ornate wooden bookshelves. Such a peaceful and comfortable room to stay in, if only I hadn't been a prisoner.

It is too cold to sit still, even in my fur coat. I walk down the stairs into the cloister, to the cemetery, towards the white marble crosses. The far corner is bare. I know that the ground holds the bones of newborn babies. Strangled, the moment they are born. Babies who were the fruits of love and seduction or the consequences of rape.

One night, I had heard cries of pain and a baby screaming. I couldn't sleep and so walked in the corridor not far from the cemetery. The baby's screams stopped abruptly, after just a few moments, and a heavy silence followed. I remained in the corridor for a while, too stunned to move. Then I heard the sound of digging, and soon all went quiet.

Why did nobody take the infants to the Pietà, the Foundlings' Hospital? It is so easy: an opening in the wall just big enough for a baby. You handed it in anonymously, and at least it had a chance to survive. How can anyone choose the other way?

Only a week ago, a young nun died quite unexpectedly. The rumour is that she had died giving birth. Two nuns have died in childbed within the past year. I wonder if it is true what the gossips say that Father Lupi forces himself on the young nuns.

Chiara, 1620, San Zaccaria, Venice

4.

Biancafiore

The heavy gates of San Zaccaria shut behind Maria Columbin. She looks across her shoulder, and, sure enough, through the small opening in the gate, eyes watch her walk away. The nuns are so bored, she thinks, they will pry into anything. Maria is careful not to slip in the thaw on the Riva, walking as fast as she can in the direction of the Arsenal. Has Ca'Morosini been flooded by the snow melting on the roofs, she wonders with dread in her heart. Is the painting Marietta wants so badly ruined? And Aunt Lucretia's house: is that flooded too and Biancafiore ill?

There is spring in the air: Maria feels it. The ice has gone at last. Gondolas and galleys again crowd the basin of San Marco. Is the Contarina among them? Maria gazes at the masts, hoping to catch sight of the Contarina's standard flying in the breeze. But no, the galley isn't there.

She turns into the delta of alleys around the Arsenal. She knows all the narrow streets. As a small girl, she used to stray into the big shipyards swarming with different nationalities: Greeks, Slavs and Turks. Even now, she senses the happy-go-lucky atmosphere. They had been seven brothers and sisters in two small rooms and that hadn't been easy. But her father had saved the day, laughing and joking through the misery.

BIANCAFIORE
THE VENETIAN SECRET, 1620

She had been over the moon with happiness when they told her that she had been adopted by the Morosinis, but living with the Morosinis had been trying. But at least they had saved her from the streets. Maria knows that her father's spirit had so impressed Marietta's uncle (the ambassador Filippo Morosini, the 'bailo' to Constantinople, the high envoy of Venice) that he had persuaded Marietta's father, Fabrizio Morosini to take her. Her poor, dear father was sent together with other shipbuilders to repair Venetian galleys in Constantinople, only to be taken prisoner by the Turks. Maria remembers how proud she had felt that he had tried to escape, even if he was killed in the attempt. She had thought that her sorrow would never end, and then her mother died only a few months later.

Maria crosses a tiny square crammed with outdoor workshops. The humble brick houses with their plain facades squeezed tightly together. They seem even smaller than she remembers. The houses had been empty for years, deserted after the last plague swept over Venice. Entire families had been wiped out. When she ran past them as a child, she believed they were haunted. She would run as fast as she could, terrified of ghosts or spirits pulling her into one of the deserted house.

Maria wriggles through the crowds of arsenalotti rushing through the gates of the vast shipyard of the Arsenal. They look the same, with their long pigtails and the stench of tar, wine, and sweat about them. She has never seen so much energy anywhere. Their tongues twist to pronounce their strangely sounding jargon. They are thick as thieves, she thinks, just like her father and his companions who stuck together in every distant outpost of the Venetian territories.

Her best playgrounds as a child had been Corfu, Cyprus, and Constantinople. Even if imaginary. Her father and grandfather had told tales of their adventures into these savage kingdoms. Maria recalls being a hostage, her father pretending to hoist her up in the masts, placing her on a high shelf in the kitchen. Once she had been disguised as a Turk, with a big white turban, and a stick for a scimitar.

When she first came to Ca'Morosini, she was certain that she had arrived in another savage kingdom. The big house was so utterly strange with so many rooms and nooks to explore, so full of treasures and riches. She wondered if the Morosinis had plundered at least a hundred galleys, like the Uskok pirates in her dad's stories. It hadn't taken her long to realize how cold and reserved the huge palace was. There was not much laughter outside the servants' quarters.

Biancafiore is already four. Not a day goes by, when Maria doesn't think of her daughter. Her pregnancy had remained a secret, and nobody had known that Biancafiore was born in the attic at Ca'Morosini. Marietta had cut the navel cord with a pair of scissors, wrapped the baby in an old cloth, and rushed off in the night to push the little body through the opening at the Pietà.

Maria feels a lump in her throat at the memory. She had cried insanely when Marietta took the baby from her arms. "Oh, Maria," Marietta had said also weeping, "I pity you with all my heart. This is what I always feared myself to hold my illegitimate child by Tommaso, only to be forced to part with it, as you are

BIANCAFIORE
THE VENETIAN SECRET, 1620

tonight."

Biancafiore would most likely have died at the Pietà, had it not been for Lucretia. Why didn't she think of her aunt to begin with? Maria's note had reached her aunt just in time. An hour later and Aunt Lucretia would have left for San Erasmo for weeks to gather sage, marigold, and all her other herbs.

Domenico. The servants' favourite. She detests Marietta's brother. He never cared one fig about Biancafiore. At the time, Maria had felt that she was a hostage once more. Only it was no game this time. Domenico had sneaked into her room and put a knife to her throat, forcing her to undress. Night after night, he had come, always locking the door behind him.

"If you breathe a word of this to anyone, you will end up as food for my dogs," he would sneer at her. Once, when she had locked the door from within, he had kicked it open, furious with her. Sometimes he had brought Uno and Due with him, and she had been scared to death by the large beasts' menacing growling. Even if the servants had told her that Domenico's behaviour was all because of his little brother, Francesco, she would never forgive the brute. They said that Domenico was only five when he watched his brother die in their mother's arms. He had been devoted to Francesco, the servants claimed. Hard to imagine Domenico devoted to anybody, Maria thinks, apart from his snarling dogs. He had grown moody and sullen afterwards and hostile to his father.

Maria smiles at the two small girls sitting on the doorstep with their embroidery. She watches the widows and married women chatter outside the houses, making lace or mending sails. Some nurse their own babies while others nurse others babies from the Pietà. Three old arsenalotti, clutching their sticks, exchange news and gossip. There is Biancafiore! Playing with her kitten in front of Lucretia's house.

"Hello Biancafiore!" Maria shouts at the top of her voice. The child lets go of the cat the moment she hears Maria's voice, and stumbles towards her. She has Marietta's face, Maria thinks, hugging the child. The same thick blonde hair and heart shaped mouth. How fortunate that she doesn't look like Domenico.

Maria walks towards Lucretia's house with Biancafiore skipping and dancing beside her. The diviner on the corner is busy, she notices. Some sailors' wives and their relatives wait patiently for their turn. When she passes, an old woman stops her to say that a galley has gone missing and it all comes back to her. When her father didn't return, her mother had taken her to the small square behind the church of San Martino, desperate to find a wise woman. A Greek or Slavic woman, her mother had said, because only women from the East knew about divination. They had found a Greek woman, who had asked an incredible price. Half a lire. The same as her father could make in a month.

The questions had stumbled from her mother's mouth: "Has he been enslaved by the Turks? Has he been tortured? Has he abandoned Christendom and become a Turk? Or has he deserted his family?" The wise woman had just stared into the smoke without saying a word. "Is my husband dead or alive?" her mother had then shouted at the woman in desperation, and the woman had nodded her head twice.

BIANCAFIORE
THE VENETIAN SECRET, 1620

Maria had been afraid of the Greek woman, and hid in a corner. All the mirrors and smoke which surrounded the woman had frightened her, as had her chanting in a low voice. The woman had sprinkled holy water on her mother from a vase painted with strange figures and animals. Maria had covered her eyes with her hands. Sitting in the corner, she had tried to sound like the Greek woman, reciting to herself in a low voice: "Please, father, don't be dead, I want you back. Please, father, don't be dead, I want you back."

In Lucretia's house, bunches of herbs hang from the ceiling and brush Maria's head as they step into the kitchen. Lucretia is busy mixing strong smelling spices for her medicines, making bundles, which she puts on the kitchen table. She wraps the spices in old rags, as Maria has seen so many times before, and marks them with small coloured signs. On a shelf are rows of little glass flasks with unguents and her aunt's famous Holy Oil.

"Dear niece, give me a few minutes, and I'll finish this." Lucretia turns her head towards Maria, breaking instantly into a smile.

Maria sits down on the worn wooden chair, and takes Biancafiore on her lap. She studies her aunt's deft movements as she works. Lucretia is chubby like her with the same black hair and almond shaped eyes.

"Biancafiore has asked me a thousand times today when you would come. Isn't that so, child?" Without waiting for an answer from Biancafiore, she adds, "Your brothers will be here any minute. There is news about the Contarina, Maria." Maria feels her heart jump, when her aunt mentions Tommaso's ship.

BIANCAFIORE
THE VENETIAN SECRET, 1620

Outside Maria hears male voices. Her brothers! She sets Biancafiore down on the floor, and rushes to the door. They have brought a friend, Arrigo, a shipbuilder like themselves. He is handsome with jet-black hair and smiling blue eyes, she thinks, feeling herself blushing. He must be twenty-five or twenty-six, like her brothers.

The next moment, her brothers' arms are around her. "How do you get on in San Zaccaria with all the pretty virgins?" Sandro says laughing. "Have you forgotten us and our simple ways?"

Maria feels exuberant, and she tousles Sandro's hair. It is the colour of polished copper, as if it's on fire, she thinks, like his temperament. She looks into his cheerful greenish eyes, and smiles. Then she turns her head, and watches Zanino. He is much quieter, small and dark like her, with clever secretive eyes. The three of them love each other; she knows that without a shred of doubt. When Arrigo smiles at her, a gap shows between his front teeth which Maria finds charming.

Maria and Lucretia set the table with plates of heavy flavoured sardines and mackerel, polenta, and onions. There is just room enough for them, and Maria loves it when they squeeze tightly together round the small wooden table.

"What news of Tommaso and the Contarina?" Maria asks, barely able to disguise her impatience for news.

"The Contarina is back at the beginning of April." Sandro says in a soothing voice. "In one or two weeks' time if God grants her safe passage and the pirates have no luck."

She feels Zanino's eyes rest on her, "Maria, I must tell you. Arrigo and I have received orders to go to Corfu to repair ships. We will be running the gauntlet through a sea of pirates too in a month's time."

"Don't frighten me so," Maria says, upset by the prospect." To have to say goodbye to you both is a terrible thought."

"Don't worry about us or Tommaso, Maria," Zannino says mildly. "The Contarina is a strong galley, and Tommaso one of the bravest merchant captains. He knows how to deal with a crisis and a few pirates, just as well as we do when on our way to Constantinople. I spoke to him sometimes when we rigged out the Contarina for her voyage. He is clever, and not someone easily fooled, Maria. He has lived half his life on the seas. Didn't you know that his father took him for long voyages when he was a boy? Tommaso will be back alright, Maria, and you won't get rid of us so easily either."

Maria wipes her eyes with the handkerchief Zanino hands her, and smiles at him. Arrigo watches her across the table, she notices. He looks concerned.

Maria starts at the sudden sharp knock on the door. A young man with a gaunt face stands in the doorway. Maria studies him. Where has she seen him before? He is tall and scrawny, dressed in filthy ragged clothes, wearing shoes so worn down that they show his toes. There's no mistaking the deep cut on the cheek, though, she thinks. It's Pietro Mudazzo.

Lucretia is already up from the table. "I've everything ready for you. Let's go into the kitchen."

"I know him." Arrigo says when their aunt and Pietro have closed the door behind them. "He is one of the thugs who loiter in the Piazza, always on the lookout for a traveller he can free of his belongings."

"Didn't he stay for a time at Segna with the Uskoks? The most savage pirates along the Adriatic coastline! I remember that he lent them a hand the last time they destroyed our cargoes and ships." Sandro's temper flares at the thought of the Uskoks.

Lucretia is back at the table in a moment. "I sent him out the back door. I hope it will be some time before I see him again."

Biancafiore takes Maria's hand and says that she kept her eyes tightly shut while the stranger was in the room. "He is probably a witch," the small girl whispers seriously. "Probably a witch," she repeats. "If you look at a witch, she casts a spell and the devil takes you." Maria starts at her daughter's words.

Biancafiore turns to Sandro. "Tell me the story of the little girl who lived next door, please. They say she could make a violent tempest sweep over Venice at will. Is it true she was a witch?"

"I think so, yes." Sandro whispers in Biancafiore's ear, but loud enough for Maria to catch the words. "The witch was actually a Turk, or perhaps an Uskok; she wanted more than anything else in the world to wreck our fine Venetian ships by raising a storm!"

Biancafiore crawls onto Sandro's lap. "I would like to make storms come at my will! Tell me the story, uncle, please."

"Lucretia," Maria says, "can I talk to you for a moment?"

"Do you have a herb which can provoke an abortion?" Maria asks when they are alone. "Cordelia, one of the young nuns, is pregnant," Maria continues. "She is scared to death. She won't tell me who the father is. She says that she was taken by force.

BIANCAFIORE

THE VENETIAN SECRET, 1620

Perhaps by Father Lupi." Maria bursts out. "He is not at all the innocent priest he pretends to be. I have noticed his lecherous smile more than once. How he gawks at the nuns! He's abandoned to his passions and the devil."

"You may be right about the confessor, Maria. I hear stories too. I have the gift of looking into souls. I know his kind and if there ever was an evil spirit, Father Lupi is one."

Lucretia reaches for a bundle of herbs on the top shelf. "This is the remedy for your friend. To cure a woman whose monthly has not come, I use sage and Devil's Root. You must grind it very fine, and tell Cordelia that she must take the paste three mornings in a row."

Maria tucks the herbs into the opening of her low-cut dress. "Like me, Cordelia worries a lot about Marietta. She loves her as much as I do. Marietta has not been well at all this winter," Maria says. "She has been coughing for months and is growing feebler every day. It became worse the day she came into her cell, about two weeks ago, and found the floor strewn with small pieces of paper. Someone had torn up her manuscripts. She had a fit and cried for days. She couldn't understand who would do a thing like that. She fell ill with a high temperature for weeks, and the coughing got a lot worse. "

"The nuns are jealous of her pretty face and her rich family, Maria. They know about her love for Tommaso. And his love for her. The Morosinis and the Contarinis belong to the aristocracy of the nobility. A mere cut of the sleeve sets them apart. It means everything."

Maria thinks of Fabrizio Morosini's wide-opened sleeves. She had noted at Ca'Morosini the subtle distinction in the quality of the cloth, the fineness of the weave, the costliness of the lace linings between Marietta's dresses and some of the visiting noble girls. So much for 'the moderation of all things', as the nobles always say.

Her aunt goes over to a small chest in the corner and takes out a metal box. She opens the lid and hands a small yellowish glass jar to Maria. "This jar contains a mixture of Nightshade and Thyme. They will give Marietta her strength back. Tell her to take three drops every morning for a month."

It is sundown: the Realtina bell chimes. Maria reluctantly makes ready to return to the convent, and puts on her heavy black mantle. She is relieved that her brothers and Arrigo will keep her company.

Maria hugs Lucretia. "Thank you a million times, dear aunt, for taking care of my precious child." She kisses the sleeping Biancafiore, wishing she didn't have to leave her daughter behind.

"Hey link-boy! Light us the way," Arrigo shouts at a young boy loitering on the corner with a lantern in his hand. The boy takes the coin from Arrigo, and walks in front. On the Riva, Maria shivers in the cold wind. She watches the splashes of foam clash against the quay, painting the ships with white fans. The galleys anchored in the lagoon follow the rhythm of the wind swinging to and fro. With not a soul visible on board, the great ships seem ghostlike, abandoned to the moaning sea, Maria thinks, just like the empty houses of her childhood. Then she feels Arrigo's arm around her waist, drawing her closer, as if to protect her from the deserted ships.

The low entrance, the sottoportego, to Campo San Zaccaria is right in front of them. The life size white marble Madonna on the corner appears to keep a lookout for them, Maria thinks.She is a sign in the dark. Maria feels safe with Arrigo's arm around her waist, and doesn't want to let go of him.

She always felt attracted to the large statue with the intense blue eyes made of the finest white and blue glass from Murano. The statue looks alive. But in the dark, the colour of the eyes loses its magic. Maria can only make out the whites of the eyeballs.

But the marble Virgin is still a miracle. Maria remembers how as a small girl she once saw tears falling from her beautiful blue eyes. She had run all the way up the Riva alone to kneel in front of the statue and confide in the Madonna that the plague had taken her little brothers.

Maria embraces Arrigo and her brothers. "Can you meet me at Vespers, two days from now, in the piazzetta?" Maria whispers in Arrigo's ear. "I have an important errand for Marietta. Will you help me?"

"Nothing I would like better", he says in a low voice blowing her a kiss as he walks away.

Maria Columbin, 1620, San Zaccaria, Venice

5.

A Marriage

Fabrizio Morosini and his four brothers are at the gates to the canal. Fabrizio feels the chill in the air, and becomes aware of the stillness surrounding him. Not a wind stirs, he observes, while watching the standards of the approaching gondolas bearing the guests for Beatrice's betrothal. The standards hang limp from the prows, reminding him of wing-shot birds.

He had given in to Manuela, and let her choose the date for the marriage. Manuela had decided that the wedding should be a week from now, on the first Sunday in April. No other day of the week seemed possible for their daughter's wedding

Fabrizio feels grave and solemn today, even sad, in spite of the festivities. He cannot stop thinking of Marietta. When he visited the parlatorio less than a week ago, she had questioned him about Beatrice's betrothal, and told him of her doubts. Was Andrea Dandolo the right match for her sister, she had asked. Fabrizio has asked himself the same question. He cannot forget the expression on her face when he admitted to the size of the dowry. She had looked so forlorn as she sat there behind the grates in her white silk dress, thinner and more fragile than he remembered. What had happened to his passionate daughter during the winter? If only he could have arranged her marriage as well. Fabrizio sighs. He knows how much she loves Tommaso

A MARRIAGE
THE VENETIAN SECRET, 1620

Contarini, and he wishes that he hadn't listened to his sister all those years ago and let Manuela have her way. Yesterday, he learned that the Contarinis have arranged Tommaso's marriage to one of the Loredan daughters. It won't be long before Marietta hears about the plans. And then what? He winces at the memory of how he had forced Marietta to sign a waiver regarding any claim to the family estate beyond her modest monastic dowry. Time has passed so quickly, and he recalls her last remark to him that day, "In here the passing of time is so painful, father. Time hurts."

Fabrizio watches the first nobles step onto the landing. The three Ducal councillors, followed by the other eight procurators of San Marco, among them his old friend and cousin, Paolo Gritti. Fabrizio makes an effort to rid himself of his speculations. He cautions himself that a wedding is politics, and this is not the time to appear absentminded.

Four distinguished Senators are next, then the heads of the Senate and the Minister of War, with the Chancellor of the Exchequer right behind him. The Head of the Council of Ten, Giorgio Grimani, passes on greetings and a message from his sister, the Abbess. She wants to assure Fabrizio that everything will be ready to receive the betrothal party at San Zaccaria in a few hours.

Fabrizio never approved of the tradition of the bride taking leave of her sisters and relatives in the convent. A cause of so much unnecessary sorrow and jealousy, he thinks.

More than two hundred nobles are waiting impatiently to see

Beatrice dance. Paolo Gritti walks slowly towards the stairs. Their wives and daughters have already arrived. He has glimpsed them in huddles in the adjoining rooms. Gritti studies Domenico looming at the top of the stairs, watching the guests as they ascend. A grim smile plays at the corners of Domenico's mouth. He appears a dark shadow against the white marble statue of Venus, dressed in purple and black velvet sash, shoes with silver buckles, and heavy gold chains round his neck. His black hair comes low down on his forehead, in an attempt to cover an old scar.

"What an arrogant youth," Paolo Gritti says aloud to himself. So superior, but the fine aquiline nose doesn't match his cunning looks. I never liked him. Always up to no good. One moment aggressive and hostile to everybody, and the next, depressed and withdrawn scowling in a corner. What a devil he was towards his sisters, Gritti recalls, Manuela always siding with him against everybody.

Gritti puts a hand on Domenico's shoulder. "I am happy for the Morosinis. I hope you will be as fortunate as your sister, and marry someone with a dowry as large."

"I'm in no hurry at all, uncle," Domenico says crossly. He shoots his uncle a cynical look, moving away from his touch. "And besides, I'm too young. Most nobles who are unfortunate enough to marry at all are old, at least thirty-five." He laughs loudly into Gritti's face.

I pity the girl who has to marry him, Gritti thinks as he hurries on towards the great hall.

The hall abounds with garlands of flowers, tapestries, and the

A MARRIAGE
THE VENETIAN SECRET, 1620

coats-of-arms of family and kinsmen. Gritti finds evidence of the Morosinis' noble lineage claiming descent from Roman senators, in the family portraits which seem to stare sceptically at the guests from the gilded frames on the frescoed walls. The light that streams in through the front windows glances off the floors of gleaming terrazzo. They are so highly polished, Gritti thinks, that, like Narcissus, you can study your reflection in the smooth surface.

The Doge's fifes and trumpets announce the bride. Gritti senses the hush descending on the men, and sees that all eyes are glued to the doors guarded by the two Moorish slaves. At a nod from Fabrizio the liveried blackamoors open the doors, and Beatrice steps in, holding the hand of the dancing master. Her gown of crimson brocade suits her, Paolo Gritti thinks, and lends a warm glow to her face. He is impressed with the way the gems on the dress twinkle, and he admires the famous Dandolo pearls coiling around the girl's neck.

" What a pretty rose," Gritti hears Giorgio Grimani whisper. "What a treasure they have kept under lock and key all these years!

But she seems to me more like a fish writhing at the end of the line than a happy bride."

Gritti searches Beatrice's face in vain for just a tiny smile. Poor innocent girl. What a waste to let Andrea Dandolo have her, given his quite opposite interests.

Beatrice listens to the applause of the noblemen. She watches timidly for a signal from her dancing master. At the back of the Sala, the string quartet starts to play. Beatrice bows to her audience, ready to dance all round the hall. Hesitantly, her eyes on the floor, she takes two small steps forward and pirouettes, holding on to the feeble old dancing master's hand. Then two steps to the left and then two to the right. Beatrice pirouettes again, and already she feels quite dizzy. The men mutter compliments admiring the new and elegant dance steps that she uses.

Beatrice is terrified when she steals a look at her future husband. She has waited so long for this day, impatient to wear the dress and all the finery, and impatient to meet Andrea Dandolo. She has only seen him once before. This is very different from what she has imagined.

She watches Andrea standing by the front windows between his father and his uncle. He is dressed in red, and looking, she fears, just a little out of sorts, even indifferent, when she bows in front of him.

What will it be like to live with an unknown man twice her age? And his father, brothers and uncles, all of them strangers. All the family crowding in Ca'Dandolo, like the nobles did everywhere in Venice. To take on unfamiliar duties in an unfamiliar household is the lot of any Venetian bride, she tries to soothe herself. Other girls have coped before, living with a large number of relatives in their husbands' homes.

She has difficulty breathing. The stays are too tight, and she is sure her heart pounds loud enough for everyone to hear. She sways a little, and squeezes Pisani's gawky arm. As an antidote, she tries thinking of her sister, who doesn't seem to be afraid of anything. She must try to be like her. How her parents can expect so much of her, when she knows so little about the world,

A MARRIAGE
THE VENETIAN SECRET, 1620

is quite beyond her.

Then the music stops, and she stands still. She watches Andrea coming towards her, tall and sleek. He takes her hand absentmindedly, without as much as a hint of a smile. To Beatrice his hand feels sweaty and soft to the touch, like a piece of dough. He slips the large diamond ring on her finger and kisses her hand, leaving traces of rouge, which she finds strange.

If only the clapping would stop. Beatrice is dizzy again. She blushes, and quickly averts her face from Andrea's. She turns around, grabs the arm of Pisani and almost pulls him through the doors to the chambers next to the great hall. Her mother and the noblewomen are waiting for her.

"They are the most handsome couple in all of Venice!" Beatrice hears the noblewomen whisper.

"Show us the ring, Beatrice!" they shout and crowd around her.

"This ring completely takes my breath away. The enormity of the diamonds is amazing," Signora Loredan exclaims. "And so beautifully set!"

"The dancing steps, Beatrice," old Graziana Loredan says, practically spitting the words in her face, "are the most elegant I've seen for many a betrothal."

When Beatrice looks at Graziana's face it becomes a blur, and only the lips remain distinct. She looks round the room for a chair. She doesn't understand why Andrea hardly noticed her, but kept whispering to the young nobleman beside him.

She crosses the room to sit down on one of the small gilded chairs in the corner. Only Domenico seems to please their mother, she thinks, when she sits down, feeling her mother's eyes resting sceptically on her. She had seen her mother turn in rage on an unsuspecting maid as furiously as she had done on Marietta. But no matter what Domenico did, even when he didn't obey their mother's strict rules, she never scolded him.

She closes her eyes to shut out her mother's looks, and remembers how they had been expected to kiss their parents' hands, saying "Good morning Signore" and "Good morning, Signora", and remain absolutely still till told otherwise. Domenico used to stick his tongue out at Marietta and kick her shins while they waited to be allowed to sit down at the table. When their mother saw him, she never interfered. Her brother always pulled her hair, and when she cried, and their mother noticed, he blamed Marietta. Many times their mother had shut Marietta up in the dark closet in the bedroom for hours. Poor Marietta, who would just remain silent and never shed a tear until their mother opened the door. Marietta used to say it was because their parents preferred sons to daughters that they only winked at Domenico's behaviour.

Beatrice is afraid of him, his hard stare, and cold fish eyes. His temper scares her too. Quite a few times since her return home from the convent, she has experienced how hot-headed he gets. She can't remember a single thing he has ever done for anybody but himself. That he should have become like this from grieving over their dead little brother is a story she never believed.

Suddenly Beatrice is aware of her mother standing in front of her. "Is anything the matter?" she whispers. "Are you ill Beatrice? You must pull yourself together this very moment and attend to your guests. Have you quite forgotten," her mother continues quickly, "that you keep your mother-in-law and new sisters-in-law waiting? Don't you dare make a fool of me, Beatrice. Marietta

A MARRIAGE
THE VENETIAN SECRET, 1620

has done that often enough."

Beatrice feels her mother take her hand, pulling her to her feet under the penetrating gaze of the women. Signora Dandolo comes up to her and embraces her.

"You look exceptionally pretty," Beatrice hears her say. "I am so pleased that you are coming to live with us in no more than a week from now. You will quickly learn to run the house." Signora Dandolo says in a gentle tone of voice.

Beatrice is uncertain how to respond. She manages a smile at her mother-in-law and to kiss her two new sisters on the cheeks. Beatrice gazes at her mother-in-law's small neat figure, resplendent in a green and golden silk dress.

"You won't have to put up with my daughters for long, Beatrice", Signora Dandolo adds in a tone that suggests that Beatrice is now her closest friend. "They are both of them getting married in May. What a relief our daughters won't have to enter a convent. You are lucky that Marietta preferred a life as a nun and saved you the tears. So your mother tells me, Beatrice."

Beatrice is dumbfounded. She is just about to tell Signora Loredan that there is nothing Marietta abhors more than San Zaccaria. But before she has a chance to open her mouth, Manuela pushes her towards a small group of women gathered in a corner. Beatrice trembles. Her mother's lies about Marietta make her feel guilty and ill at ease, unreal, like a sleepwalker, stumbling in and out among the brocade dresses at her mother's bidding.

"What beautiful pearls, Beatrice!" Tommaso's mother, Amelia Contarini, says. "We are planning a wedding too, you know.

A MARRIAGE
THE VENETIAN SECRET, 1620

Tommaso is to be married to Livia Loredan in less than a year."
Beatrice is suddenly awake. She feels as if someone has slapped her face with a cold leather glove. All she can do is glare at Tommaso's mother.

"Don't just stand there gaping," her mother says, her voice like a drumbeat. Beatrice can only look steadfastly at her silk shoes.

"The excitement has been too much for her, Amelia," Beatrice hears her mother say by way of apology. Beatrice isn't used to so much attention."

"Tommaso will be home soon for just a short while. Come and see us, Manuela, before he sets out again for Constantinople. They will be married on his return, a year from now. That is a match made in heaven. Livia brings with her a dowry so large I won't even mention the amount."

What will happen when Marietta hears of this? Beatrice prays that she is the one who tells her sister. Please, Blessed Virgin, don't let it be one of the others. She knows that rumours spread with the speed of lightning in the convent. Most likely, Marietta has already heard the terrible news.

Surely Tommaso would never marry anyone but Marietta. But how Marietta and Tommaso can possibly stop this wedding from taking place, she can't imagine.

A MARRIAGE
THE VENETIAN SECRET, 1620

6.

A Bridal Visit to the Convent

"The gondolas are waiting!"

The sound of her mother's voice makes Beatrice start. Reluctantly, she descends the staircase to the portego and steps into the gondola. She takes her seat outside the canopy, on the elevated chair covered with the soft carpets. The gondolier dips his oar in the water, and the boat slides lazily into the shallow canals. A cold breeze toys with her dress, chilling her to the bone. She turns her head to watch the guests, who follow in their gondolas. She feels a sense of profound sadness. She watches the crowd wave and cheer on the embankment, and find their joy and happiness out of place.

Six gondolas loaded with food, barrels of wine and gifts for the Abbess and the choir-nuns glide on the even sea in front of her. Lulled by the water, a fierce image crosses her mind: that Marietta will contemplate, from behind the grate, the expensive gifts and food carried into the parlatorio, while longing for Tommaso. If only her sister doesn't know of the wedding plans yet. Beatrice closes her eyes listening to the gondolier's oar. If only she could exchange places with Marietta. There is nothing she would rather do.

At the landing stage, Beatrice watches the guests crowd through the gate to the large parlatorio. Andrea stands beside her now smiling formally. She doesn't like his tight rouged mouth, and she shrinks from his touch when he takes her arm to follow the guests.

It is unreal to be a visitor, Beatrice thinks. She is afraid to enter the parlatorio on Andrea's arm. She remembers the triumphant brides she has watched so many times from behind the grate; perhaps she is the first bride to feel sad at leaving the convent. She watches the nuns in their pretty dresses of the latest French fashion, their earrings, pearls, little curls prettily arranged behind small pearly veils, flowers round their waists, most of them longing to be her, wanting to change places with her. She hears Giorgio Grimani whisper to one of her uncles: "The nuns look more like nymphs to me than sacred virgins."

She looks around for Marietta. There her sister is, looking pallid in the rose-pink dress. Beatrice smiles apologetically at her and disengages herself from Andrea's arm. She pushes past the servant nuns who are unpacking the pastries and marzipan. Beatrice sits down as close as possible to the grate, opposite her sisters and Giulia. She takes Marietta's hand, and kisses her cheek through the grilles.

"I'm not sure I can go through with this, Marietta," Beatrice whispers.

"You will be fine, Beatrice," Marietta says softly smiling at her, "I know you will." Her sister speaks with such confidence.

Beatrice squeezes her hand, and looks around. Their mother keeps an eye on them. "Marietta," Beatrice says quickly, "I don't want you to hear this from anyone else. The Contarinis have planned for Tommaso and Livia Loredan to marry in a year's

A BRIDAL VISIT TO THE CONVENT
THE VENETIAN SECRET, 1620

time."

Beatrice watches Marietta's face, and knowing her sister so well, she has no doubt that this is the first time she hears of Tommaso's marriage.

"Don't worry, Marietta. Tommaso will find a way. He always did in the past, when something didn't agree with him. He'll never go through with it. Remember, he follows his own mind."

Marietta doesn't say a word, and suddenly their mother stands beside them.

"Rose-pink suits you, Marietta," their mother says mockingly, "I am glad to see that you thrive." She smiles a little at her eldest daughter. Beatrice studies her mother's face. How can she say that Marietta looks thriving when, in fact, her sister looks pale and thin? Why does she hate Marietta so?

"What makes you think that? You always only see what you want to see, mother," Marietta says coldly.

Their mother doesn't pay attention to her answer. She hasn't been to see Marietta for years, as far as Beatrice remembers. Their father pulls a chair to the grates and sits down close to Marietta. Beatrice notes how he smiles apprehensively at her sister.

"How beautiful you look, Marietta, in your silk dress. Quite as beautiful as Beatrice." He obviously feels ill at ease, and Beatrice can't help thinking that her father looks as heartbroken as Marietta.

Beatrice looks around the parlatorio. Everybody, nuns as well as guests, is eating and drinking. The musicians play a cheerful tune, and they appear, absurdly, to be a happy gathering. Their mother turns towards the twins. "Tell me about your lessons. How are you doing?" But Beatrice notices that her mother's

A BRIDAL VISIT TO THE CONVENT
THE VENETIAN SECRET, 1620

attention wanders from the twins' eager faces to the guests.

"We like the singing lessons best, mother, much better than reading." Elena and Angela speak at the same time. Their mother doesn't pay attention.

Beatrice studies her father, who contemplates his wife's perfect features, her slim body, and the mass of blond hair arranged into curls and plaits. So peculiar, Beatrice thinks, to possess such a callous soul and this extraordinary beauty too.

"You know what Father Lupi told me before I left, Marietta?" Beatrice whispers to Marietta. "That a married woman is entirely subject to her husband's will, and even the slightest thing may stain her honour. The priest's words obviously don't count for our mother. "

"I wish you could live in Ca'Dandolo with me." Beatrice is anxious. Marietta hardly speaks at all. "I'm afraid to go on my own. Andrea didn't even look at me when I danced.

All the Dandolo family members living in the house are strangers to me, and I don't know how to be the mistress."

Again Beatrice feels their mother's eyes resting on them. Suddenly Manuela gets up from her chair without warning.

"Illustrissimi, dear friends, it is time to leave for Ca'Morosini. Dinner is waiting. It is getting late, and the time has come for Beatrice to take leave of her sisters and relatives." Beatrice thinks their mother's loud voice cuts the room in two.

She watches Domenico talking to Lucia Loredan. He leans up against the grate whispering to her. She hands him the red carnation from behind her ear. Beatrice is disgusted when Domenico sweeps Marietta a mocking wide bow, before leaving the parlatorio for the waiting gondolas. She is the last one to

A BRIDAL VISIT TO THE CONVENT
THE VENETIAN SECRET, 1620

leave. She looks back at Marietta and waves at her pale sister. She has never seen Marietta like this, and feels her stomach churn. As Beatrice steps into the gondola, she ponders what Domenico's relationship is to Lucia Loredan.

A BRIDAL VISIT TO THE CONVENT
THE VENETIAN SECRET, 1620

7.

A Letter Arrives

At Ca'Morosini, a servant is stationed on every step of the grand staircase, holding a torch to illuminate the dark. In the salotto, the table is covered with fine embroidered cloths. The silver and gold candelabra shine beside the enamelled bowls. Liveried moors bring in oysters, truffles, sausages, hams, and sturgeon from Ferrara, eels from Binasco, sausage from Modena, quail from Lombardy, goose pate from Romagna, pasta from Genoa, pastry, and every kind of fruit.

Paolo Gritti takes his seat next to Manuela. He regrets that he didn't get the chance to talk to Marietta today. He feels a pang of remorse when he recalls how desperate she had been. Gritti will never be able to forget it. She had begged him to help persuade Fabrizio to change his mind, insisting that she couldn't possibly become a nun. Ah, he always liked the girl – so bright, so confident. But there was nothing he could have done. Not that he hadn't tried.

Gritti sighs at the thought of the letter. He had hoped to make Marietta understand the necessity of her sacrifice, but she never answered him. He turns to face Manuela. "Has Marietta come to terms with her destiny?"

"Funny you should ask. In fact, she has. She has finally found her vocation. It seems she takes comfort in religious life." Manuela smiles sweetly at Gritti.

"Then her attitude has completely changed over the years?" Gritti finds it hard to believe. He had seen how pale and sad Marietta looked today.

"Marietta wouldn't wish for any other life now," Manuela replies. Gritti is surprised and wonders if his letter did help Marietta after all.

Manuela looks away from Gritti. Today she couldn't face Marietta without thinking of Francesco, her dear lost son. Marietta, spoiled by Fabrizio, allowed to attend Domenico and Tommaso's lessons. She had said no, but Fabrizio had still granted her the right. Marietta had gone to the schoolroom triumphantly. A mere girl being taught maths and law didn't make sense.

That Marietta had come home, when she was tied to her bed, had been Fabrizio's idea. The mere thought annoys her. She would have preferred anybody but Marietta, even silly old aunt Fantina. But her pains had been exasperating, and she couldn't find the strength to argue with Fabrizio. Luckily, Marietta hadn't spent much time with her, but disappeared whenever possible.

Manuela studies Signora Loredan. Finally, Marietta will have to give up her dream of marrying Tommaso. She contemplates Beatrice across the table, far from certain that she will live up to her expectations. Manuela had noticed Beatrice whisper to Marietta today. Of course, Beatrice would have whispered of Tommaso's wedding.

Fabrizio's low-pitched voice distracts her. He discusses the Doge Antonio Priuli with Nicolo Contarini and Leonardo Dandolo.

A LETTER ARRIVES
THE VENETIAN SECRET, 1620

Her husband wants to become the next Doge. But why can't he understand that he isn't of the right age? He is only 65, even if he looks older. Watching him talking and smiling, she remembers her own betrothal. It is not a memory that she treasures. She wants to push it to the back of her mind. It hurts to remember, even now, to think of his chilliness towards her. He always kept his distance, and sometimes she had cried herself to sleep. But Francesco's death had changed everything. She had fallen out of love with Fabrizio. Now she merely despises him and his soppy ways with Marietta.

"It is more than generous of you to have made Casino Morosini part of Beatrice's dowry. It is the most beautiful villa on Murano, a splendid retreat for delights and pleasures," Leonardo Dandolo says smilingly to Fabrizio.

Fabrizio nods, feeling a little sad at having parted with the small house. He has always loved the villa for its frescoes and lush gardens.

"Andrea looks forward to inviting his friends for literary evenings," Dandolo adds.

"Yes, it is an earthly paradise with such a particular sweetness of the air," Fabrizio replies distractedly. He prays that there is no truth in the rumour he has heard recently, that Andrea has a young nobleman as a lover. Only yesterday, ornamented and perfumed young nobles displaying their bare chests had paraded round the city. Sodomy attracts the wrath of God, he thinks.

"We expect Tommaso to be back in Venice in no more than a week," Contarini says, sounding delighted. "He might be here in time for Beatrice's wedding."

A LETTER ARRIVES
THE VENETIAN SECRET, 1620

At the mentioning of Tommaso, Fabrizio feels unhappy and turns towards his peer, forcing himself to smile.

"The Contarina returns with a valuable cargo of silk from our firm in Constantinople. Tommaso has become an invaluable tradesman, Fabrizio. I have made up my mind that of my four sons, he shall marry. Not an easy choice, you know, but I am convinced that the family's possessions will be safe in his hands. I've high hopes in Tommaso, and every possible trust."

Contarini sounds so solemn, Fabrizio thinks. Still, he wishes that he could talk like that of Domenico.

"Don't think that I am not aware, Fabrizio, of the love Tommaso had for Marietta for years," Contarini says a little ill at ease. "I pray that he has recovered from his infatuation with your lovely daughter, now that Marietta has become a nun. Do you know if she has ever heard from him?"

"Marietta doesn't confide in me these days," Fabrizio answers forlornly, "She can't forgive me."

"Forgive you what, Fabrizio?"

"For returning her to the convent."

"We haven't told Tommaso yet that he must marry Livia Loredan." Contarini continues seriously. "However, as soon as he arrives, I shall tell him. I will have to send him back to Constantinople, though, to take care of urgent business in our silk factory. The workers demand a considerable pay rise. I trust Tommaso to deal with it. He won't return till the end of December. When will Domenico marry, Fabrizio?"

"I don't know. We haven't decided anything yet. I hope he will settle down to his duties soon because he will be twenty-five

A LETTER ARRIVES
THE VENETIAN SECRET, 1620

in a month, like Tommaso. In fact, there is something I've wanted to ask you for some time," Fabrizio continues hesitantly. "Is it possible to buy a post for Domenico as a bowman on the Contarina? I want to get him out of Venice for a while."

It is Fabrizio's hope that Contarini hasn't heard too much of Domenico's vile behaviour. Domenico risks getting arrested, even banishment from Venice, even though he is a noble. Fabrizio is aware that his son has been kissing and pawing at young girls in church, breaking up betrothal parties and extorting money. Fabrizio also knows that his chances of being elected Doge will diminish considerably if Domenico doesn't mend his ways. He blames himself for allowing Manuela to spoil Domenico. But she had been devastated when Francesco died, and Domenico became her darling.

"Perhaps a sea voyage could improve Domenico's understanding of his duties."

"Of course, Fabrizio, Domenico shall be welcome on board the Contarina."

Suddenly Fabrizio becomes aware that someone is standing behind his chair, calling his name in a low voice. He turns around, and there is Maria pointing a letter at him.

"Please, Signor Morosini," she says nervously, "could you read this letter from Marietta right away?"

"Maria, how you startled me. Is anything the matter?" Fabrizio's hands tremble as he reaches for the letter.

"No, no, Signor Morosini, don't be alarmed. Marietta is fine." Maria smiles nervously.

Fabrizio gets up from his chair abruptly, almost knocking it over, making excuses to Dandolo and Contarini, ushering Maria out through the doors and into his study.

Fabrizio breaks the Morosini seal and tears the letter open:

San Zaccaria, March 1620

Illustrissimo Father,

Can you imagine my sadness today seeing my sister in her wedding dress? I missed Ca'Morosini more than ever, and I thought, as I often do, of the painting of Rosalba and our games of chess. The hours we spent together in your study are my most treasured memory. Now I ask you to give me the painting of Rosalba to keep in my cell as a memory of those happy times. No one will miss it, covered as it is in cobwebs, forgotten by everybody. You just have to tell Maria if the painting is still in the portego, and she will bring it here tonight.

You must know that I was told today that Tommaso is going to marry Livia Loredan. Bearing my grief in mind at this news, I have no doubt that you will grant me my wish. I have one more thing to ask of you. I miss Fini. It would be a great comfort to me, as well as to the twins, to have our old dog here. Can Maria bring him with her tonight?

Your obedient daughter,
Marietta Morosini

"Do you have any idea, Maria, why Marietta wants the painting

A LETTER ARRIVES
THE VENETIAN SECRET, 1620

so badly? She says it is for the fond memories she has of it. Still
I find it strange." Fabrizio is concerned. What is it that Marietta
has remembered about this long forgotten painting?

"No, Signore, I don't know. Marietta never said why she wanted
it."

"Take the painting," he says reluctantly. No doubt, Fantina's
stories have left an impression on Marietta. Didn't his old aunt
always claim that the painting contained a secret? He wonders if
his daughter knows about Rosalba and her destiny. But he realises
that he has no choice but to give in to his daughter's wish. "It is
still in the portego. And take Fini too, Maria," he says hurriedly,
much troubled at Marietta's wish to summon up Rosalba.

Domenico notices Maria at once. What is she doing here? Talking
to his father? He is mystified when they disappear through the
door together. Why would Maria be at the house, if not on an
errand for Marietta? He becomes curious. What is Marietta up
to?

He is bored sitting at the table having to come up with plausible
answers to all kinds of questions from Giorgio Grimani. He
decides to find out what is going on. He makes an excuse to
Grimani, leaves his chair, and follows Maria at a distance down
the stairs to the portego. Why would she disappear into the
furthest corner of the portego? Slowly he creeps up behind her
and grabs hold of her arm. With the other hand he deftly muffles
Maria's cry as he pushes her up against the wall.

"What are you and my dear sister up to this time, darling Maria?"
Domenico squeezes her arm roughly, feeling his finger sink into
her soft flesh.

A LETTER ARRIVES
THE VENETIAN SECRET, 1620

"Let go of me, you hurt me!" Maria shouts and spits in his face when he removes his hand from her mouth. "I have your father's permission to be here."

Blind with rage, Domenico rips the front of her dress open and gropes for her breasts with one hand while the other holds her firmly. She kicks him, and he feels the intense pain when she bites his hand. Maria tears herself loose and runs towards the gates, trying to gather her torn clothes in one hand. Domenico catches up with her and takes hold of her shoulder. He hears the sound of running feet behind him, and turns around still clutching Maria. He is surprised to see an Arsenalotto coming towards him followed by Fini, who yelps maddeningly.

"Take care, Arrigo," Maria cries, "he carries a knife!"

Domenico's hand snatches the glass stiletto from his belt. He strikes angrily at the Arsenalotto and watches how Arrigo's sleeve turns from the purest white to crimson red. Domenico laughs when Arrigo lets out a cry of pain and clutches at his arm while the blood trickles onto the floor.

"Next time I won't let you off so easily. Intruders I usually hand over to the Council of Ten, or to my dogs." Domenico bows mockingly to Arrigo, and wipes the stiletto in a handkerchief that he crumbles into a ball. He throws it at Maria's face before he turns his back on them and walks towards the stairs, still laughing.

"What a coward. I never expected that I had to be armed picking up a painting and an old dog," he smiles wryly at Maria.

Maria tears off his sleeve making a bandage of it. "Thank God, it is only a flesh wound."

A LETTER ARRIVES
THE VENETIAN SECRET, 1620

Maria hurries to the end of the portego and finds the old door. The painting is there, covered in dust. She carries it to the landing. It is large, but no bigger than Maria can manage, and with the help of Arrigo's sound arm they get it into the boat. She glances at the painting mystified, wondering why Marietta finds it so very important.

She picks up the old dog. It licks her face and seems happy to see her.

"Hopefully Fini won't mind living a religious life," she says smiling at Arrigo when they are ready to go. They pull at the oars, moving slowly through the dark canals. "I rowed with my brothers as a child," Maria says. "If it hadn't been for you, Domenico would have killed me."

"Yes, he is a madman. I heard that he carried a woman out of a gondola a few days ago and threw her husband into the water," Arrigo says.

Together they manipulate the boat through the turns and twists of the canals, finally arriving at the Riva.

"I'll meet you tomorrow in the piazzetta. I pray that your arm will be better by then." She kisses him several times on both cheeks. "See you at noon." Maria steps onto the landing stage and lifts the painting carefully from the boat onto the Riva. Arrigo hands her the small dog, and Maria puts it on a leash.

Fini yelps at the few passers by as they cross the Riva walking towards San Zaccaria. The frame makes the painting heavy and, out of breath, Maria arrives at the gate.

"It is me, Maria Columbin," she calls. "Open up."

The gate opens. Sister Pax stares at the painting that Maria has

A LETTER ARRIVES
THE VENETIAN SECRET, 1620

wrapped in a sheet of old cloth from the portego. The small dog is biting at the hem of the nun's habit. Fini is having great fun, Maria thinks. She sets the painting down beside her, finds Marietta's ducat in her purse, and hands it to Sister Pax. The old nun takes the gold coin without a word and slips it in the pocket of her habit. Maria studies her in the light from the lantern. Sister Pax has a mean face, she thinks, like a prison warder's, or someone who is accustomed to have power over others – who thrives on it. Her habit is merely a cloak of cunning.

Maria stoops to pick up the painting. She pushes past Sister Pax, dragging Fini behind her, up the staircase to Marietta's cell.

Maria likes the atmosphere of the convent at this hour of the night because she imagines that sleep has smoothed away the lines of sadness and discontent from the young choir nuns' faces.

She knocks carefully at Marietta's door before turning the handle. The candles in the silver candelabra are alight and Marietta and the three small girls wide awake, waiting. Maria lets Fini run to the bed where the girls shower him with kisses. Marietta hugs Maria briefly and rushes to uncover the painting, placing it up against the wall. She takes one of the candelabras and holds it close to the golden frame.

"That's Rosalba!" she exclaims while her fingers lovingly follow Rosalba's contours on the canvas. They stand silently in front of the painting studying the enigmatic girl in the glow from the candles.

"Oh, thank you Maria. The painting might save my life. My old aunt always said so!" Maria can't see how, but she doesn't say

A LETTER ARRIVES
THE VENETIAN SECRET, 1620

anything. She leaves Marietta to contemplate Rosalba and the man in black.

*　*　*

I go over the painting once again. Rosalba appears as sad and beautiful as I remember her in my father's studio. Why does she gaze at the beholder instead of concentrating on the game of chess? And why does she point to the black king? I turn the painting around and study the back of the canvas. I read the tiny letters which spell 'Rosalba', recalling my father and his words about adding up all the details in a painting to get at the meaning. Beneath 'Rosalba', I distinguish the miniature letters of 'p' and 'c' written in pale red, but they don't mean anything to me.

This painter has a magic touch. The way he masters draperies and transparent shadows, and his use of brilliant colours is elegant and rare. Such refined brush work! I am enthralled by the man in black with the grim face, severe eyes, and unsmiling mouth. He plays the black pieces. In his right hand he clasps the white knight tightly, so tightly that his hand is drained of blood.

I give up. I am tired out and go to lie down beside the sleeping girls and Fini. When I fall asleep, I dream of Rosalba. I see Rosalba beckon at me to enter the painting. I rise from the bed to follow her invitation. I go over to the canvas, take yet another step, and find myself in the luxurious room of the painting. I stand beside the chair with the beautiful girl in red. Rosalba points to the paintings on the wall behind the man in black and smiles sadly at me. She gets up from her chair by the chessboard and takes my

A LETTER ARRIVES

hand, leading me across the room to the wall where the paintings are. Six in a row.

Rosalba stops in front of the first painting. I recognise the crypt with the tessellated floor underneath the chapel and the mosaics in a circle depicting imaginary animals. I see the man at the chessboard has turned around, scowling at us. He waves his fist at us, dropping the white knight on the floor. It turns into a white horse that Rosalba and I mount. In the night, we gallop swiftly through the narrow streets of Venice, where naked women lay drunk, smothered in acid vapours, reeking, and I cling to Rosalba's red dress. The horse gallops across the piazza, stops abruptly, and rears in front of the Ducal Palace. Rosalba kicks its flanks with her heels, and it prances up the stairs into the hall of the Council of Ten.

All ten members are present, but none of them seem to notice either the white horse, with its neck darkened with sweat and nostrils flaring or the two women. Rosalba turns her head to smile at me and points to the wooden ceiling decorated with canvasses framed in gold. I know the pictures that celebrate the glories and triumphs of Venice, the goddess Juno showering gifts on the city and Jupiter hurling thunderbolts. Rosalba's face is everywhere in the paintings. In the face of Juno, Jupiter and even the reclining girl beside the old man wearing a turban. I feel dizzy and the room begins to spin. Suddenly Juno and Jupiter are descending on me like angels from the sky. I let out a cry of terror.

Fini growls and I sit up in bed, gasping for breath. Now I recall the name of the painter! Paolo Cagliari, the Veronese. My father

A LETTER ARRIVES
THE VENETIAN SECRET, 1620

had taken me as a child to the Halls of the Great Council and the Council of Ten. There I had seen the paintings on the ceiling, which Rosalba showed me tonight.

Paolo Veronese. He painted The Chessplayers. I light my candle and get out of bed, kneeling in front of the painting. Yes, that is the crypt at San Zaccaria in one of the small paintings on the wall behind the man in black, just as Rosalba pointed out to me in the dream. I will go to the crypt in the morning after Matins when the chapel is empty, and I have everything to myself.

A LETTER ARRIVES

THE VENETIAN SECRET, 1620

Fabrizio Morosini, 1620, Ca' Morosini, Venice

8.

Rosalba

A faint knock on the door to my cell wakes me up. The three girls beside me are still sound asleep.

"Marietta!" Sister Agnese calls out in her crisp voice.

"Agnese! The bells have not tolled dawn yet."

She must be the oldest nun there is, I think. I have lost count of Agnese's age, but she must be 106 at least. She is still sound of mind, but so small and shrunken that she seems out of this world.

Sister Agnese stands in the doorway leaning on her stick and holding the twins' prayer books in one hand.

"They left them in the schoolroom. And it isn't the first time," Sister Agnese croaks. "My eyes are still as sharp as they ever were, thanks be to the Almighty God," she continues, placing the books on a chest. "The boarding girls leave everything lying about," she complains, but stops short when she notices the painting. She gropes for the glasses in the pocket of her habit, puts them on, staring at Veronese's work without saying another word.

She pulls the footstool in front of the canvas, and sits down.

"God be praised for all He does!" Agnese exclaims. "To think that I should see Rosalba Morosini again this side of the grave!"

ROSALBA
THE VENETIAN SECRET, 1620

"You knew her?"

"Of course I knew her! How could I not?" Agnese yelps. "She was a choir nun here for a short time, and my favourite too. A gentle soul and beautiful, like the Madonna. I used to think that she was an angel sent by God to help us."

"When was that?" I say, getting impatient. "What happened to her?"

"Wait a moment, child. I have to go back a good many years and, unfortunately, my memory is not as sharp as my eyes. But I do remember that it was on the first of May 1572 that Rosalba came to this convent: The Pope died on that very same day. Rosalba: your great aunt. Don't think I didn't know." Agnese nods her head slowly several times. "Yes, the sister of your father's grandmother. I never mentioned her to you, Marietta, because it was a great scandal to your family and the convent. Hushed up at the time. Can you imagine, an escaped nun! The disgrace. The Magistrates were here to question everyone. Even the Patriarch came. We sounded the alarm when Rosalba was missing; the bells were chiming for hours. Everyone in Venice knows what that means," Agnese pauses, peering at me above the thick lenses.

"Many have wanted to, but few have had the courage to go against Christ. In my time, only Rosalba and two others have disappeared from our convent." Agnese stares very hard at me now. "Alas, my girl, where to go? And how to survive in a world that is quite unknown to us. Just think of the agony of the soul! I have often asked myself what happened to Rosalba. I pray that she doesn't suffer God's punishment and is not tormented in the Abyss for her sins! I have prayed for her over the years. You remind me of her. Look at the painting, my dear. Can you see how much you resemble her? Only you haven't got her angelic expression," Agnese sighs.

"I thought that maybe you knew what had become of her?" I am disappointed.

Agnese ignores my question and asks: "How did you come across the painting?"

"It is a present from my father. Maria brought it yesterday from Ca'Morosini."

"How very odd that he should give you that painting, Marietta."

"Please, Agnese, do tell me everything you know!"

"Rosalba was meant to be married," Agnese continues, making sure the girls are still asleep. "It was then discovered that she had a love affair with someone else. Or at least, so the rumour goes. I never spoke to her about it and she never told me anything. You cannot imagine her beauty, my dear. Not even this painting does her justice. I have never seen anyone so beautiful in the hundred years I have been here, serving Almighty God. He does indeed move in mysterious ways.

During the few months she lived here, I often found her sitting under the orange flower tree in the orchard crying. I tried to comfort her and pray with her, but she became more and more remote and sad with the passing of time. Her father sent her here because her betrothal was annulled. That much I do know. The Abbess, and most of the choir nuns, voted in favour of accepting Rosalba. Her father paid for the wooden chairs with the beautiful carvings in the choir and donated a substantial sum of money to the convent."

"What happened on the day she disappeared, Agnese?"

"I always kept a look out for her, and when I didn't see her at

Matins or in the refectory for breakfast, I told the Abbess. The Abbess went looking in her cell and found her white habit and veil lying on the floor, trampled on and torn to pieces. We searched the church and convent but found not a trace of Rosalba."

"Is that really all you know?"

"That was rich pickings for the gossips who claimed that the Medici family helped her escape. But you know the gossips," Agnese says severely. "I never understood how Rosalba got away. The gates were locked and the gatekeepers there. They were questioned by the Magistrates and the Patriarch, and they swore that Rosalba never passed through the gates of San Zaccaria. You know, child, I sometimes fear that the devil himself took possession of Rosalba's soul and turned her into a witch. Perhaps that was how she escaped. Flying across our high brick wall, an agent of the devil, to turn others against God! My poor angel!" Agnese hides her face in her hands and cries. "The memories, Marietta," the old woman says between tears, "are more than I can bear."

When Agnese has closed the door behind her, I stay in bed studying the colours on the canvas. The dragon red of the dress glows, gold shines in the blond hair and the deep blue of the sapphires in Rosalba's bracelet sparkle. The colours seem vibrant against the shades of grey and white used to depict the six paintings hanging in the room behind the man in black. What do they represent? One really does show the crypt beneath the church, where the relics used to be. Another shows the white stone altar with the angel. Looking carefully, I clearly distinguish the mosaics which form the circle of animals. One of the paintings shows a dark passage. But I can't be sure. I tear myself loose from the picture. I wash quickly, splashing water from the bowl over my face. When I open the small window in my cell, I sense a mildness in the air, which seems to carry with it a scent of hope. Only a week from now and it will be the first day of April. The date predicted for Tommaso's return to Venice.

ROSALBA
THE VENETIAN SECRET, 1620

9.

A Ship on the Horizon

Maria is breathless from running.

"Marietta! The Contarina has arrived!" Maria has to stand still to catch her breath. Then she stumbles to the ground beside me on the grass in the orchard.

"And …Tommaso?" I suddenly have difficulties pronouncing the name.

"Don't worry, Marietta. He is in good health and unharmed. He whispered to me that you must be in the parlatorio after Vespers today".

"Was he much changed, Maria?"

"Only more handsome than ever, and gentle as of old," Maria says reassuringly.

"I only saw him for one brief moment. He had just embarked on the Riva, which was thronged with people cheering the galley. He caught my eye at once, even though I was constantly pushed about in the crowd like a small helpless animal."

"Oh, how to wait till after Vespers, Maria?"

"You have waited for so long. A few more hours will make no difference."

* * *

I spend the time until Vespers writing in my cell.

A SHIP IN THE HORIZON
THE VENETIAN SECRET, 1620

"My sisters will become nuns because I want to be rich!" I write in my new notebook, remembering how Domenico repeated this sentence as often as he could to anyone who cared to listen. It infuriated me as a small girl, and always made me apprehensive in case it might be true. I asked my father if there was any truth in what Domenico said, and he answered evasively. "It is quite natural that Domenico should want to be rich. The desire to grow rich is as normal to the nobles of Venice as the desire to live."

"But can't boys and girls share the riches?" I asked him, wondering that there should be this difference. "Don't girls want to be rich?"

My father had smiled and said that there was no need as girls were taken good care of, either by their husbands or in a convent.

If Tommaso lets me down and marries the Loredan girl, I won't stay. Why would he choose her?

Why do people choose each other? I won't live the life many of the others do. They always blame their fate; plot their escape, building castles in the air, not wanting to die in this prison. They never do anything. But not me. I shall find a way out, if it is the last thing I do.

I will marry someone and have children. Or become a prostitute. I don't care. Perhaps a courtesan in Florence or Milan, or an actress. There are lots of travelling troupes. Tommaso will soon see that I can take care of myself. They won't keep me behind locked doors for much longer.

To know that he once loved me, and that I would never see him again, would be more than I could bear. Every day to know that he was with someone else would be a deadly grief.

A SHIP IN THE HORIZON
THE VENETIAN SECRET, 1620

I give up writing. I can't concentrate. I go to my cell to change. I can't decide which dress to wear and open a chest. There is the pretty dress I wore on the night of our pledge. The one made of green satin with flowers in gold. The silk stockings and the embroidered velvet slippers are there too. I pick up the white lace handkerchiefs that we used to wipe off the blood, sealing our pledge when the two bloods mingled.

As soon as Vespers is over I am in the parlatorio. Tonight the big hall is full of visitors; I go to the furthest end, which is still empty, to sit as close to the grates as I possibly can. I watch the door to the parlatorio open. Tommaso is in the doorway looking for me. As he comes towards me, I size him up in a second. He smiles at me with such tenderness that I nearly jump for joy. His face is exactly as I remember it, refined, only more weather-beaten. His black hair is much longer, reaching for the shoulders; it covers his high brow and makes it hard to discern his eyes. A white scar, the shape of a small crescent on his pointed chin, is new.

Tommaso sits down in front of me. He takes my hands through the narrow openings in the grates and presses a small object into my palm.

"Keep your hand closed till I have left," Tommaso says looking serious.

"I can't stay long, no matter how much I want to, despite having thought about nothing but you for so long. You never left my thoughts. I often imagined that you walked beside me in Constantinople.

I am expected at Ca' Contarini in just a little while. I had to make up a story about going to fetch some papers off the ship. But I'll be back tomorrow. Early. Right after Matins."

His lips are warm against mine. Then he gets up and is gone.

Was he really here at all? The only thing that seems real is the fact that I hold something hard and smooth in my hand.

Someone is watching me. I feel it. I look around. Of course, Suzanna, Livia's cousin, is glaring at me. I keep my hand tightly closed. What will Suzanna make of Tommaso's visit, I wonder. Suzanna, with a vicious tongue that likes to stir things up, watching through her cold eyes, greedy for slander. Livia Loredan will probably know everything about his visit in no time.

I rise slowly from my chair, passing close by Suzanna. The next moment, I find myself lying on the floor. Suzanna stuck her foot out, tripping me on purpose!

My hand is empty and my hip aches. My eyes search the ground— and there, on the floor just in front of me, is Tommaso's gift. I grasp it just as Suzanna's boot hits my hand. I pull my hand away and get up, hardly able to see, my anger blinding me as if a fog suddenly clouds my vision.

"Get out of my way," my voice comes out in angry bursts as I thrust Suzanna away from me.

"Don't think I didn't see!" Suzanna shouts. "Just you wait, you stuck-up Morosini!"

When I am alone in the cloister, I open my hand. The diamonds sparkle in the light from the oil lamps. The Ricordino! The Contarini betrothal ring! He never ceased to love me.

A SHIP IN THE HORIZON
THE VENETIAN SECRET, 1620

10.

A Passing Shadow

I can't sleep. I keep thinking of Tommaso. One green eye and one brown. I know no one else who has eyes like that. His eyes fascinated me as a small girl and I used to imagine that the green eye was the colour of the seas his father wanted him to sail, and the brown I found impenetrable, hiding from the world his most secret desires and his love for me.

I touch the ring on my finger, and feel the gold and finely set gems. I know that the ring has been in Tommaso's family for generations, as the most important heirloom. What will happen when the Contarinis notice it is gone? I toss and turn in bed beside the girls. All I want is to be with Tommaso. My whole being cries out for him. My heart beats too fast and I feel a nervous flutter in my breast. To have seen him so briefly after years of longing is devastating. I think of the painting and wonder if it is true that it can help us, as Fantina claimed. I will to go the crypt this very moment. It is a perfect time because the chapel will be empty at this hour.

I pick up my green silk dress from the floor, slip it on, and put on my black velvet mantle. I take the candle and tip toe into the corridor. I hurry down the stairs into the chapel and descend the few stony steps to the crypt. As on most days the crypt is flooded, water is seeping in everywhere, and the low vaults and columns reflect in the water. The reflection of the vaults looks like empty boats: gondolas waiting to carry you off across a still sea of mirages. A beautiful sight.

The water permeates my silken slippers. My stockings are soaked, the mantle and skirt of the dress too. I am in water up to my calves and the smell from the clammy walls makes me cough. The mirages dissolve as I move slowly through the water. I go from one vault to the other, lifting the candle to hold it close to the walls. It is hard to distinguish anything clearly for everything is immersed in the dark. I have only the single flame for a guide.

Is it the eight Doges' breathing I can hear? It sounds as if their quiet respiration seeps like water through the sarcophagi. I force myself to turn my back on the graves and look at the white stone angel on the altar in front of me.

I study the floor through the water and move into the apse of what was once the old church. The circle with the animals must be right beneath me. The two strange deer-like animals in black and white squares are on my left. This may be the spot Rosalba pointed to in her dream. But it is impossible to be sure. I can't see anything clearly due to the water. I feel disappointment in my throat like a hard lump. I had really hoped to find something, believed that Rosalba's secret would be revealed to me. But no, I have to examine the crypt by daylight.

I know that light from the large windows in the chapel finds its way down here. When the tide isn't in like tonight, I will be able to study the floor. What if I didn't get Rosalba's sign right?

A PASSING SHADOW
THE VENETIAN SECRET, 1620

What if she had actually pointed to the sarcophagi, and Rosalba's secret is entombed with the doges?

I decide to return the next day, hoping the water will have receded. I drag my wet dress through the water towards the staircase to the chapel.

My heart almost comes to a stop. At the top of the stairs, my way is blocked. A silent, black figure looms large in front of me. His gown reaches the floor and most of his face is hidden by the hood.

But I know who he is. There is no mistaking the hawk's nose, the fleshy lips.

"I can't say how surprised and dismayed I am to find you here, Sister Cynthia," the confessor, Orsolo Lupi, says. I search my mind for a plausible explanation.

"My sisters forgot their prayer books," I say quickly, thinking I'll just have to stand my ground. He is the kind of man who will know weakness, and how to take advantage of it.

"It is far too late to walk in the chapel on your own. The night bell sounded a while ago. You should be nowhere but in your cell."

"That may be." I stare hard at the black figure in front of me. He looks like a bird of prey, I think, which, spreading its wings, shrouds everything in darkness. How I despise him. I take a step forward hoping that he will step aside, but he doesn't move.

"Excuse me," I say as sharply as I can, and find myself so close to him that I can smell the wine on his breath. I have to take a step back down the staircase. Lupi seems to loom even larger standing above me, staring down at me.

A PASSING SHADOW
THE VENETIAN SECRET, 1620

"I see that you are not dressed according to the rules. Your dress is a scandalous colour. God will punish you for wearing it." Lupi's face is contorted. I remain silent. "If you fall ill, it is not due to your wet clothes, but a sign from Him that your diseased soul has infected your body. Mortal sins cause mortal disease!"

* * *

What was the girl up to in the crypt, Lupi wonders angrily. Something she doesn't want others to find out about. He realizes that he hardly knows anything about this girl. About most of the others he does. Their secrets are his treasure. All their thoughts, all their longings, all their weaknesses, they have let him have in the confessional.

Even if he can't discover why she is here, the situation alone can be turned into something valuable. Intimidation and accusation – he knows what works. He will smoke her out, as they do with the rats. He continues in a low voice:"Tell me why I have hardly seen you in the confessional since I first came here? Only once have you confessed your sins. And as far as I recall the sins that you confessed didn't amount to much. You must be close to sainthood having that little to confess?"

"To be honest, Orsolo Lupi, because I do not trust you."

He senses how the girl tries to keep her fury under control, but her voice comes out in a rush of malice. Lupi knows she has a desire to just push past him. She probably knows the punishments he can sanction, but how much does he dare to do. She's a Morosini, even if she has lost her freedom. His lineage is not noble like hers. His name was never in the Golden Book. He is put off a

A PASSING SHADOW
THE VENETIAN SECRET, 1620

little by her answer, but keeps his unwavering eyes on her face.

"I have watched you in chapel. You neither incline your head, nor make the reverend gestures. It is your duty to be confess and be relieved of your sins at the beginning of every month.

I will inform the Patriarch if you keep away. The rules of this order are sanctified, and to go against them is to challenge the devil himself."

He watches the nun's face. She is holding back, he can see that. He continues, waiting to see how far she will take this.

"I expect to see you in my confessional before the week is up. I'll make sure that we have plenty of time. I will, of course, have to report your strange behaviour to the Madri di Consiglione, the Abbess' closest advisers."

"Father, I offer to do the reporting of this incident myself. That will save you the trouble. You don't have to waste your valuable time more needed to save souls. I'm well acquainted with such procedures since my family employed several priests at Ca'Morosini. What would you want me to put in my report as the reason for your being here at this time, Father –are there new hours for your confessionals? I think it's late for both of us don't you?"

Without another word, Orsolo Lupi stands aside and the girl walks past him. He is furious, scared by her words and threats. To have to take that from a mere woman, and a girl of nineteen at that. Something will have to be done, he swears. He'll find a way to deal with her.

A PASSING SHADOW
THE VENETIAN SECRET, 1620

11.

Silent Cries

I lie down beside the girls. I watch the flame of the candle burning brightly, never wavering and not once flickering in the dark. Will we escape? Nuns have been caught before and imprisoned. But I must try not to anticipate the future in terms of the past.

My sister's marriage is recorded in the Golden Book. Mine and Tommaso's will never be. Beatrice's sons will grow up in Venice. Ours won't. They will probably never even see Venice. When I watched the women among Beatrice's wedding guests in the parlatorio, I felt I was looking at shadows of persons I might have been, or lives I might have lived. How does it feel not to love your own child, I wonder, the image of my mother's hateful expression before my eyes.

During the first few months I was back at San Zaccaria, I had a distorted sense of reality. I kept praying that my parents would change their minds. I even tried pleading with my mother.

"Why would you prefer married life to life in a convent?" my mother snapped. "What is so attractive about being married to a nobleman, living in his house, having to put up with his brothers in all kinds of ways, dealing with the affairs of his house and attending never ending ceremonies? When you are a nun you don't risk your life giving birth and won't have to suffer the grief of losing a child."

My mother never had to grapple with the possibility of becoming a nun being the only daughter. Her life is so full of trivialities. She wakes up late, drinks chocolate in bed, sits at the toilette for hours and then gets dressed with the help of her maids. She spends the time before dinner with her pet dog, reclining in the soft cushions of a couch. After dinner, she returns to the looking-glass, admiring her figure, fan, mouth, and eyes.

My mother goes into studied hysterics if anything does not go her way. We were brought up as if we were creatures devoid of thought and feeling. It never mattered to her if we got beyond the first letters of the alphabet. When she caught me with a pen in hand, she tore it away from me as she tore my life away from me on the day I was sent to the convent.

I walked beside my mother and father to the church of San Zaccaria, relatives and all the important nobles following. I wore the traditional long white silk dress for the ceremony. On my head was the crown of virginity, roses and violets. The church was crammed. Walking down the aisle everyone looked at me like a lamb going to the slaughter. Someone cried out, "What a pretty bride for God!" A young man sitting close to the aisle shouted, "What a waste! Such a lovely girl! A beautiful nun is always a tragedy." The old man beside him croaked, "She will end up as prey for some priest!"

Tommaso had been in the church and I felt his eyes resting on me. Lying on the church floor, my lips had touched the cold stones;

a black cloth was thrown over me and lighted candles placed at my feet and at my head. The litanies were sung, everything suggesting that I was dead. I felt like a witness to my own funeral. I cried silently under the black cloth. The priest told me to rise from the floor and kneel at the high altar. There I was sprinkled with holy water. My outer clothes were removed and Francesca Grimani cut off my beautiful long hair. I was dressed in my nun's robes and my face veiled. The heavy oaken doors swung open and the Abbess and choir nuns came to claim me.

"You belong with us now," the Abbess whispered in my ear.

"Our daughter has caused a great deal of worry, Reverend Mother. We are happy that she is safe now, away from the temptations of this world," I heard my mother saying to the Abbess, Francesca Grimani in the parlatorio afterwards.

In vain, I had hoped for mercy and understanding. I had begged Paolo Gritti to help me, but his letter made me give up: "Marriage preserves the decorum of society.

But if one looks closely, one will find more thorns than roses, more reason for despair than happiness." And so on and so on. It seems that only Rosalba can help us now.

SILENT CRIES
THE VENETIAN SECRET, 1620

12.

Tommaso

The moment I enter, I see him sitting on the edge of a chair by the grate, his body betraying the familiar restlessness. At the sound of the door slamming, he turns his head quickly and smiles at me. As I hurry towards him and the frills of my silk gown make little rustling sounds like whispers and sighs, pushing me forward. I feel confident and glowing, restored to love, no longer condemned to a life in the shadows.

His silhouette looks hazy in the early morning light. Broad at the shoulders, narrow at the waist. Coming close I distinguish the fine features, the singular expression of one green and one brown eye, and the pointed nose. I sit down on the chair, my heart pounding. I am afraid to touch him, lest he should dissolve like a dream and disappear like yesterday. He is so close that I can feel his warm breath on my face. His white shirt collar is open and I glimpse his smooth bare flesh. I remember that was how he looked standing by the oar in the gondola, wearing his black velvet breeches and wide sleeved shirt.

Tommaso takes my hand with the Ricordino, the beautiful betrothal ring, knitting my fingers through his own, pulling me closer. The sensation of the touch of his hand and lips, the sweet taste of his tongue, make me forget time and place.

"We'll go away," he whispers, his lips close to my ears now.

"A sea voyage with my father made up my mind long ago." Tommaso speaks urgently. "Did I ever tell you?"

"No, you haven't told me. Tell me now."

"When I was seven or eight years old, we returned from the Levant on a convict galley. Our own ship had to have repairs done to the main sails. I always felt sad for the lives of galley slaves. My father told me that three hundred men are condemned to the oar every year. One day, when my father was busy reading the charts, I decided to go to the benches. I wanted to understand what it meant being clapped in irons, chained to the bench, forced to follow the beat of the oars for hours on end. Without anybody noticing, I crept up to an old man, and slipped in between the oars. I sat down on the bench between his legs and leaned up against his gaunt body. He never uttered a word, just kept up the steadfast rhythm. I followed his movements as he bent forward and pulled the oars towards him. I knew the danger I exposed him to if he couldn't follow up. The foul odour of sweat and dirt made me vomit. I sensed his exhaustion and pain as the drum struck up the rhythm. I noticed a young boy in front of me falling behind. My pulse beat a little faster because I was aware of the consequence of this. The next moment a whip leapt across his back and blood trickled from the wound. An awesome blow. He never let out a sound, but just continued to row." Tommaso becomes silent for a moment, and draws in his breath sharply.

His words impress me. I feel respect towards him, as I know most people are living lies.

TOMMASO
THE VENETIAN SECRET, 1620

"But first, I must go back to Constantinople on the Contarina for a time," he says quietly before I can say a word.

"Tomorrow morning?"

He looks serious, yet sad also. Sadder than I have ever seen him.

"I often thought of the day you were consecrated. Seeing you in the church made me feel so lonely. What a relief it is to see your determined face now. There is something else." He continues in a low voice. "I must pretend to the world that I intend to marry Livia Loredan. She will be hurt when she realizes the truth, but it will be nothing but hurt pride. She doesn't care for me."

My face falls, and he lifts his hand a little to stop my words.

"Don't say anything. You know I have to. And I wouldn't leave tomorrow unless I thought I had to help my father one last time. He has hired a batch of new sailors and freemen. It seems our firm is in trouble and matters are grave. The workers left the looms over a squabble," Tommaso says as he caresses my hands. "Keep the ring a secret, Marietta. Hide it. I wish the jewels could reveal the things still to come."

I take the ring off and put it in the tiny pocket of my belt. Of course, I know he is right. I just got carried away.

"When will you be back, Tommaso?"

"By the end of December, at Carnival time."

"A painting might help us escape," I whisper, happy to share my hopes with him.

"A painting?" Tommaso looks bewildered.

"Yes, I am certain that my painting of Rosalba keeps a secret."

"Who is Rosalba?"

TOMMASO
THE VENETIAN SECRET, 1620

"My father's aunt. My father kept Paolo Veronese's painting in his studio when I was a small girl. As a young woman my great aunt was trapped in this convent till she found a way out."

"It is strange to hear you mention the name. You remember my childhood friend, Lorenzo Medici?" Tommaso says. "He is our guest at Ca'Bovolo Contarini right now. I have confided our plans in him and know, I can trust him. He has promised to take us safely to Bacchereto, the Medici's hunting lodge. Some time ago he told me that his grandmother's name was Rosalba – Maria Grazia Rosalba."

I have never heard that the Medici and the Morosinis were related. All I know is that the families were friends at the time Cosimo Medici was in exile in Venice. And that was two hundred years ago.

"Lorenzo said that everything concerning his grandmother's past was hushed up. You said 'trapped for a while.' How did she escape?"

"I don't know. Perhaps across the ice. If the lagoon freezes again, we can walk to the mainland. People have done so this winter."

"The ice is treacherous, Marietta. There are holes, and floes might be torn loose by strong undercurrents."

"But it is the easiest way to go, Tommaso, in spite of the danger. There will be danger no matter what we do. We have to take Giulia with us. She will die here. I have seen how she suffers and she is such a delicate and melancholy child. I couldn't abandon her."

"Giulia won't have to stay on here forever. Being my only sister she will marry one day."

"She won't last that long. Seven or eight years will have to pass before she marries. And only seldom do your parents come to see her. It hurts her so."

"But to take a child, and a timid one at that, will be immensely dangerous."

"I can't leave her behind. She dotes on me, Tommaso. And she loves you too."

He is silent for a moment before he says, "She can come if you think it right. But it will increase the risk. Don't forget there are other dangers. Domenico will be on the Contarina tomorrow morning. Our fathers have arranged for him to go with me to Constantinople as a bowman and to learn navigation. My father thinks that your father fears that Domenico will end up in prison or be banished from Venice if he stays."

Domenico on the Contarina. My brother who is capable of anything. "But how can you be sure he'll go?" I am terrified at the idea.

"Because," Tommaso explains, "your father has threatened to disinherit him otherwise. And your mother has agreed because she is afraid her pet will come to harm. I don't like him – nor his two black dogs, his evil spirits. I told him to leave them behind.

13.

Fears

I forgot to give Tommaso the heart shaped medallion with my portrait. I want him to wear it on this voyage. Maria must take it to Ca'Contarini tonight. In the cloister laughter, children shouting, and the sound of running feet take me by surprise. Five or six boarding girls are playing hide and seek, crying out in excitement. Francesca Grimani is hurrying towards them.

"Stop it!" The Abbess cries. "Return to your lessons immediately." But the girls don't pay attention.

"The way the girls behave!" she says to me in passing, turning her back on the girls. I watch Francesca Grimani's fat body disappear down the staircase and can't help but pity the ageing woman. She always feared confrontations.

At the end of the corridor, I discover a small pale child curled up, holding two dolls tightly in her arms. Giulia. When I reach her I stoop down and lift the child to her feet.

"Why is it not always daylight, Marietta?" Giulia asks sadly, looking up at me.

"So that we can sleep, Giulia."

"I'm afraid of the shadows of night," Giulia whispers, hardly audible staring hard at the marble floor.

"Why don't you play with the others?" I ask, stroking her hair, hugging her.

"Because there was something important I had to ask my parents," Giulia explains, hiding her face in my dress. "They have to consider what I said before they answer, my mother told me. I must wait here." Her voice is muffled because of the cloth of my dress.

"Do you want to tell me what you asked them?" I feel at a loss. I bend down and look at Giulia's troubled face.

"I asked them what I have done wrong."

"But, Giulia, you haven't done anything wrong. Whatever makes you think that?"

"I must have. Or they wouldn't have sent me away." Giulia looks at me as if she wonders why I don't understand something so obvious.

"Your parents have sent you here to learn all kind of things, like reading and singing. Not to punish you or because they think you have done something wrong," I say as gently as possible.

"I'll be back in a little while when I have found Maria." I wrap her cloak tighter around her.

I enter the bakery. Everything is in a frenzy. They are preparing for the grand dinner for the Doge on Easter Sunday. Maria waves at me from the other end of the kitchen. She's standing next to Elisabetta Corner and her clique. I make a sign to Maria to go into the storeroom.

"Domenico is sailing with the Contarina tomorrow." I watch the expression of liveliness disappear from Maria's face.

"Arrigo and Zannino are going too! To repair ships in Constantinople. Arrigo and Domenico will skin each other alive!"

FEARS
THE VENETIAN SECRET, 1620

"Tommaso will know how to handle Domenico, Maria, don't worry!" I hug her as I hugged Giulia just a moment before.

"Please, Maria," I say, "Could you give Tommaso this letter at Ca'Contarini tonight, and the medallion bearing my portrait, the one Adriana did last winter?" I hand Maria the little piece of jewellery dangling from the golden chain. "I want him to carry it as a lucky charm."

"The likeness is incredible, Marietta," Maria says, studying the portrait before she tucking it away in her apron.

As we step out of the storeroom Adriana hugs me, her arms covered in flour, and my yellow dress is spattered with white dust.

"The doctor has just arrived for the abbess," Adriana whispers.

"Francesca always pretends to be ill. I think she only wants the doctor to feel her body and touch her underneath her skirts."

Adriana's laughter is contagious. I wonder where my friend finds her reservoir of cheerfulness. Perhaps in her art, in painting, as I sometimes forget everything when I am writing.

"Lupi confiscated my drawings of the Seven Deadly Sins yesterday," Adriana says mockingly. " I saw him leave my cell. When I went in the drawings had gone. I had used priests as models for Gluttony, Vanity and all the rest. He must have seen me making the drawings in the orchard." She laughs again.

"Orsolo Lupi does what he wants in this convent."

"I know, Marietta, I realised that some time ago. He tried all kinds of tricks on me in the confessional yesterday, feigning sincerity."

"He is a parasite, Adriana. He nourishes himself by sucking the life out of others, extracting our secrets, and using his knowledge against us. His soul is as black as his robes."

FEARS
THE VENETIAN SECRET, 1620

"The Madonna will unveil him eventually and deliver him to damnation."

Adriana laughs again but stops short when she notices the ring on my finger. Sometimes I put it on for a little while and then forget to hide it away.

"There, you had nothing to worry about, Marietta. I knew Tommaso would never let you down." Adriana embraces me. A tender embrace. Loving and caring Adriana, I think, grateful that she exists, a light in the dark sea of faces.

Before returning to the library, I go by my cell to fetch my notebook. I stop in front of the painting of Rosalba. I can't believe what I see. Someone has slashed the canvas with a knife. There is a deep cut across the painting, right through the chessboard and Rosalba's red dress. I kneel down in front of it. The damage is serious; a small shred of canvas is torn off and on the floor. It is a fragment of the white pawns that are dressed like the nuns. I pick it up. Can I mend it by sewing everything together? I must save the painting. I look at the wall. Someone has scribbled in charcoal one of the rules of St Benedict: "To keep the possibility of death every day before our eyes".

14.
Letters of Importance

*P*iazza San Marco is crowded. The lagoon is a sea of colours, Maria thinks, with the painted sails of the fishing boats, orange and white, scarlet and blue. She stands still for a moment, gazing at the naked bronzed limbs of the seamen, before going past the vegetable stalls and second-hand book dealers.

She stops in front of a shop selling paintings of birds, fruits and animals. They appear more real than life. She would much rather have one of these than the big gloomy canvas Marietta is so crazy about. She continues towards the campanile past the money-changers' wooden stalls, thinking of Biancafiore, wishing she had the money to care for her. She hurries by the bakers' shops wondering why they are situated next to the reeking latrines and the decrepit hostelries.

In the calle towards Campo San Maurizio she stops again for just a brief moment to look into her favourite jewellery shop, gazing at shelves overflowing with glass beads, rubies and emeralds. She plucks up her courage and asks to try on a ring with blue and orange beads, admiring the look of her finger. Perhaps Arrigo will place a ring like this on her finger one day, she thinks returning it to the shop dealer.

The muddy streets are swarming with people now. An artisan pushes past her, and she smiles shyly at a few handsome Dalmatian soldiers who make way for her as she runs up the marble steps of the bridge. A Greek with hair the colour of ivory flashes a smile at her, and she returns it briefly, pushing past him. She hastens past some senators in scarlet robes and feels sorry for the haggard pale prostitute dragging herself along the walls.

She is in Calle di Mandola. In a few steps, she stands in front of Ca'Contarini del Bovolo. She hears music and the sound of voices trailing through the open windows. She looks up the winding staircase with the white marble balustrades. It looks like a huge conch, she thinks. The House of the Money Chests, she knows it is nicknamed, and wishes that Tommaso could bring one or two with him when the time comes for him and Marietta to leave.

She knocks on the wooden gate which is eventually opened by an old manservant. "Is Tommaso Contarini in?" she asks, a little out of breath.

The old man must be deaf, Maria decides, because she has to shout the words at him several times before he understands.

"I have an urgent message for Tommaso Contarini", she cries into his ear. Finally he understands and beckons her into the courtyard. "Wait by the two marble statues" he says and shuffles off.

She goes to stand beside the Madonna between lush plants and blue and yellow flowers.

She hears steps on the narrow staircase. There's Tommaso's face in the light from the torch.

"Hello Maria. I am glad to see your face again. I have thought of you often, grateful that you keep an eye on Marietta. "

"Thank you, Signor Contarini."

"Do you have a message for me?"

"Yes, I do. A letter from Marietta." She hands him the letter with the Morosini seal and the medallion.

"Thank you, Maria. You are the only one here we can trust."

"Signor Contarini, Marietta has told me that you set out tomorrow morning early for Constantinople," Maria says, feeling immensely shy.

"True, we set sail at sunrise."

"Please take care, Signore." Maria has to summon her courage. She has to warn him of Domenico.

"With Domenico Morosini on board I just thought you should know that he and Arrigo," she stops to breathe, "who is going too, are deadly enemies." Maria feels embarrassed talking like this about one nobleman to another. But surely Tommaso Contarini will understand.

"I promise to keep an eye on Domenico. And between us, Maria, I never liked him either."

"Don't turn your back on him, please Signor, ever."

It is dusk when she walks out the gate, and the contours of the city are fading away. Maria hates to walk the streets at night alone. She turns into the silence of the black narrow alleys towards the piazza, feeling apprehensive. She hurries along a canal, where a single oil lamp swings from a hook in front of a house, and she watches the shadows in the dark. No moonlight at all. Anything can happen under cover of the darkness.

She hears the sound of heels tapping against stone and realizes

LETTERS OF IMPORTANCE
THE VENETIAN SECRET, 1620

that someone running fast is coming straight towards her. The sound of a dress brushing against the ground makes her heart pound and she swiftly retreats into a doorway. In the faint light from the lamp, Maria distinguishes two figures: a man in a long cloak following a young woman. Before Maria has the time to say an Ave Maria, the man has embraced the woman. It looks quite peaceful, she thinks, but then she hears the woman let out a long sigh and fall to the ground. The next moment, the woman's body is floating in the canal. She watches the masked man standing still a moment before turning around and hurrying close past her. Maria holds her breath. No, he doesn't notice her. She catches a glimpse of his face as he passes realising it is a face she knows well. No mistaking the scar on the cheek.

Maria remains in the doorway waiting for her heartbeat to quieten. She takes a few steps towards the brink of the canal to get a better look at the floating body. The locks of hair, like seaweed in the foul canal. She quickly turns her back on the body, weeping, unable to stand the sight. She notices the handsome hair-brooch with the jewellery which she has seen many times before. It is the body of Nicola da Mula, the boarding-girl who left San Zaccaria to be married only two months ago.

On the edge of the Fondamenta are two crumbled pieces of paper which the murderer must have dropped and she bends down to pick them up. The letters carry a seal and are stained and covered in greasy fingerprints. Maria looks around her in all directions, before putting them into her pocket, but the calle is still empty. Then she runs for the piazza.

Maria is through the gates and up the stairs, nearly swept off her feet by the smell of food in the corridor. The Corner clique dining in one of the cells. The door is ajar, and Elisabetta's voice penetrates the silence.

"You know what happened to young Lucia Loredan today?" Elisabetta has lowered her voice to a confidential whisper. Maria moves closer to the door.

"When Father Lupi was taking confessions, he thrust his organ through the curtain and sprayed his semen all over the girl!"

Serves him right that Marietta put him in his place that night in the crypt. Last week, when he thought himself alone, she had seen him in the chapel with his hands all over the Madonna's white marble breasts.

Maria quietly slips into Marietta's cell and sits down on the bed beside her friend. She takes the sullied letters from her pocket.

"Where did you find them, Maria?" She can see how mystified Marietta is at the sight of the crumbled sheets of paper.

"I found them on the Fondamenta. Pietro Mudazzo must have dropped them. He is a foundling my aunt Lucretia wetnursed years ago. And a murderer too. Tonight I saw him kill poor pretty Nicola da Mula with a knife. He pushed her into the canal." Maria feels like vomiting.

"Nicola da Mula, the boarding-girl who left to get married a little while ago?" Marietta is as incredulous as Maria

"The very same."

Marietta opens the letter Maria hands her, reading aloud in a low voice:

1619, 13th January

LETTERS OF IMPORTANCE
THE VENETIAN SECRET, 1620

To the most illustrious and most honoured lords, my masters, Presidents of the Ten.

Your faithful servant, Pietro Mudazzo, offers my services to you, most honoured lords. I can kill all the enemies of our state in the most secret manner possible. I use both slow and rapid poisons.

In particular I use a poison which I myself have invented with the help from a famous poison brewer. He has distilled a liquid expressed from the spleen, buboes and carbuncles of the plague-stricken. Therefore my proposal to you, my masters, is as follows:

On the success of my experiment to kill any person your Lordships wish me to, I shall receive five hundred ducats a year for life. If the noble lords wish me to operate on the persons mentioned, the annuity shall be raised. For the Grand Turk, 500 ducats; for the King of Spain (exclusive of travelling expenses) 150 ducats; for the Duke of Milan, 60 ducats; for the Marquis of Mantua, 50 ducats; for his Holiness, only 100 ducats. As a rule, the longer the journey and the more valuable the life, the higher the price will be.

Your true servant,
Pietro Mudazzo

1620, 4th March
To Pietro Mudazzo, true servant of the Republic.

The Presidents of the Council of Ten have received your letter of the 13th January 1619. We have considered and accepted your proposal.

"Do the Ten employ poisoners?" Maria is stupefied.

"If the letters are real they must be among the most secret papers."

"Can it be true that the Ten answered Pietro's letter? It seems odd." Maria is nervous and wishes she had left the letters alone. "What to do with them?"

"We would be accused of treason if we mentioned the letters to anyone," Marietta says.

"I'll keep them hidden away," she adds to Maria's immense relief. "I'll find a safe place for them. Who knows? They might prove useful one day."

"But Nicola's murderer, Marietta?"

"We can't denounce Pietro to the Ten considering the letters and the fact that they employ him. They might claim that the letters are nothing but forgeries. If you gave evidence, Maria, you would probably end up like Nicola da Mula. We can't denounce Pietro anonymously because, as I am sure you know, the Ten never pays attention to anonymous letters."

"Can't we do anything at all?"

"I will write a letter to Giovanni Tiepolo telling him of the murder. The Patriarch will keep the letter in mind even if it is anonymous."

15.

Viva Il Dose

Doge Antonio Priuli feels the weight of the heavy toga and the many layers of brocade. Ermine is unsuited for sunshine, he thinks. Walking along the Riva like this would be impossible without the parasol. Today he feels his years. The slow pace of the procession is tiresome; the pointed shoes are far too small. Last year's Easter Procession hadn't been such a strain, the air had been chilly and the sky grey: an Easter Sunday more to his liking.

Before setting out, Priuli had studied himself in the palace's large mirror. He was pleased that his dark hair has only a tint of grey. Not many can boast that at the age of 83. Surely, he was almost as slim and as good-looking as he used to be, with his faculties still intact. Yet it has become harder sitting for hours on the Great Council. Fatigued, he takes to losing himself in Paolo Veronese's painting of Rosalba: her face always smiling at him from the wall opposite his throne. The painter never tired of her as a model.

The crowds on the Riva cheer him and the shouts echo "Viva il Dose! Viva il Dose!" Hats are thrown into the air and children run from one end of the long procession to the other. "Viva Venezia, our good mother!"

It makes him proud to see the standards flutter in the wind:

VIVA IL DOSE
THE VENETIAN SECRET, 1620

the winged lion of Saint Mark against the blue of the sky, the evangelist guarding their republic under his wing.

A Senator offers his support as he climbs the steps of the next bridge. Only a few more bridges to go. Soon he'll be out of the heat and inside the cool church. But today is not just about duty.

There'll be the nuns' heavenly voices. To hear Vespers at San Zaccaria truly moves him. To watch the faces of so many beautiful young women will take him back in time to the one most dear to him. He is getting more sentimental every year.

"Almost there, Your Serenity," the Senator says.

On the corner of the gateway to Campo San Zaccaria, adorned with the white marble Madonna, two small girls sing and dance for the Doge. The statue's blue eyes startle Antonio Priuli. Not many Venetians know the secret of the Madonna and, once again, he wonders if Rosalba found some happiness when she disappeared from the convent fifty-three years ago.

Their attraction to each other was immediate. He was thirty and she seventeen, nearly eighteen. It had been the year of 1567, on Ascension Day on board the Bucintoro.

The last time his father had married Venice to the sea.

She was lucky to have married a Medici, for no one could have protected her better than the powerful family. But even the Medicis couldn't stand against death, and just at twenty years old.

Walking through the sottoportego and across the campo, still waving and smiling at the cheering crowds, he again plays over the question of who had really been the father of Rosalba's child. The painter or the Medici? Or somebody else?

As always, the entrance to the church is decorated with garlands of red oleanders. When he sets his foot into the building, the organ sounds. He walks down the aisle towards the High Altar, the long procession winding its way like a caterpillar behind him.

Priuli sees Francesca Grimani through the grate of the choir, and greets her with a faint smile and bow of the head. The ducal seat is close to the altar and the nuns' choir, and he grasps hold of the carved armrests as he settles in. Momentarily, he is distracted by his hands. The skin is thin, white as parchment, and the delta of blue veins distinct. Were they like this last year? Looking up he sees the Abbess with her ingratiating smile. How fat she's grown. Much fatter than last year.

Behind her are the choir nuns wearing long tight dresses of white silk under the mantle and tiny transparent veils. Like a flock of lambs, he thinks.

His hands gradually release their grip on the arms of the chair, and he leans back against the soft cushions, carried away by the nuns' beautiful voices. He looks at the faces behind the grate.

One amongst them attracts his eye and causes him to tighten his hold on the armrest. The blond hair behind the veil is the same. The face with its frank blue eyes, the heart-shaped mouth, and the expression too. She must be a Morosini.

All of a sudden, he remembers everything vividly. The light at sea had been particularly fine that day. The Bucintoro had been packed with noble families. Galleys, barges and gondolas had followed in its wake flying a hundred flags. The bells of the city had rung out and the cannon at the piazza thundered at intervals every five minutes. Rosalba had been standing together with the

Nani family, amidst the tritons and satyrs of the Bucintoro.

She was Filippo Nani's bride-to-be. He had already heard rumours of her loveliness. He knew that Paolo Veronese had been on his knees before her father to be allowed to use her perfect face for the sketches of his grand painting 'The Triumph of Venice': the painting now in front of him every time he headed the Council in the Great Hall.

He still recalls what falling in love was like. The ecstasy of it all. Rosalba had been his first and only love. He had been swept away by her courage as much as her beauty and her recklessness. No rules but her own decided what Rosalba did. He would have risked anything for her sake.

As it was, he had run great risks for her.

The world had changed from the day he had met Rosalba. Other people went about the humdrum of everyday life, but his sense of invincibility and almost painful exultation had set him apart. People smiled at him for no reason at all. The resonance of love had seemed to strike a deep cord within them. Looking at her and listening to her voice had been the greatest happiness of his life those few months it had lasted. He had lived only for their few brief meetings.

On that first day, Rosalba had glanced in his direction several times. He had caught her eye and she had looked straight into his. She had smiled coquettishly before hiding her mouth behind her small fan. Rosalba wore a rose-coloured brocade dress and enamelled flowers, pearls and rubies in her long fair hair.

How could she not appeal to Veronese's sense of sumptuous colours? No wonder the painter had fallen in love with her too. In all Veronese's paintings of Rosalba, the love for his model is obvious. Indeed, Veronese had told him years later that sincerity in the expression of feelings in paintings transcends everything else.

When his father had thrown the golden ring into the sea accompanied by the ritual words "With this ring I marry the sea to Venice" he had moved close to Rosalba while everybody had watched the ceremony. He took her hand and kissed it and she had traced a finger along his chin and neck. He can still feel it. In a whisper, she had asked him to meet her at midnight the following night, outside Ca'Morosini on the corner by an old hidden door. That had been the beginning.

Veronese had probably always been his rival; they had both loved her. Poor Filippo Nani: her fiancé only in name.

Priuli looks at the small withered man with the thin wisps of white hair on the bench across the aisle; his rival for the dogeship. Filippo Nani, who had done so well in his foreign employments. But he was stiff and sensitive, and had been only sixty-three at the time of the election. Nani had been devastated when his family called the wedding off. The transaction between the Nanis and the Morosinis came to nothing.

Paolo Veronese had been in and out of Ca'Morosini for about a year at the time he met Rosalba. She had told Priuli of their painting sessions, and how she had persuaded her old nurse to leave the two of them alone. Jealous, he had wondered if Rosalba and Veronese had been lovers, or were still. They had lived on borrowed time. He never doubted that Rosalba would marry Filippo Nani. But against all the odds, he had had some hope.

There was no way he could have anticipated their relationship's abrupt ending. Even if he had heard rumours about Rosalba and Veronese, he hadn't believed them. Of course, there could be mutual admiration, even fascination, between the model and the painter. But more than that? After all, she was betrothed to be married in a few months. Veronese had married the year before.

At the time, Veronese had been working on the paintings for the church of San Sebastiano. Driven by curiosity he had gone to the church one day. They had talked and Veronese had been friendly and easy to get along with. They had discussed the use of harmonious colours. Veronese had explained his use of saturated colours in the foreground and light pastels in the background. Carbon black, malachite, copper carbonate green, ultramarine, azurite, vermillion, orpiment, lead-tin yellow, the names of the pigments haven't escaped Priuli.

Veronese's paintings were a mirror of the perfection of Venice: coordinated, balanced, consistent and in blazing colours. He had felt some envy and jealousy at the talent – genius even – of the painter. How could Rosalba not feel fascinated, seeing Veronese produce these wonderful works?

He finds it difficult to take his eyes off the young nun who resembles Rosalba, and she in turn looks his way from time to time. At dinner, he will know her name.

Priuli had liked the painter. They had met on and off, even though they had been wary of one another. Rosalba's name had been mentioned only once. Talking passionately about light and colours, Veronese had said that on sunny spring days a rare light suffused her room. It was particularly fine when seen through the thin ultramarine hangings. Veronese had looked at him through the corner of his eye, realizing that he had made a slip of the tongue. Priuli had pretended nothing was wrong.

Priuli knew well that these hangings were placed around Rosalba's bed. She herself had described her quarters to him. But he had pretended nothing was wrong, turning instead to the sheaf of drawings, leafing through them whilst Veronese had studied his face. Priuli had thought then that what Veronese's pen had done was to caress Rosalba's lips, the curves of her cheeks, and catch the seductive look in her eyes. The rapid nervous pen sketches were voluptuous. He had recognized the expression on her face. An expression, which he had thought until then was only meant for him.

Later, when the painter had left the church to buy pigment, Priuli had seized his chance, going through a series of drawings left in a corner. They had stunned him. They were drawings of Rosalba posing naked on a couch.

Then one morning it had been all over the city. The Nanis had called off the wedding. There were accusation of a secret love affair, and to protect the family honour Rosalba would have to be examined by the state doctors. Veronese's name was never mentioned in public, only in the letter. A letter from Filippo Nani's father, that Priuli had seen on his father's desk in the ducal apartment:

Paolo Caliari, the Veronese, a man most arrogant and impudent, destroyer of the honesty of families, has violated the security of my house, betraying and deflowering Rosalba Morosini, my future daughter-in-law, carrying off her virginity and the honour of myself and my entire family, which has always been more dear to me than life itself.

VIVA IL DOSE
THE VENETIAN SECRET, 1620

The case caused a huge scandal, and Priuli's love affair with Rosalba ended on that same day. Before long, her future was sealed. From the Giants' Staircase in the Ducal Palace the state doctors had pronounced their verdict in front of the crowds. Rosalba had been deflowered. On hearing the proclamation, the nobles had shuddered at the infamy and dishonour to the Nanis and Morosinis. His own name thankfully had not been mentioned. Still, he could only feel love for her. He was sure nothing she had done had been for anything but love.

In a matter of weeks, the Morosinis had paid the dowry for Rosalba to enter San Zaccaria, and

Veronese had been exiled to the Church of San Sebastiano for a whole year. For a time, Priuli

had felt a strong urge to see Rosalba in the parlatorio. But the thought of seeing her trapped behind the grates was too much.

One day, some time later, a small boy had brought him the letter. He can still see the boy before him. Completely out of breath from running, standing in the doorway panting, like a dog.

Antonio, Please help me, Rosalba had scratched the words on the paper in a hurry, and inkblots had made it difficult to read. *I won't survive convent life. Help me find a way out of here. Bring me a poison that sends me before God quickly, if need be. If I am caught escaping that will be the only way.*

16.

A Face From the Past

The Doge's sharp eyes travel round the church, resting on Fabrizio Morosini on the nearby bench. Fabrizio Morosini looks particularly serious today. Perhaps he is thinking of that vile son of his. Fabrizio, who aspires to become doge. Yet Domenico will bring scandal down on Fabrizio before long, Priuli thinks, and Fabrizio's dreams will evaporate with Domenico's deeds. He follows Fabrizio's gaze to the young nun in the choir. She must be his daughter. Priuli looks from father to daughter. He has seen wretched nuns before. With the passing of time, they either fade away or break down altogether.

Thank God for the influence and the power he had when Secretary to the Ten. Without it he would never have been able to save Rosalba or gain access to the hidden passage built to save the relics in case of a siege. He had been amazed when he discovered where the tunnel ended. Not in a million years would he have guessed. The white marble Madonna had indeed granted him a prayer. He had never told a living soul about the passage. Only Rosalba knew.

Passing the guards had meant risking his life to get at the Ten's poison cupboard. He had been shocked by the contents of the letters. The numbers of tenders for assassinations and contracts

for the removal of enemies of the state by means of poison.
What a mess the cupboard had been: poisonous substances scattered about among the shelves. No labels telling what kinds of poison, nor the dose. From the shelf marked "quick poisons" he had taken a small emerald green flask. Immediately, he had sent his servant with the flask, hidden in a small ivory box, and a copy of the drawings of the passageway to Rosalba. In the end Rosalba got help from Veronese's friends among the Medicis.

Ah, the memories. The events of this period of his life had come to him only in fragments over the years. To see the painting had been distressing. Years later to come upon their old rivalry quite by accident. The Grimani family had commissioned four paintings titled 'The Allegory of Love' for the ceiling. In 'Unfaithfulness' Veronese had surpassed himself; the tints and the brushwork alone had been magnificent. It must seem such a strange picture to everyone not familiar with the events. Rosalba with her back to the viewer and her face turned towards himself. Naked, sitting right in the centre of the painting. Between him and Veronese. They were both holding her hands, she secretly slipping a letter into his hand. Veronese had even written a few words in red pigment, but Priuli had not been able to distinguish them. Veronese had presented himself looking directly, entreatingly at Rosalba, pulling at her arm in an attempt to drag her closer to him. And himself so young! What a sad expression on his face. He appeared lost, looking past Rosalba towards the sky. Later he had asked Veronese what was written in red in the letter. "...*if you have one...*" Veronese had answered, smiling sadly.

Priuli becomes aware that the singing has stopped, and that the

A FACE FROM THE PAST
THE VENETIAN SECRET, 1620

organ has begun to play. The abbess is opening the massive oaken doors to the nuns' church. One more duty to perform before the grand dinner. If only the crypt isn't flooded like last year; he had been lucky not to catch a cold even though his feet had been wet all through dinner.

Only the six ducal councillors follow him into the nuns' choir. How I wish I could go straight to the parlatorio like the others, he thinks, walking beside Francesca Grimani towards the chapel and the crypt. He cannot help noticing the sour smell from her habit, barely cloaked by the scent of perfume. When she turns around and smiles, he observes the thick layers of rouge upon her cheeks.

"The crypt is quite dry today, Your Serenity. Not at all like last year. Damp and chilly still, but the floor isn't flooded." Francesca Grimani's voice seems to reach him from afar. Priuli nods and thanks her for her consideration.

In the chapel, San Zaccaria and John the Baptist seem to greet him from the frescoed vaults. At the high altar, the chandeliers gleam in the late sunlight from the tall windows. A gold cloth embroidered with a scene of the Resurrection adorns it. On the wall hangs a cloth of turquoise damask with the cross, the Madonna, and St. John decorated with small and large gold tassels.

Priuli glances at the inscription on top of the altarpiece: In this chapel above the blessed martyr of Sabina we have some of the blood of our Lord Jesus Christ in a vial. It never ceases to move Priuli to be so close to Christ's holy blood. To be so near to the dawn of Christianity is compelling. He remains there a little while in silence. In a flash, he sees the young nun's face before him. Doge Antonio Priuli whispers a prayer for her. Then he turns toward the councillors and Francesca Grimani.

They go down the small staircase to the crypt. It is steep, forcing him to concentrate on every step. At the bottom of the stairs, he looks up at the sarcophagi with the bones of his early predecessors. This is how he will end up himself before long. He looks round the crypt in the light from the oil lamps on the walls. For the briefest of moments, his eyes rest on the beautiful circular stucco ornament on the stone altar.

He is relieved when they are back in the chapel, walking into the cloisters. When Priuli enters the parlatorio and sees the ducal chair at the top of the table, he realizes how much he has longed to sit down and rest his legs.

The odour of sweat mingles with the aroma of the food and strong spices, worrying the doge. Foul odours are carriers of disease. By now the room is crammed. Some of the state visitors and priests will have to dine standing up.

Priuli looks at the nuns gathered behind the grates. Can he go to the grates later and ask the young nun about her life, if there is anything he can do for her? Suddenly he feels young and reckless. He is again the young man in love with Rosalba; he feels the dust of decades swept away by a surge of passion.

Where is she? There. He can see her talking to Fabrizio Morosini, and all the while she doesn't smile. Not even once. Priuli takes a deep breath and goes to his place at the top of the table near the fireplace. He is pleased to sit down on the soft cushion in his ducal chair. His heartbeat slackens and he is once more an old man contemplating the dreams of his youth.

A FACE FROM THE PAST
THE VENETIAN SECRET, 1620

The lay nuns serve his favourite dishes:Spanish bread, cream, oranges and salted tongue, boiled calf's feet, tripe, roast veal and turkey, delicious green sauce, dessert custards, cream cheese, prunes and dried chestnuts.

The Doge observes the nuns' confessor, Orsolo Lupi. He sits opposite the abbess ingratiating himself with the prelates. What a sly face. Priuli doesn't care for the way he leans towards the Patriarch in that toadying manner, smacking his tight bloodless lips as he chews his food. Lupi with his sanctimonious air. Lazy too. Could be because he had priesthood forced upon him and had grown up with a bully for a mother. Priuli remembers distinctly that Lupi's father left everything to a younger brother. Now his ambitions have to be reached within a convent, but he doubts if Lupi's desires are altogether spiritual.

He cannot help being curious. He listens to Lupi's wheedling voice when he addresses Giovanni Tiepolo. Priuli can see that the Patriarch is annoyed having to listen to Lupi. Giovanni Tiepolo doesn't care for that priest, Priuli thinks. He sees right through him. The priest turns pale, and Priuli smiles to himself. He is pleased that the priest is told off. He wonders if it is on purpose that Tiepolo uses words like "safe-deposit" and "security" when speaking to Lupi: there are rumours that the priest has stolen money from the convent's strong-box. A steward collecting rents for the nuns had whispered in the Patriarch's ear that the confessor stole the keys from the abbess. The rumours might be true. But then again, Lupi doesn't enjoy much popularity.

Tiepolo had approached him after his visit to San Zaccaria.

A FACE FROM THE PAST
THE VENETIAN SECRET, 1620

The Patriarch explained that the record-book, at all times kept under lock and key, had gone missing. Now it was impossible to compare the amount of money left inside the box with the withdrawals that had been made. Tiepolo had desired that the convent magistrates keep an eye on Lupi. Other more serious rumours about the nuns' confessor have reached Priuli too, and he wonders if Lupi's days are numbered.

He looks towards the grate once more, still surprised at the surge of feelings he experienced from seeing the girl. He is pleased that he can see Fabrizio's daughter from this angle and turns to the procurator who sits beside him.

"What is the name of your beautiful daughter?"

"Marietta, Your Serenity," Fabrizio answers in a tender tone of voice.

"I wonder if your daughter is pleased with her life here. She looks melancholy to me."

"I very much hope she is content." Fabrizio sounds sad.

"If a young woman doesn't feel a vocation, her loss of freedom can be ruinous." Priuli feels sorry for Fabrizio as he says it. And for the girl too. It is easy to see how much Fabrizio cares for his daughter.

He sips at his wine, its colour in the light from the candles like that of rubies. Nowhere do you get finer wines. He wonders from which of the nuns' many vineyards it comes. The nuns' enterprise impresses him; their presence travels far beyond the convent walls. Even if they are enclosed their investments in property are wise and profitable.

The abbess' face looks as red as the senators' robes. She has been

A FACE FROM THE PAST
THE VENETIAN SECRET, 1620

drinking far too much, Priuli thinks.

Priuli empties his glass of wine and looks for Marietta. She isn't behind the grating any more. He wonders where she is gone.

A FACE FROM THE PAST
THE VENETIAN SECRET, 1620

17.

What the Painting Revealed

Why did Antonio Priuli look so intensely at me all day? Not like a Doge at all. Sitting behind the grate, I suddenly caught a glimpse of the man behind the robes of our formal Doge.

Now is my chance to explore the crypt. I will have it all to myself as everybody is busy eating and making deals. Looking at the painting through the magnifying glass this morning, I had discovered something new. I recognised the ornament on the stone altar in the crypt in one of the small paintings copied into 'The Chessplayers.' The secret might not be in the floor at all. In the dream, Rosalba could have pointed to the tessellated floor in the crypt to make me aware of a circular ornament.

I hurry into the chapel and down the steps. It is chilly in the humid crypt; the silence broken only by a clinking sound when drops of water hit the scant puddles on the floor. The oil lamps are still burning, now low, and a few are burned out. A vague scent of perfume and spices mixes with the musty smell and the stench of smoking wicks.

In the dim light, I can just make out the ornament on the altar. In Veronese's painting, I had noticed a band of light encircling it. I take one of the oil lamps from the wall, and when I get close, I see the circle is the size of the wellhead in the courtyard. Within the big circle, a smaller one looks like the sun with fine lines of rays of light.

I put the lamp down beside me, and let my fingers travel slowly across the circle. It doesn't feel like stone, but rather like stucco. The flame from the lamp flickers and I feel a slight draught. I tap the circle with my fingers. It sounds hollow, like tapping on wood. Suddenly the ornament swings open, and stands at right angles to the wall.

I make out two stony steps, which lead down to a dark passage. A rank stench of rot penetrates my nostrils. It is obvious that the tunnel has not been in use for a long time. What is the purpose of the passage? I know the convent's relics were kept in the crypt before the time of enclosure. Was it a means to save the relics in case of danger? I feel the ornament again. It is made of wood and stucco, only it looks exactly like stone.

Where does the tunnel take you, I wonder. Is this the enigma of Veronese's painting? The secret my aunt Faustina tried to impress on me when winking incessantly? Is this how my beautiful great-aunt got away in the end?

I am just small enough to squeeze through the opening. Carefully, I place the lamp inside on the top step. I can't stand upright. I will return with Fini to scare off the rats and see where the passage leads. If, indeed, it leads anywhere at all. I leave the lantern inside the doorway. No one will miss it. I go back and give the doorway a gentle push. The door shuts, and the ornament is once again one with the altar. No one would ever suspect this to be an opening.

I stop in front of the staircase to the chapel. Is that the sound

WHAT THE PAINTING REVEALED
THE VENETIAN SECRET, 1620

of heels against the tiled floor? Someone is running fast, now stopping, but only briefly. Tap, tap, tap. The person is leaving. I tiptoe halfway up the staircase and peek into the chapel. A tiny figure dressed in a jerkin, a tall hat, knee breeches, and trailing a cloak in one hand is hurrying towards the door. The jerkin looks like the one we use for our plays. I can't be certain in the vague light, though. Then the figure disappears into the darkness.

WHAT THE PAINTING REVEALED
THE VENETIAN SECRET, 1620

18.
Farewell to a Life of Corruption

It is late when the Doge and his procession leave. The empty parlatorio falls silent, dirty plates and crystal goblets are left on the tables. The garlands of flowers droop from the walls and the floor is scattered with red shell-shaped petals. Francesca Grimani has said to leave everything until morning. The gold and silver brocade hangings must be returned to storage, and the trestle tables and folding chairs dismantled and put away.

In the kitchen, the mortars for grinding and mixing the boiled crayfish and the green sauce are reeking of unpleasant odours, blending with the fragrance of thyme, mint, basil, garlic and rose vinegar for the sauce. Every year the nuns exceed themselves: the bread chests are empty and one sack of flour is all that's left in the pantry. Terracotta pots for the braising of pork are piled in the sink and heaps of spits are on the floor beside the fireplace.

In the cloisters, Chiara stops to wrap the black velvet cloak around her and tie the black ribbons securely. She remains in the dark for a few moments to summon her courage. The night is cold, so she hopes no one will find her mantle conspicuous. She puts a hand inside it and fingers the many small wooden buttons of the jerkin. It feels comforting, like touching her Rosary. Ten

Hail Marys for ten buttons interspersed with bigger ones for Our Fathers.

She hopes the Virgin will concede miracles to her for her devotion. Behind the collar of her shirt she feels her Agnus Dei medallion, bearing the image of the Lamb of God, and with a lock of her mother's hair. She knows it has been blessed by the Pope on another Easter Sunday years ago. It is her most treasured possession and has protected her against the corruption of San Zaccaria.

The smell that emanates from the clothes makes her dizzy. The wig is warm and too tight, and her head itches. But there is nothing for it; her short cropped hair would only give her away. Her disguise is reeking of male. It disgusts Chiara because it is the same smell as Orsolo Lupi. When they happen to pass each other in the cloisters, he comes close to her, so close that his robes brush against her habit. He even took hold of her hands once. She had torn her hands away from his tight grip, bowed her head so as not to meet his eyes, and run off. Lupi has more concern for the shame of the world than for fear of God. Perhaps the priest is some kind of divine test, she wonders. She cannot fathom the ways of the Lord in this.

She hates to think that a man has worn her costume. A slight scent of perfume arises from the jerkin too. Has the man been with a woman, embracing and kissing her? Chiara flushes. What makes her think like this? She had felt terribly shameful looking at the chest with the costumes in the attic. Covered with decorations of naked little boys holding up the Grimani coat of arms. Why are the nuns allowed to put on plays and sing profane songs? Chiara knows that the performances cause great confusion in the minds of the nuns and great scandal outside. The abbess calls it 'honest recreation', but Chiara believes it is because Francesca Grimani likes to perform in male clothes in front of their confessor. The friars revel in the performances in the parlatorio during carnival. She has heard them shouting, drunk with wine and sometimes playing at cards with the choir nuns, even grabbing at them through the grates.

Last year it had been a comedy. A wicked one. She is pleased that the Blessed Virgin ordered her to seize the copies of the play and burn them. They never found out who did it. The Virgin had thanked her because there had been no more performances.

At the Visitation, she had believed that the Patriarch would take her words to heart when she whispered to him of the nuns' sins. Giovanni Tiepolo had listened seriously and promised to put an end to all "undue corruption". But it had been nothing but empty words.

In the chapel, when she thanked Santa Marina for her holy inspiration, she had felt so peculiar, dressed just like the saint during her life in the monastery. Chiara looks at the breeches. They are creased and tatty, but the green cloth feels soft against her skin. The vermillion green silk stockings too. The worn leather shoes are too big and awkward. Santa Marina must have suffered too, wearing men's clothes. But a true Christian must make sacrifices. If only this was all behind her and she was safe in the monastery in Padua.

Chiara has studied an old map of the convent in the library and knows that she must walk along the wall up to the Lagoon. Then she must turn right toward San Marco, as she has heard

FAREWELL TO A LIFE OF CORRUPTION
THE VENETIAN SECRET, 1620

the gossips say, and there she'll find the mail boat for Padua. She must look for a red lantern. She has heard that the boat leaves every night at midnight.

Chiara moves slowly towards the gates. She keeps as close to the wall in the cloisters as she can, clutching her Agnus Dei for good luck. Marietta let me down too, she thinks. The thought makes her legs tremble; she stops behind a column to calm down.

Marietta's writings still upset her: ridiculing priests and famous theologians. These thoughts keep rushing through her head and she can barely concentrate on her flight. She had been merciful to Marietta, taking the sheets of paper from their hiding place and tearing them up. The twins had been right to tell her where to find Marietta's manuscripts. In her vision, God had ordered her to destroy blasphemous papers. Now Marietta would not lie down in bed with manifestations of sin on her soul.

It had also been her duty to ruin the painting, slashing it with the knife. It should have been burned. If only she could have made a bonfire of vanities in the courtyard and thrown all the nuns' illegal possessions into the flames where they belonged, the Lord would have thanked her.

Suddenly, Chiara feels miserable. She is fond of Marietta in spite of her mistakes: Marietta who nursed her through her long illness in January. The day in the chapel when they had talked about escape, she had felt close to Marietta: closer than she had ever felt to another human being. After all, Marietta detested the convent too.

The moon is out, but still the sky is a myriad of stars, and the cloisters are swathed in moonlight. Chiara tiptoes towards the gate. The shoes are soft and don't make a sound. She stops when she sees the two nuns guarding the gate. Sister Dorothea is so fat that she is sitting on two chairs, and Sister Zuana so small that her legs can't reach the floor. They are both asleep. The potion has worked.

Immediately after the Doge and all the other guests had left, Chiara had gone to the kitchen and offered to bring food and wine for Sister Dorothea and Sister Zuana. All she had had to do was to empty the small flask of green liquid into the terracotta jar with the wine, and now she congratulates herself on her slyness. The nuns always served the best wine from their vineyards for the Easter Procession. She had told Sister Dorothea and Sister Zuana that this was the very wine that had been reserved for the Doge. This way she was certain that not a drop would be left. They were greedy, always eating and drinking to excess. She had searched among the numerous jars in the pharmacy for the right sleeping drug. The small flask of strong herbal medicine for killing pains had been hidden away at the back of the shelf.

Chiara says a prayer, hoping that she hasn't used too much of the drug. Her vision reassures her because, in her mercy, Santa Marina has shown her the way. She must keep faith in her vision and go through with the plan just as Santa Marina has told her to do.

Slowly she moves closer to Sister Dorothea. She stops for a moment to listen to the nuns' even breathing. The fat Dorothea moves on her chair and starts to snore. The noise makes Chiara almost faint. There it is. The key to the gate. Chiara is trembling. Can she go through with this? She closes her eyes and touches the buttons. The big iron key is fastened to a thick leather string

FAREWELL TO A LIFE OF CORRUPTION
THE VENETIAN SECRET, 1620

attached to Dorothea's girdle. Chiara feels for the small kitchen knife in her pocket. Slowly, carefully, she lifts the leather string with the key towards her with one hand, and with the other she starts cutting the string. It is harder and tougher than she expected and seems to take forever. Chiara has trouble breathing; her heart is beating fast. Dorothea's mouth is open, and her foul breath makes Chiara feel dizzy. Will this string never give in? Cold perspiration is on her forehead as she imagines Dorothea suddenly opening the tiny slits she has for eyes and grabbing her harshly by the arm, never letting go of her.

Dorothea snores louder, stirs in her two chairs. Chiara summons what courage remains and is through the leather at last. She has done it... the heavy key is in her hand. Zuana shifts in her chair, twitches and grunts. Her leg kicks out in her sleep and she only just misses Chiara. Chiara freezes. She is convinced that Zuana will wake up and ring the bell. But Zuana's head in the black cowl tilts to the other side. Still asleep.

Chiara turns the large key in the lock. She tries putting it back in Dorothea's girdle, fumbles tying a knot. How clumsy she is... There... At last it's done. The key for the gate to the Riva she puts in her pocket. If only this was the end of it. But it has all only just started, and there's no turning back now.

Carefully she opens the heavy gate and in front of her is the campo lit by only one lamp.

She is outside, and it frightens her.

She hasn't been on this side of the gate since she was seven. Was she not better off inside? She is confused, feeling hot and cold at the same time. The houses are unfamiliar and seem to watch her, their windows like huge black eyeballs. Chiara feels like falling. Is this dying? Has her heart given in? She panics, and her legs feel limp. She touches the buttons, tears running down her cheeks. The way her legs tremble makes walking difficult but she must hurry to the Riva. No time to lose. When will they discover that she is missing? In her mind, she can hear the chimes of the huge bronze bells blending in with every other bell in the city. Even the solemn strokes of the bells of San Marco will claim her. An inferno of sounds reverberates in her head. The bells will talk of my escape all over the lagoon. Chiara has heard stories whispered in the corners of the convent of the punishment awaiting escaping nuns.

CH-I-A-R-A! Is somebody calling her name? CH-I-A-R-A! Does the call come from within the gate? CH-I-A-R-A! Who would be shouting like that? CH-I-A-R-A!

She holds tightly on to her small leather bag, fumbles for the key in her pocket, and unlocks the gate to the Riva. She leaves the key in the lock and closes it quickly behind her. She runs as fast as she can through the sottoportego and onto the Riva, afraid that the devil will be lurking in the dark waiting to grab her. She stops.

A white marble Madonna. Chiara gazes at the Madonna's eyes that shine in the light from the candle. The flame wavers and the Madonna seems to tremble. Is she trembling because of me? Chiara is stupefied; is she trying to warn me? Is it a sign? Blessed Virgin, help me, she whispers. She makes the sign of the cross before turning, looking around her.

The lagoon is right in front of her. No wind stirs. The moonlight makes the water look like a silvery mirror stretching infinitely

FAREWELL TO A LIFE OF CORRUPTION
THE VENETIAN SECRET, 1620

before her. She stops stunned by the sight. Two galleys leaving together look like giant sea monsters. She hears the soft dipping of oars. Commands fly through the air. The outside world is not what she has imagined. She never gave it much thought till now. Why should she? It had nothing to do with her life as a bride of Christ.

Chiara runs for the row of houses lining the Riva. I'm safe here, she thinks. No moonlight.

As she turns right to continue towards San Marco, a small boy comes up to her. She starts, and to avoid the light from his lantern she turns her head towards the windows catching a glimpse of her reflection in a windowpane.

She can't pay attention to what the boy says. In the convent she never looked at her own face. How unfamiliar her face looks. The wig and hat make it look even stranger. For some reason, she always imagined that she looked like Marietta. Now she sees that she doesn't. Why must she go through all this? She doesn't deserve it. Everything is so complicated? Is this her Via Dolorosa?

She pushes past the boy, barely avoiding tripping over her own legs, trying to rid herself of the reflection of her face. She mustn't cry.

She stays close to the wall, hearing the boy shouting behind her. Her zeal will impress the friars, she thinks, trying to soothe herself. The times she has crept from her cell at night and remained on her knees in the dark chapel, lit only by the sanctuary lamp, reciting the entire Office of the Dead, then a Rosary and many a De Profundis. She had stayed until she was so terrified that she could scarcely move.

She feels lost and lonely among the people passing by. Chiara

FAREWELL TO A LIFE OF CORRUPTION
THE VENETIAN SECRET, 1620

looks at the numerous boats moored along the quay looking for the red lantern. There it is! Showing the red and gold of the Lion of San Marco. It must to be the mail boat. She starts walking towards it. She won't run, afraid to attract attention.

Chiara stays close to the houses. A few rats dart past her and disappear into holes in the walls. Scattered crowds of people are walking on the broad quay, and the strangers give her a choking sensation. She keeps her eyes fixed on the lantern, walking towards it. She walks faster. The boat mustn't leave without her. What will she do if she is not on it? She cannot imagine where to hide all night. And tomorrow, what will happen when day breaks? The nuns will surely miss her at Prime. Her escape will be disclosed and the bells chime.

She mustn't cry. The saint will help her through it all.

Two figures come right towards her. They are women, and Chiara sees their breasts are bared. She grabs such a firm hold of the buttons that one comes off. Wicked and sinful women! Nothing could be more indecent in the sight of God. Again her face feels hot and the choking sensation returns. Her stomach churns and she feels a lump constricting her throat.

Chiara keeps her eyes glued to the ground.

"You look like a pigeon ready for plucking. Come on, handsome boy. We'll pluck you, but gently."

Their shouts and laughter terrify her, like the loud cooing noises they make. She must ignore them. Not give herself away. She walks faster to avoid them, swerving towards the water away from the safety of the houses.

"Don't run away, handsome. A kiss won't cost you a soldi. If you pay a lira, we'll take you to our bedroom and grind two sacks of

FAREWELL TO A LIFE OF CORRUPTION
THE VENETIAN SECRET, 1620

grain." Bursts of laughter ring in her ears as she runs. "You know what?" they shout, "Don't be so holy. A whore doesn't cheat convents or husbands; she is like a soldier paid for doing evil. She doesn't pretend to be virtuous!"

She runs and runs, and doesn't stop till she is completely out of breath. Right in front of her, she hears loud singing. Five young men chant 'Ave Maris Stella,' adding shameful insults. One of them starts to recite 'Sancte Petre', and Chiara hears the others respond using the most infamous words in contempt of St. Peter's name. She remains standing, frozen to the spot, not knowing what to do. She does not dare go past them. They stand right in the middle of the quay and might easily grab hold of her when passing. She must wait for them to leave. She starts crying with relief when they disappear into an alley off the Riva.

Through tears, she stares steadfast at the red lantern right in front of her. The boat is docked. There's still time. She can see the standard with the lion of San Marco hanging slack from a small pole at the bulwark. A short stocky man in a turban and an enormous dark beard is quarrelling with the boat's crew. Beside him are two big barrels. Chiara gazes at the jewel he has in one ear lobe. This man must be a Turk; Chiara shudders at the thought. She looks at his baggy trousers. She recognises them from the gossips' description. She has heard frightening tales of the Turks' cruelty, how they ravage Venetian ships. They have honey in their mouths but hatchets in their hands, the gossips say. Coming closer, she sees he has a sword hanging from his belt. Chiara prays that the Turk won't be among the passengers. She looks at the boatman gesturing and shouting at the Turk. The boatman is a terrifying sight, with his hooked nose and loud voice. She has never been on a ferryboat and has no idea how to behave. Marietta once told her that Tommaso had been seasick in a storm and the waves had been gigantic. But she doesn't have to worry about being seasick tonight. The lagoon looks calm, the air is still and the stars are out.

Chiara feels for the ducats in her pocket. Will one ducat be enough? Will they ask to be paid or must she offer? What would she have done without the money from the strong box? It was an act of God that the key had been right there on the hook with the crucifix above Francesca Grimani's bed. She had only been in the Abbess' apartment for a moment when she saw the key. She is relieved that she threw the account book from the box into the well. Now they will never know how much money has disappeared.

Chiara hesitates. What now? Three men in long cloaks are waiting to embark. Chiara reluctantly walks up to stand behind them. From their conversation, she understands that they are fan-makers. They are only going as far as Giudecca to pick up some ivory and tortoise shell or the handles of fans. They are annoyed by the Turk, who takes up their time, delaying them. Apparently, the Turk wants the mail boat to take the two heavy barrels to Padua. But he can't agree with the boatman on the price.

One of the fan-makers turns around and smiles at her, revealing a run of half-rotted teeth. Chiara feels faint being so close to a man and looks away.

"At last," the fan-maker says, "I think the captain has agreed on a price with the bloody Turk and we can start loading. Otherwise, I would have knocked his turban off."

FAREWELL TO A LIFE OF CORRUPTION
THE VENETIAN SECRET, 1620

The fan-makers push ahead and the Turk struggles to get his barrels on board, paying the oarsmen to help him. Chiara is relieved that she stands last in line. She watches the others pay their fares clutching a ducat in her hand. She stretches out her arm towards the boatman and opens her hand.

"A ducat! Do you want to buy the boat, boy? Don't you have less than a ducat, boy? I don't have the change. What do you expect? Wait till Padua."

Chiara feels the boatman's probing eyes resting on her. He looks at her suspiciously, stooping down trying to see her face. The fan-makers' conversation stops.

"I'm not so used to sailing," Chiara mutters looking at the ground. She is so scared that she could die right there and then.

"Not used to sailing? Here? Ha-ha!" The boatman takes Chiara's arm as she crosses onto the boat. "Go and sit down beside the barrels," he orders her.

The fan-makers have already taken their seats on one of the small benches. The Turk's barrels take up a lot of room in the small boat, forcing Chiara to wedge herself in between the fan-maker with the rotten teeth and one of the stout barrels in the back of the boat. The smell of decay from his mouth when he turns towards her, staring at her, makes her feel nauseous. She presses up against the hard barrel. Squeezed in between the fat fan-maker and the barrel, she can hardly breathe.

The boatman releases the ropes from the thick wooden poles, and Chiara feels the boat moving. She listens to the slap of oars in the water. The two men at the oars are working hard. Her journey has started. The sounds from the Riva gradually disappear as they move quickly away from Venice. Soon she sees

FAREWELL TO A LIFE OF CORRUPTION
THE VENETIAN SECRET, 1620

the receding facades of the houses with lighted windows on the Riva, the Ducal Palace and the two tall columns in the Piazzetta. She looks for the convent. She sees the black contours of the bell tower rise high above the roofs.

Chiara tries to breathe normally. Sailing makes her feel worse. She hasn't been on a boat since she was seven when her father took her to San Zaccaria. The dark water scares her. She trembles at the thought of what it might hide. She fingers the remaining buttons of the jerkin mumbling prayer upon prayer.

Further down the basin of San Marco, she hears the gondoliers chanting the stanzas of Gerusalemme, one answering the other. She has heard the gondoliers' songs through the high windows in the workroom. She still remembers a few old Venetian songs from when she was a girl in the big house on Murano.

Chiara feels the fan-maker pressing against her with the rocking of the boat. He looks at her from time to time. Chiara can feel it.

"Poveretta mi", she keeps whispering to herself. "Poveretta mi, poor me".

""Poveretta!" Are you a girl, boy? Funny clothes for a girl!"

She never realised that she used the feminine form of the word. She shrinks away from the fan-maker's inquisitiveness, dropping her eyes. She just stares at the bare wooden planks at the bottom of the boat. She feels completely at a loss. Has Santa Marina let her down? She has no idea how to answer his question.

"Where are you going? To Giudecca? Stra? Or Mira?"

Chiara feels the tension in her chest increasing. She hides her face in her hands and cries. She is clutching so hard at the Agnus Dei that the chain breaks. The medallion hits the planks with

FAREWELL TO A LIFE OF CORRUPTION
THE VENETIAN SECRET, 1620

a small sharp noise. When she bows down to reach for it, the broad brimmed hat falls off. The next moment, everything turns dark and she feels the wig across her eyes. She pushes it back in place.

"Poveretto!" Chiara hears the fan-maker roar with laughter at his own joke.

"Look, Gobbino," he says. He turns towards his small hunchbacked colleague beside him.

"I'll be damned if this isn't a girl dressed up as a boy! What do you think, Gobbino? You always were the clever one."

"I think you are right, Zuan. And it isn't just any girl dressed up as a boy, you know. I'll wager it is a nun, masquerading as a boy! I saw her short cropped hair underneath that wig of hers."

The fan-makers stare at Chiara. Her stomach is tight with fear now. They know she is not a boy. What will they do to her? Chiara can't stop sobbing and her eyes hurt. She hears the fan-makers' voices rising. Through her tears she looks at the small scary hunchback they call Gobbino.

"What's the matter, Gobbino?" Zuan wants to know.

"I smell money coming our way, Zuan, don't you?"

"Which money would that be, I wonder?" Zuan asks. Chiara sees how his lips curl in a small malicious smile. She can hardly breathe now. It doesn't matter if she will be crushed to death between the barrels and Zuan.

"The reward, Zuan, for handing in escaping nuns. A handsome amount too, I'm told. I think this girl is running away, don't you?"

"A judgement from the Heavens, Gobbino. You are right as always." Zuan croaks, his thin lips revealing only gums.

FAREWELL TO A LIFE OF CORRUPTION
THE VENETIAN SECRET, 1620

"What to do with her, Gobbino?" the third fan-maker asks the hunchback.

"Hand her in, Francisco, hand her in, you fool." Gobbino says, sounding annoyed.

Chiara's face is filmed with sweat. In her head is her vision of the Madonna and the letter that She had dictated to Chiara about her escape. The Blessed Virgin has abandoned me, Chiara mutters to herself. Santa Marina too. What has she done wrong?

"Tell us where you come from, my pretty," the one they call Zuan says.

Chiara can only cry. She holds tightly on to her bag. Her relics. She will never tell them what is in her bag, nor let them touch her treasures with their unclean hands. The pure white linen handkerchief trimmed with lace that has a thread from Our Lady's veil. It had been her mother's. And the letter dictated to her by the Madonna; the miniature painting of her beloved Beata Francesca who had raised three people from the dead.

Through the bag's soft hide she can feel the outlines of the white alabaster vase her father has given her, the one that once belonged to Mary Magdalena and possesses strong healing powers.

Gobbino's eyes stare greedily at Chiara's bag.

"Leave her bag alone, Gobbino, it will only get us into trouble with The Ten." Zuan snaps.

"Let's just take her to the Inquisitor's prison, shall we? And collect the reward."

Chiara hears the hunchback's words distinctly. Prison, he said. Why prison? "No, no, please don't, please!"

Chiara panics. This must be the devil testing, tempting me, she thinks. It is his poisonous influence, which wards off the Virgin

FAREWELL TO A LIFE OF CORRUPTION
THE VENETIAN SECRET, 1620

Mary and Santa Marina. She is certain that the devil has taken the shape of the small hunchback they call Gobbino. If I show courage, Chiara thinks, Our Lady and the saint will come back to me.

Is this a test? The Infernal Enemy cannot inhabit my body if I keep my faith in Christ and the Blessed Virgin. Chiara makes the sign of the cross several times and prays to the Virgin.

"She looks as if she is in a trance," She hears Gobbino say to the others. "Captain, won't you turn the boat around?"

"Turn her around? That's impossible, Signori, I have the mail to consider."

He points to the badge with the lion on his cloak and to the standard of San Marco to make certain they know in whose service he rows.

"I'll have trouble with the Council if the mail is not in Padua on time. The tide won't wait for me or the barrels, Signori. I'll have grave problems with the Turk's scimitar if his valuables don't arrive on time."

Have her prayers been heard? Have they reached the Blessed Virgin? Does She talk through the boatman? Is he Her vessel? Now the devil will shrink back.

"But think of the ducats, Captain. We'll share the reward with you. Just turn her round. It won't delay you much." Gobbino tries in his most persuasive tone.

"What would the republic think of helping an escaping nun?" Francisco asks.

"You can just go in and leave when we are ashore," Gobbino adds. "We'll seek you out when you are back and give you your share."

"Don't listen to the words of the devil!" Chiara falls to her knees on the wet planks in front of the boatman. She must make it clear to him that he is negotiating with the evil one.

Chiara sees that the boatman hesitates. "The devil will weaken your stomach and addle your brains. The devil will enter your body if you pay attention to him."

"Avarice is one of the Seven Deadly Sins," she cries at him. "God will punish you and strike you dead." Her words have made an impression on the boatman. He makes the sign of the cross. Gobbino looks afraid too.

"Don't let her words scare you." Zuan stares hard at the others.

"The reward is big enough for us to share and still get our money's worth," Francisco looks from one to the other. Chiara is crying silently now.

"Alright," the captain says at last, "I'll turn her around."

The oarsmen pull the rudder and the boat swings towards the Ducal Palace. As soon as it comes into dock, Gobbino and Zuan grab a firm hold of Chiara. Closely followed by Francisco, they walk across the Piazzetta. The mail boat is already leaving for Giudecca.

Chiara hugs her bag tightly. She doesn't note the Ducal Palace, nor the Basilica of San Marco as they pass. She is oblivious of her surroundings. She can only think of how alone she feels, now that the Blessed Virgin has left her. She must be possessed by the devil. She has failed the test somehow.

The fan-makers tug and yank at Chiara. They close their fat palms around her arms, which are crossed tightly on the bag. She has gone limp and Gobbino and Zuan have to drag her along between them, like a criminal to the gallows. Her feet do not even touch the ground. They pass the sacristy of San Marco and cross the courtyard to the private chapel of San Teodore.

Gobbino knocks on the door to the jailor's apartment. They have to wait and are just about to knock again when the door opens.

"Who knocks at this late hour? Don't you know this is the Holy office of the Inquisition?" A tall gaunt man looks suspiciously at them from behind the door.

"We bring in a nun dressed up as a man. She tried to escape to Padua," Zuan says and pushes Chiara towards the jailor.

"What is your name?"

"Zuan, fan-maker and honest citizen from Castello doing my duty."

"Looks like a boy to me."

"Why don't you see for yourself? Look beneath the wig!"

The wig and the hat are in the turnkey's hand before she knows it. Chiara feels a chilly wind against her scalp. She has only uncovered her head at night alone in her cell, never in the company of anybody; she feels naked. What might be the Virgin's intentions?

"She is a mere shrimp without the wig and the hat," the jailor exclaims staring at her short hair.

"I'm a bride of Christ and consecrated to God. You can't touch me or look at me without my veil," Chiara sobs.

He lets go of her arm and steps back.

"If you touch a nun, God's wrath will strike you down." She screams at the jailor.

"What might be the reward for bringing her in?" Zuan pulls the jailor aside.

"Wouldn't know about that, fan- maker, you'll just have to wait and see. I'll ask the tribunal to look into the matter," he adds. "If you are wrong you'll be in deep trouble."

He takes hold of Chiara's arm again and pulls her inside the door.

Their shouting reaches Chiara through the door. Zuan's voice cuts right through her. "We'll never get a lira; it was all for nothing. The jailor will probably keep the reward for himself."

"I'll take you to your cell. Won't that be almost like home?" The jailor seems to have got hold of himself now. "Ha- ha-ha." His laughter echoes in the basement vaults and to Chiara it sounds like voices of damnation taunting her, mocking her.

A cell. Suddenly Chiara is not afraid. The thought of a cell is a comfort. It is like home, as the jailor says. Safe. Away from the world and the fan- makers.

"Give me your bag," the jailor says and takes the bag from her. He looks into it, and sees the relics. He seems scared, she thinks, when he returns the bag to her.

"Take it with you," he says gruffly. "This way," he says, and pulls at her arm again. He raises the taper in his hand a little and lights the steps for her. The taper throws shadows like coiling serpents, she thinks. They stop and he opens a door. "In here," he grumbles. The jailor holds forth his hand with the candle and she steps in.

FAREWELL TO A LIFE OF CORRUPTION
THE VENETIAN SECRET, 1620

She is in a small room with a straw mat along one wall. Nothing else. She hears the door being bolted, and then everything is darkness.

19.

A Hearing at the Holy Office

The Patriarch Giovanni Tiepolo snuffs the candles on his desk. He sprinkles sand on his last note, places his pen in the tray, closes the lid on the inkpot and gets up from the chair. He walks across the polished terrazzo floor in the Red Room and flings open the windows.

It is a beautiful morning. The light coils in the water like white silken ribbons, and the sunshine is like a smile from the Virgin blessing the city. As he leans a little out of the window a gust of wind caresses his cheek, bringing with it the sweet smell of roses. But roses are nowhere in sight. This is surely a sign from Our Lady.

Time to leave. Tiepolo puts on his black robes for the tribunal and glances at the pile of letters on his desk. They all carry the nuns' seal showing the Saint Zaccaria with the image of the lamb and a veiled nun. He has spent the early hours of the morning reading Francesca Grimani's letters again, to be prepared for today's hearing in San Teodore. The letters have kept coming almost every day for the past three weeks. He picks up the letter in which the Abbess implores him to remember how very pious Sister Celestia is: I do believe that Sister Celestia is a budding saint. But she is weak from fasting and easily confused. I implore you, Reverend Patriarch, to bear in mind that her father is only four weeks dead; this has affected her terribly. Her father went down with his merchant galley and the family fortune at the bottom of the sea.

But no, Tiepolo thinks, pretence of holiness is a grave matter and must be kept under the strictest control. If not, the church will suffer and heresy, like a howling wind of darkness, will rock its foundation. He must show no weakness in spite of his compassion for the nuns.

He had felt sorry for Sister Celestia at the Visitation in January. She struck him as a little disturbed, as the abbess says in her letters. If she is, the evil humours in her mind will inevitably descend and corrupt her entire body.

Approaching the Fondamenta della Canonica, Tiepolo watches the Nuncio, who has already arrived from Palazzo della Nunziatura. Vespa cuts a statuesque figure, his long robes chiselled into dramatic folds. He is waiting in front of the church, looking at Paulo Erasmo, whose face is shaded by the cowl, as he steps out of his gondola from his monastery of San Domenico di Castello.

Tiepolo gathers his heavy robes and smoothes his long grey beard. He walks across the small courtyard towards the others. He looks into Vespa's severe looking eyes and bids him good morning. Vespa is tense, Tiepolo notices. Tiepolo doesn't try to shake Vespa's hand. Neither does the Inquisitor. Tiepolo has never seen the Nuncio shake the hand of anyone.

Shaking the hands of Venetian nobles makes them put on airs, Tiepolo had heard the Nuncio say to the cardinal. Tiepolo knows that Vespa considers himself the most prestigious member of the tribunal. He thinks this vanity a mortal sin.

Tiepolo shakes Erasmo's hand. It is cold and bony to the touch. He finds the face unattractive with its small, calculating eyes, thin tight lips and a look of self-righteousness. Does he carry this expression because the Pope has granted inquisitors full remission of their sins?

Tiepolo walks beside Vespa into the modest chapel at the Church of San Marco; Erasmo follows behind. In front of the golden altar, they stop to offer a prayer. Today Tiepolo prays for Sister Celestia's soul. They walk towards the raised platform and take their seats along one side of the long rectangular table.

"Time to summon the Three Savi." Tiepolo turns towards Paolo Erasmo, who gives a sign to the door keeper to let in the Senate's representatives.

When the three Savi enter, Tiepolo greets the lay deputies with a solemn nod. The chancellor and the five assistants follow and take their seats. The chancellor sits down at the short end of the table. He removes the lid from the inkpot, dips the pen into the golden substance and begins writing on a sheet of thick white paper:

The Venetian Holy Office. Interrogation of Sister Celestia, San Zaccaria, May 25th. Anno Domini 1620.

A door creaks on its iron hinges and the tribunal turn their heads to watch the tiny person coming towards them. Chiara stops for a moment, staring at the twelve grey stern looking men at the long table. Seeing the Patriarch's face, a slight gasp escapes her, and she clasps the small leather bag even tighter against her

A HEARING AT THE HOLY OFFICE
THE VENETIAN SECRET, 1620

breast.

"Approach the Holy Office," the Inquisitor's voice cuts through the air in the chapel.

Chiara's eyes are fixed on the floor as she approaches the platform. In his sharp impatient voice, Paolo Erasmo orders her to take the seat facing the tribunal. Chiara drops onto the empty chair, still clutching her bag, her legs dangling in midair, head bowed.

"You must inform this court of your name and age," Erasmo yelps at her.

"My religious name is Sister Celestia. I have lived for 17 summers."

"Your place of residence?"

"The convent of San Zaccaria."

"I must warn you, Sister Celestia, it is necessary not only to freely confess the truth of your deed, but also your belief and, recognising your error, to repent from the heart. In this way you ask mercy of God and the Holy Church," Erasmo says looking severely at Chiara. "Sister Celestia, tell us your reasons for leaving the sacred enclosure of your convent," Erasmo begins his interrogation, while the chancellor scrawls the words for his report down rapidly. In the silent room, the noise from the scratching pen sounds like a small hissing animal trying to ward off a terrible enemy.

"I...I wish to live the most austere life possible...I believe... that... this mortification of the body pleases the Lord." Chiara doesn't dare look at the men across the table. Her eyes are glued to the floor. "I want to live my life according to the holy vows I have taken. I never desired to escape to a life outside the convent."

"Sister Celestia, you live in a sacred convent already quite in accordance with your holy vows. You must explain why you left."

"Religious life in San Zaccaria …suffers…the rules are not obeyed…and… the choir nuns don't attend the services. The Blessed Virgin and…and Santa Marina helped me…they …they appeared before me… and showed me the way to holy friars' monastery." Suddenly Chiara starts weeping, her small body convulsing in bouts of crying. She loses the grip on her bag, which hits the floor with a noise of splintering glass.

"A sign from the saint!" her outburst stun he men behind the table.

They look uneasy and the chancellor hesitates for a brief moment before his pen hisses: *The defendant lets out a series of loud cries for a period of a Miserere; her face is distorted, her eyes are red, and she keeps crying.*

"My relic... Maria Magdalena's alabaster vase….," Chiara screams. "Shattered like my aspirations. The saint has left me …I have let her down …I've failed to follow the way she showed me."

Chiara collapses on the chair, sobbing silently now. Her constant tears, Tiepolo meditates, must come immediately from God.

"Sister Celestia, I must ask you to calm down or I will have to send you back to your cell," the Inquisitor says, looking with disdain at the odd creature before him.

Waiting for Chiara to stop crying, Erasmo reads a few lines in the Spaniard Juan de Torquemada's manual from 1435, opened in front of him. The Spaniard was shrewd. He knew how to test revelations,and what questions to ask in these cases. He browses through his notes of Teresa of Avila's 'Life' to remind himself of how divinely inspired visions can be distinguished from diabolical ones.

Tiepolo watches how Erasmo studies his notes nervously. He is undecided, Tiepolo thinks, like last time. He should have paid attention to my letter. Every nun in Venice is under my jurisdiction. Erasmo exposes our convents to great scandal.

Chiara has stopped crying.

"Did you ever experience visions?" Erasmo wants to know.

"Yes," Chiara answers quietly. "Since I was a child I've had visions of Our Lady and the saints. Once I had a vision of an old man bearing a cross with which he touched my chest."

"Have you been visited by the devil and transfigured into an angel of light?"

"No, I have never had that kind of vision." She raises her hand as if to ward off a demon.

"Have you ever encountered animal figures enticing you to fornication?"

"Madonna!" Tiepolo exclaims and he and several of the others look at the ceiling moving in their seats uneasily. What kind of question is that, Tiepolo thinks. Why can't Erasmo show just a little sophistication and not scare the life out of the girl? He glances at Vespa. Even the Nuncio sighs audibly and has a hard time concealing his disapproval. Tiepolo sees that Chiara's face is flushed. She is not fit to stand trial, he thinks, but Erasmo doesn't realise it. His insight into the human mind is indeed limited.

"No," Chiara whispers.

"Did you feel a burning in your heart or pains in your side?"

"Only when I was taken seriously ill in January."

Erasmo isn't quite sure what to make of Chiara's answer. Is this a question of religious delusion? Is it the devil's hoof prints he sees, or could the pains be due to the illness the girl mentions? Most likely, she is nothing but a pious fraud. He isn't certain if he should probe deeper into this matter; he has had that kind of pain himself once.

"Have you ever craved communion as your only food?"

"No, illustrissimo Inquisitore, but I've often fasted to cleanse my soul and in honour of the Virgin and Santa Marina."

"Have you performed false miracles, or believed yourself to understand the highest mysteries of the faith?"

"No, I never aspired so high. I've only acted on the simple messages I received from Madonna and the Saint."

"Do not presume to be an intimate friend of Our Blessed Lady or the holy Santa Marina! Messages, you say! Remember that the Virgin Mary did not consider herself a peer of the angel Gabriel! Those who aim to raise themselves higher than their status permits will slip and fall!" Erasmo forgets himself and shouts the words at Chiara, whose tiny body begins to shake again.

Vespa leans towards the Inquisitor and whispers something in his ear. For a moment, Erasmo looks troubled by the Nuncio's words.

"What messages were they?" Erasmo resumes his questioning taking care to sound calm.

"They were manifold. Of late to destroy the blasphemous manuscripts of Sister Cinthia, Marietta Morosini that is, and the sacrilegious painting in her cell depicting the nuns as pawns in a game of chess."

Erasmo makes a note of Marietta's name. Forbidden paintings and blasphemy; he must look into that, even if Tiepolo has

A HEARING AT THE HOLY OFFICE
THE VENETIAN SECRET, 1620

warned him that the nuns are the Patriarch's responsibility.

"Santa Marina showed me how to dress up like a man and live among the friars in Padua. But I must have failed her."

Perhaps she feigns holiness in public. Eramo doesn't believe the nun's explanations.

"Remember Saint Jerome's dictum Sister Celestia, 'Of the two evils, it is less wicked to sin openly than to simulate holiness.' Are you a wolf in sheep's clothing?"

"How could I not have been inspired by the saint?"

The Nuncio nods towards the door to their chambers. Tiepolo, the Inquisitor and Vespa rise and walk into the chambers behind the chapel. Tiepolo looks at the Nuncio. How will he vote? Will he recognize that the nuns are his jurisdiction? Or will he stand by Erasmo? What a fool Erasmo made of himself. As long as he doesn't learn to control his temper, he'll never make an inquisitor.

"Illustrissimo Patriarch," Erasmo says. "Would you oblige me with your opinion of Sister Celestia's condition?"

"I believe that women are more prone to melancholy than men, a malady at the root of many visions and temptations. It is my experience that women fabricate visions more readily than men, and Sister Celestia appears to suffer from a devastating sense of disappointment with her life in the convent. Therefore, I see no reason to suspect pretence of holiness. It is Sister Celestia's poor dishevelled soul we hear crying out for help."

"My own opinion differs from yours, Giovanni Tiepolo. I am certain that Sister Celestia is consciously and deliberately feigning holiness," Erasmo says not too loudly. The Nuncio frowns at Erasmo.

"The nun is a poor bewildered soul, Paolo Erasmo. I think that you should strive not to over indulge in pursuing your immediate ideas when questioning a defendant of such a fragile state of mind," Tiepolo says. The Nuncio is silent.

"The nun is a weak subject paying attention to the flattery and fraud of the Evil One!" Erasmo persists.

"Your Excellency, the three of us have witnessed the feeblemindedness of this nun. We all want to end this case as quietly as possible." Tiepolo says.

"In my experience, women often talk of strange spiritual encounters inspired by their imagination. The reason lies in the inferiority of female nature." Tiepolo looks at the Nuncio as he speaks, hoping that today Vespa will agree with him.

"This could be the reason for Sister Celestia's delusions," the Nuncio says looking pointedly at the Inquisitor. "We must not forget that women's bodies, inherently cold and damp, are prone to internal disturbances, which they are too feeble and foolish to fight off. Women are naturally inclined to all seven deadly sins and unable to withstand the onslaught of temptation. This you may read in all the manuals we use in court. It is my express wish that she be returned to her convent. Can we agree to that?"

Erasmo's temper flares up again. "If we do not give her a severe sentence, confined in the prison of the Holy Office, it could result in grave prejudice and disrespect towards honest people, Christian life and faith itself! Escaped nuns, if apprehended, must be confined to the convent prison and disciplined according to the provisions of their order's rule."

The Nuncio gives the Inquisitor a look of warning. "In my

A HEARING AT THE HOLY OFFICE
THE VENETIAN SECRET, 1620

opinion, Sister Celestia should be sentenced to remain for three months in her cell in the convent. She must strive to mortify her will and the notion that she is in any way special."

"Sister Celestia must be exorcised again. The confessor at San Zaccaria, Orsolo Lupi, has exorcised nuns before. To my knowledge he is competent and experienced in these matters," Vespa says, ignoring Erasmo, asking Tiepolo what he thinks.

Tiepolo doesn't like the thought of the priest as Sister Celestia's exorcist, but the wisest thing is to agree with Vespa.

The Nuncio stares hard at Erasmo. "Do you agree with us, Inquisitor?"

"Of course, Illustrissimi," Erasmo says, taking a deep breath

A HEARING AT THE HOLY OFFICE
THE VENETIAN SECRET, 1620

20.

The White Madonna

"There were pools of blood all over the floor," Beatrice whispers with her mouth close to the grating. "I never saw so much blood in my life. I thought he would die right there and then." She stops to breathe. "The wine glass was on the floor beside the couch where he was lying with Massimo. He must have slipped from the couch and fallen right onto the glass. It broke, but left the stem standing sharp as an icicle. It went in deep just below his right arm. The doctors say he might not live," Beatrice says. "If it hadn't been for the Jewish doctor at Murano, Andrea would never have seen daylight again. You remember the Sala d'Amore, Marietta? Only a few moments before I had surprised them there, entwined on the couch, reciting poetry and drinking wine."

I have no difficulty recalling the Sala d'Amore. Sometimes, when I met Tommaso secretly at night, we went to Casino Morosini. I stole the key from the Egyptian vase in my father's studio. In my mind's eye, I see Andrea lifeless on the floor, blood gushing from his wound.

"They had been sitting in the shade of the arbour all day drinking wine. They were singing love madrigals and telling bawdy tales, laughing at what to watch out for in a wife and quoting proverbs, like boys of sixteen, rather than men of thirty-five."

"I heard that Andrea had these appetites before you were married. I tried to tell father, but he merely told me that mother wanted the fortunes of the Dandolos and the Morosinis united, and nothing I could say would change her mind. 'Don't forget, she is a Conaro- woman, a descendant of Catharina Conaro, the queen of Cyprus. Money and descent go hand in hand when it comes to marriages,' father mumbled, as if to explain away his defeat."

"Mother spent a long time warning me what would happen on the wedding night," Beatrice continues. "How I was expected to be obedient to my husband and do nothing to displease him. I vomited on the floor when she told me how the hymen would break and the blood there would prove it. I was so terrified that I sewed my nightgown together, like a sack. But I need not have worried, Marietta, because Andrea stayed at his side of the bed all night, and we never touched. Only once have we touched in the four months we have lived in Ca'Dandolo. One night he suddenly threw himself on top of me and tore my nightgown open. But nothing ever came of it. I think his father had ordered him to make me with child." Beatrice looks downcast.

"That night," Beatrice goes on, "Andrea told me that his confessor had warned him against frequent sexual activity. Intercourse, he said, drained natural male vigour, and could lead to early death. Mother never mentioned this; I wondered whether it might be true, until I caught him with Massimo. From then on he slept in his own room."

"You never said anything in your letters, Beatrice."

"How could I when Andrea's servants read my letters? There is no one I can trust. They are all strangers, even enemies. Not

THE WHITE MADONNA
THE VENETIAN SECRET, 1620

my friends for sure. They have quite a different agenda from mine, don't forget that Marietta. I wasn't even allowed to bring my beloved Zusanna as my chambermaid. I've been locked up in our apartment in the house for a long time, and his servants spy on me. One night I escaped the house and went home. I was so terribly miserable. But mother wouldn't let me in. She came to the door when Zusanna announced me and said, 'you have your own house now, Beatrice. Remember, there is always a period of adjustment. Make your face up and go home to your husband; we can't have Andrea hunting you down, can we?' Isn't that just like her? For a long time I was alone with my secret fears before the truth finally dawned on me when I saw Andrea embracing Massimo."

"Father was always in a hurry when he came for brief visits. Every time Andrea was there kissing my cheek, so I couldn't say a thing. And how could I complain to father of my husband, thinking of the dowry he has paid for me? I always worry and fear scandal; Andrea's male friends come to the house every day. If only you could see his toilette Marietta, full of silver-backed combs, rouge pots, pins, curling-tongs, brushes, all kept with delicate neatness. There are more items than I ever saw on mother's toilet table."

"Where is Andrea now?"

"He is at Ca'Dandolo. His mother and the doctor are there. But I had to come and see you, Marietta, and tell you. And to give you the letter from Tommaso. Three months for that letter to reach you from Constantinople. Marietta, I've missed you every day since I left San Zaccaria. I haven't found freedom or happiness at all in my new life. It is not what I thought when I danced in the great hall in all my finery. I am buried alive behind a different

THE WHITE MADONNA
THE VENETIAN SECRET, 1620

set of locked doors, more alone and helpless than ever. I don't know what will happen to me if Andrea dies but I don't think my life can't get much worse."

"I have missed you too, Beatrice. If Andrea dies, the Dandolos will return your dowry, unless the two families decide that you marry one of Andrea's brothers to avoid handing the money back. But listen", I whisper, gently pulling Beatrice closer to the grates. "If that happens, you can go with me, Tommaso, and Giulia."

Beatrice doesn't understand my words. "What do you mean?" She looks questioningly into my eyes. "I recognise that familiar glint of agitation," she says.

"I've found it. The secret passageway. Just like Rosalba showed me in her dream. I've solved the riddle of the panting from father's studio." I know I sound impatient. "And there's something else that I have found."

"What passageway? And what did you find?"

"Four months ago, on Easter Sunday, I slipped out of the parlatorio and went to the crypt. In father's painting, which I now have in my cell, Veronese has painted the ornament on the stone altar in the crypt. Do you remember the ornament, which looks like a sun with rays of light?"

"Yes, I remember." Beatrice looks a little confused at my agitation.

"It is a secret door to a low, dark passage leading to the Riva. Built to rescue the relics. But the most incredible thing happens at the end of the tunnel. You find yourself inside the white Madonna, you know, the statue on the corner of the Riva and the sottoportego. You can watch the Riva and the lagoon through a small hole in the Madonna's navel! Inside the Madonna, at the bottom, are two rusty hinges, and if you push, a small door opens. If you squeeze through the narrow opening you find yourself on the Riva!"

"Marietta, are you going to escape through a tunnel? I have prayed at the altar in the crypt so often. I adore the beautiful white stone angel. I can't imagine opening the circular ornament to enter the passage!"

"Yes, when Tommaso comes back. At Carnival time, on St. Stephen's day in December. At midnight. Nobody will miss us till the morning and we'll be far away by then. Do you remember how we trained Fini when he was a puppy to carry notes from one of us to the other? And how proud he was to do it? Rushing up and down the stairs with letters in his mouth?"

Beatrice nods. "Yes, I remember. The small clever dog wagging his tail eagerly when delivering the letters. But what has Fini got to do with this?"

"I brought Fini with me the day I went to explore the tunnel. To scare the rats off. He ran in front of me barking and growling, back and forth in the dark tunnel. Suddenly there he was wagging his tail, a letter between his teeth. He must have found it chasing rats. It is a letter from Rosalba, Beatrice."

I produce the letter from my sleeve, wrapped up in a piece of lace. I unfold the yellowing paper carefully, and hand it to Beatrice.

Venice, August 1567

I hope that one day these jewels will come to the aid of a young

THE WHITE MADONNA
THE VENETIAN SECRET, 1620

woman of the Morosini family, like me, forced to live behind these walls and, like me, wanting to escape this bleak life of captivity.

I am going towards an uncertain and lonely fate. But with the help promised me, I believe that I will not need the money tcious jewels would provide Two of the rings are extremely valuable; the one with the rubies, pearls and diamonds bears the Morosini coat of arms. The stones are set by the Florentine painter Alessandro Botticelli. The second with the sapphires, bears the Priuli coat of arms. It was given to me as a token of love.

I long to be free, and am not afraid of a life away from Venice. I am certain that I will find happiness wherever I go. Like me, you must have faith in the future. Maybe you have heard of my fate, maybe not, but whatever it has been, it will have been happier than my existence here, which cannot be called a life. Even if I will have to swallow the poison I carry.

Rosalba Maria Grazia Morosini.

Should you fail along the way, I have hidden a potion of strong swift working poison in the small chamber at the back of the Morosini ring.

Beatrice watches me carefully remove the lid of a small dusty case with the initials RM stamped in gold on the black velvet. She stares at the collection of jewels.

"Marietta, the size of the rubies and diamonds are immense! The blue of the sapphires is so deep. One of these will buy you half a palazzo!" Beatrice whispers finally. "That must be the missing Morosini ring mother is on about, the Botticelli ring.

THE WHITE MADONNA
THE VENETIAN SECRET, 1620

I remember her looking for it in the jewel cases and chests at home many times. Once, she even had the couch in the salotto torn apart, because she got it into her head that the ring was lost in the lining."

"Yes, that's the same, but I want you to pawn it with the Jews in the Ghetto. But keep the Priuli ring."

Beatrice takes the two rings and slips them into a small pearl embroidered purse. "With Andrea ill, I can go to the Jews without anybody spying on me."

"Beatrice, do you think I look like Rosalba?"

"Very much so, as I remember the painting from father's studio. But then, of course, I was just a small girl.

"Do you also remember that Aunt Fantina sometimes called me Rosalba?"

"Yes, but I always thought she just was a silly old thing."

"I think I know now why the Doge kept staring at me all through Easter Sunday. The ring, Beatrice. I wonder how Rosalba came into possession of the Priuli ring. Strange, don't you think?"

"Yes...the stones being so very valuable."

"I can't imagine what might have taken place between Antonio Priuli and Rosalba, or how she got the ring, I say."

"Do you know what happened to Chiara?" I ask her.

"No. Please tell me. I never heard what became of Chiara after she was sent back to the convent."

THE WHITE MADONNA
THE VENETIAN SECRET, 1620

21.

The Priest Will Take Care of Her

Marietta's account

*C*hiara suffered solitary confinement in her cell for three
months, from May to July. The Holy Office had decided that only
Orsolo Lupi could see her, in order to exorcise and confess her. The
lay nuns were allowed to bring her food and empty her chamber
pot. They reported to Francesca Grimani of Chiara's constant
weeping and tried to plead with the Abbess. There was nothing she
could do about it, she said. How could she possibly go against the
Inquisition of Venice?

When Maria asked permission to stay with Chiara for a few
moments, the Abbess declined it. 'The priest will take care of her,'
Francesca muttered.' 'He knows the art of inducing penitence in a
sinner.' She slammed the door to her apartment in Maria's face.

Chiara had been crying since the Inquisitor pronounced her
sentence. She had begged to be sent to an observant convent
where the rules were adhered to. But no. I watched Lupi come
and go to Chiara's cell through the hot summer months and heard
Chiara weeping when passing her cell. Most days I slipped a note

underneath her door hoping to lift her spirits. I knew which lay nuns had the key, and I paid for Maria to take the tray with food to Chiara's cell.

"She is a sorry sight, Marietta," Maria told me one day closing the door to Chiara's cell behind her.

"She is thin, worn out from crying and lack of sleep. I think her mind is going. She paces back and forth crying. She mutters 'Order will come out of chaos' constantly. When the bell rang for None, she whispered, 'It's the gong of doom, Sisters be vigilant.' No wonder. She has been alone for more than two months."

"Didn't she know you?"

"Not at first. She just stared at me with a vacant expression. It's me, Maria: don't you recognise me, I said. Then she looked at me, took my hand, whimpering, kissed it and pointed to stains of blood on the sheets. 'Do you want me to change them, Chiara?' But she trembled and shook her head, looking distracted. She went over to the washstand and started rubbing her arms with the rough soap."

I opened the door and paused on the threshold. In spite of Maria's words, I was quite unprepared for the sight of Chiara. Chiara's head was bare and short wisps stood out like a caterpillar's spine-like hairs her veil was on the floor and the skin on her arms red and bruised from the washing. I went over to stand beside Chiara at the washstand. She looked at me, and a wry smile lighted her face. I took her in my arms and led her the few steps towards the bed.

"Not there!" She whimpered.

We sat down on the floor close beside each other, our backs against the wall. I put my arm around Chiara's shoulder.

THE PRIEST WILL TAKE CARE OF HER
THE VENETIAN SECRET, 1620

"*I'm sorry about your manuscripts and the painting, Marietta. Santa Marina ordered me to destroy them. When I told the twins of the saint's anger, they showed me where to find your writings.*"
I was speechless. Beatrice! I went all tense for a second. Did Chiara do it? She's deserved everything she's got then, I thought. My manuscripts... how could she? But the next moment, I felt infinitely sad, and all my anger had gone. Poor Chiara, these strong visions distorted her life.
"*Never mind, Chiara,*" I said. "*How could you possibly disobey the saint?*"
When I looked at the floor in front of me, I discovered small signs of the cross imprinted in the dust.
"*Did you make all the crosses, Chiara?*"
"*He ordered me to lick the crosses. It is required,' he commanded.*"
Chiara's voice sounded so weak, and it made me feel sick to think of Lupi ordering her about like this.
"*Why can't we sit on the bed, Chiara?*"
She started to whimper again, rocking back and forth, clutching her knees.
"*Was it him? Please, tell me, Chiara, and I'll make him stop.*"
"*It still hurts, Marietta. It was the devil who did it.*"
"*Try not to worry about the priest, Chiara,*" I said to her. "*I'll write some letters today and, rest assured, Lupi will be suspended before the Marangona has sounded tonight.*"
"*But Marietta, not even you can stop the devil. He conquered Santa Marina and the Blessed Virgin.*" Then Chiara got up and went over to the washstand. She started rubbing her chest with the soap.

"*Please, Chiara, stop it.*"

THE PRIEST WILL TAKE CARE OF HER
THE VENETIAN SECRET, 1620

"But the stain on my soul is still there. I've got to try," she muttered.

I hurried to my cell and wrote letters to Tiepolo, Antonio Priuli and father. I stated the accusations against Lupi and the testimonies I had gathered from the young choir nuns during the summer. In the letter to Priuli I added: 'Two letters have come into my possession by accident, not so long ago. They bear the seal of the Ten and speak of poisoners in their employ. Were these letters to become public, I have no doubt that they would cause great scandal and severely harm our state. The moment Orsolo Lupi is relieved from his duties, and I have your Serenity's word that the Ten have instigated investigations of my accusations against him, I shall return the letters to you.'

"Please take these letters to La Serenissima's Messengers at once," I said to Maria. "Tell them to deliver one letter to the Ducal Palace, one to the Patriarchal Palace at San Pietro and one to my father at Ca'Morosini immediately."

On the morning of the 25th of August, a letter arrived from the Holy Office. Chiara had been pardoned and was free to resume the religious life.

A letter from the Patriarch Giovanni Tiepolo informed us that Orsolo Lupi was relieved of his duties. He had been taken into custody for questioning by the Ten. Another priest would take his place as soon as possible.

Everybody talked of scandal and hoped that Lupi would fry in the 'piombi', : the smallest low-ceilinged cell beneath the lead roof of the Ducal Palace. 'The scorching sun will crush him,' they all said. 'He will be consumed by the flames of Hell before his time. Serves him right, and good riddance.'

THE PRIEST WILL TAKE CARE OF HER
THE VENETIAN SECRET, 1620

Francesca Grimani wrung her hands and grieved in her apartment for hours on end, neglecting her responsibilities. I was told that when they met the following day in the Chapter Room to discuss the situation, the Discreet Ones revelled in the Abbess' much too blatant sorrow at the loss of our confessor. They hadn't forgotten how she danced in front of Lupi in men's clothes when we performed a play in spring. Nor her peals of girlish laughter. Or the gifts she sent father Lupi every so often, not to mention the frequent meetings with him in the sacristy or the confessional.

Francesca Grimani's eyes were swollen and red from crying, and her rouged cheeks streaked with tears. She went about in the cloisters, dabbing her eyes with her grimy handkerchief, sniffling through her tears.

"Do face it, Francesca," one of the Madri di Consiglio snubbed her, "Orsolo Lupi has burned his candle at both ends. We have all had our suspicions for some time now. We will await the verdict of the Ten. I have never seen you shed a single tear for Sister Celestia,Francesca. She is really the one in need of compassion, not the priest. We must decide what to do."

The Abbess had blushed a little, and put her handkerchief away in the sleeve of her habit.

"What is the matter with Sister Celestia?" she said, trying to sound calm. "I saw her at Tierce today quietly praying in the chapel."

"You can't have been very observant, Francesca. You must have had other things on your mind," Sister Pax said. "I was sitting next to her in the chapel. Quite near to you too. How could you not notice how she kept turning the pages of her prayer book, even when there were no more pages to turn? All through Tierce, she whispered, 'the angels will meet me, they'll know the light again,

THE PRIEST WILL TAKE CARE OF HER
THE VENETIAN SECRET, 1620

when they see me.'"

"We might have no choice but to send Sister Celestia to San Servolo. They are skilled in treating disorders of the mind," Aunt Paulina said.

At Matins, Chiara suddenly ran to the altar and prostrated herself. She moaned and sighed, 'somebody go and find Santa Marina!' Then she ran into the cloisters with her hands over her ears shrieking,' don't you hear the cries? It's the devil's voice trying to lure me into the abyss amid the flames with him! I'm damned in all eternity.'

She cried out for the Madonna and fell to her knees in the courtyard by the well.

'I'm an angel of light,' Chiara screamed. It is hard to image a sadder sight, Beatrice. 'I'll rise from the flames and go to Paradise!' poor Chiara went on. 'The eye of the devil makes me tremble. I'm lost – take the crucifix away! I'll lick the crosses at your command!' Chiara pressed her head against the wall repeating. 'It's the Tempter – it's the Tempter!'

When the bell sounded the Hour of Prime, at the first rays of day, a scream travelled through the tranquillity of the cloisters. The sound waves seemed to flood our cells and break against the stone walls.

I watched the nuns at the gate peek into the campo through the small opening. Chiara's naked body was pierced by the points of the iron railing that surrounds the old grave of some former Abbess. The bell tower rose high above it, shrouding the bursts of blood in its shadow. The nuns stepped into the campo hesitantly, unsure to leave the enclosure.

The following day, Francesca Grimani performed a brief memorial

THE PRIEST WILL TAKE CARE OF HER
THE VENETIAN SECRET, 1620

service, and the nuns gathered in the chapel to pray for Chiara's soul.

*"Let us pray for Sister Celestia, the frail victim of delusions."
Francesca Grimani said.*

Turning to face the altar, the Abbess let out a small scream. It turned out that Chiara had drawn a man's private parts, crowned with a halo, on the white altar cloth. The Abbess took the Bible and covered the charcoal drawing swiftly, before resuming the service. She made a sign, and the nuns' voices rose with 'Te Deus Laudamus'.

As soon as the service was over, the servant nuns were put to work erasing Chiara's other scandalous and sacrilegious drawings on the walls in the cloisters. Tittering, they washed the walls of drawings: penises urinating into chalices; horny devils with human faces sticking out their tongues; and church bells, with the rope attached to testicles, drawn on four of the columns and the door to the parlatorio.

At the burial, a lay nun fetched the white silk bag with the cuttings of Chiara's long auburn hair from the cupboard in the Chapter Room. The Abbess arranged the auburn locks around Chiara's face in the coffin before closing the lid.

"A beautiful Bride of Christ she'll make in Paradise," Francesca Grimani sobbed, looking at Chiara's peaceful face.

Beatrice cries as I end my sad story. I take her hand, thinking of Chiara that day in the chapel when she had first told me of her escape plans. How bold Chiara had been then.

I finger Tommaso's letter in the pocket of my dress. Is he safe with Domenico on board and pirates plundering the seas?

THE PRIEST WILL TAKE CARE OF HER
THE VENETIAN SECRET, 1620

Tommaso Contarini, 1620, La Contarina, Venice

22.
News of Tommaso

I close the door to my cell and turn the key in the lock. The girls are asleep, Giulia hugging her china dolls as always. She is coughing and tossing, crying out from time to time. Her breathing is uneven and troubled.

Clutching the unopened letter in one hand, I kneel down next to the bed listening to the child's breathing, caressing her hot brow, smoothing the damp hair clinging to Giulia's face. The medicine with the ginger and the cinnamon potion hasn't done much good. It worries me that Giulia is ill with a cough in the middle of a warm September.

I take the taper from the wall, sit down on my footstool, resting my back against the wall. I have had no news of Tommaso until now and have difficulty keeping my hands still when I open the letter. The pages are densely scrawled in his bold, wild handwriting. The letters seem to move along the paper like rebellious spirits out of a fantastic tale.

Constantinople, 20th June 1620

Sweet Marietta,

I am safe in Constantinople. I miss you every hour of the day. As I go about my father's business, I conjure up your lovely face. You have been with me every night in my restless sea dreams full of longing for you.

The painting of Rosalba has been on my mind too. I hope you will have found her secret when I am back in Venice at Christmas. If not, don't despair, Marietta, we will still find a way.

It probably won't come as a surprise to you that your brother's presence on the Contarina has been a nuisance. He has been aggressive every bit of the voyage, in everybody's way, or moody, the way we know him. Arrigo and Zannino were always wary of him and with good reason.

It was all on the pretence that Domenico was going to learn about sailing. He is not interested in knowing about charts, or anything else about navigation, for that matter. You know how Domenico hates taking commands from others, particularly from me as the captain, his peer and childhood companion. Your father's hopes of making a trader of your brother will come to nothing. However, I do not think your father will be surprised or even much disappointed. Furthermore, I have once again experienced how his temper can explode and what a coward he is.

When we left Venice, we had a few days of uneventful sailing. Even if the republic claims to have finished off the Uskok pirates, we kept as far away as possible from the coast. The Uskoks always seem to know when a merchant ship passes. I

NEWS OF TOMMASO
THE VENETIAN SECRET, 1620

have seen their heads mounted on the Proclamation Stone in the piazza many times. I should have known better than to believe that these pirates were finished when I saw their bloody faces exposed in this way on the day of my departure.

The Brazzere, the Uskoks' small boats, came upon us a few days' sailing from Venice. So much for the reassurance of the republic. The men on the watch had seen nothing due to the fog. Many of the sailors have very little experience and no training for the sea. When the Uskoks boarded our ship, several of the crew hid below decks for fear of their lives, including your brother. Arrigo and Zannino saved the day.

As the last Uskoks jumped overboard, Domenico appeared from below deck together with the two carpenters, the cook, and five of the sailors. He looked pale and ill at ease.

"The chickens have left their coop, Captain!" Arrigo shouted.

"Keelhaul the bastards!" the rest of the crew cried.

Your brother, like the others, claimed that they went below to get their weapons.

"Are you accusing me of cowardice? How dare you!" Domenico sneered at Arrigo. Then he drew his pistol and shot Arrigo in the left hand.

I had Domenico arrested for cowardice and assault, and placed in the ship's prison.

Thank God, Arrigo's hand has mended now and he is able to use it as well as before.

Our casualties were serious: five dead and eight wounded. I found myself the commander of a crew of injured seamen.

NEWS OF TOMMASO
THE VENETIAN SECRET, 1620

I was hit by an arrow in the attack. My wound became infected and I came down with fever. I had to turn the command over to the steersman. While we sailed on I was lying shivering in my cot in the dark. My head was swimming and I was hallucinating for days. I dreamed that a dark ship was sailing close by, casting a dark shadow that loomed over the Contarina. In my dream, a white butterfly went by. It seemed to break the shadow dancing in the air, as if inviting me to follow. I have thought ever since that is was you, who came to save me

When I woke up the next morning, the fever had miraculously left me. I got out of my berth, and stumbled onto the deck, light at heart. I had been senseless for five days and nights, and all the time Zannino had looked after me. Arrigo told me later that Zannino stayed with me at night, drying the sweat from my brow, and forcing me to drink. Lucretia has taught him to use healing herbs, and he had brought many different kinds for our voyage. I am now fully recovered thanks to Zannino, apart from the scar, the only reminder of the Uskoks, and as good as new.

A northerly wind blew behind us all the way to Constantinople. This was the first time I arrived in command of a ship. We got there at dawn on the Sultan's birthday, May 15, without any more trouble.

Your uncle released Domenico from the ship's arrest; being the Bailo, he has the authority. At least I am rid of Domenico. He left with your uncle to stay at his house, where seven young noblemen from Venice are his guests. I know a few of them. They have come to learn about Constantinople under your uncle's protection. I wonder how Domenico will get on with them. When I said goodbye to him on the ship, he was angry and depressed. Like when we were children. One moment in high spirits, bragging about his cleverness, and the next aggressive and low. What a relief that he is going back to Venice with your uncle. If he doesn't come home, I will not shed a tear.

Our warehouse has kept me busy. When I returned, the workers had left over a squabble about money. It has taken me weeks bargaining with them, persuading them to return to their work. Now I spend my time buying raw silk from the Imperial Silk Factory to bring back to Venice. I am to take supplies of corn for the granaries as well. Most days I go through the vast Bazaar on my way to the silk factory. Here are traders from all over the world: Persia, Afghanistan, India, Russia; Slavs, Armenians, Syrians, Negroes, and Jew; the Rialto market at home seems quite ordinary in comparison.

Your uncle had an audience with the Sultan a week after we arrived, and asked me to accompany him, as I didn't go last time I was in Constantinople. He thought it essential to the success of my trading and said that life would be a lot easier if I paid my respects at court.

Our relationship with the Turks is full of ups and downs. One moment, the Venetian merchants are honoured guests and allowed to trade anywhere, and the next moment our ships are seized and our properties confiscated. The Turks are experts at the granting and withdrawing of favours; they are bloodthirsty too, always on the rampage. Perhaps their temperament is forged by the never-ending wars, as the Ottoman Empire

NEWS OF TOMMASO
THE VENETIAN SECRET, 1620

survives only because of the Turks' constant warfare.

I decided to go with your uncle to the palace. As the Venetian Bailo, he is much respected in Constantinople. But I think his character is like your brother's, if you don't mind my saying so. He is cunning and sly. But that is a great quality in this city if you are a diplomat: it is a dangerous job. Who knows, with Domenico's temperament, perhaps his future lies in Constantinople?

White Arabian stallions were waiting to take us to the palace, beautiful horses standing on the quay impatiently pawing the ground. An escort of Janizaries accompanied our suite, and your uncle's servants carried the presents of the Venetian silk and damask for the Sultan. Francesco's horse looked particularly handsome, draped in a tabard of fine Venetian crimson velvet that swept the ground, and Francesco himself, imposing in his long cloak of crimson satin.

On our way to the palace, we rode past the Hippodrome, the arena where the four golden horses of San Marco used to be. As they stand in pairs of two, on the façade of the Basilica now looking undauntedly towards the Piazza, unbridled and free, the thought of the horses left me full of hopes for our future together.

The palace, the Bucoleon, which is much larger than our Ducal Palace, is a vast labyrinth of corridors. I only wish I could have showed it to you, you would have marvelled at the magnificence of the wonders there. Four of the Sultan's bodyguards, fierce looking Janizaries, took us through splendid halls and galleries to the audience chamber. When we entered, artificial birds twittered on golden branches, and mechanical lions roared, beating the ground with their tails. The Sultan sat on a throne of gold and jewels, dressed in silk and brocade of every colour. When we made our obeisance, he was suddenly whisked into the air to the sound of organs, only to descend the next moment in more glorious robes. There he sat, motionless on his golden throne: his eyes on the ground, and his hands in his lap. We were forced down on our knees and given a corner of the Sultan's robe to kiss. Francesco was placed opposite the Sultan with his back against the wall. As he made his address it was translated by the Grand Dragoman, the interpreter. The Sultan looked bored, pretending he didn't hear. All he said before we left was 'Giozel'- that is ,'Very well.'

"No one ever dreamed of such a tyranny," Francesco said to me afterwards. "The Sultan puts his subjects to death at will, and they accept their fate without resistance."

The Sultan owns those responsible for carrying out his desires. They are all slaves: Christian-born peasants captured as children and brought up in the palace. Your uncle also told me that hundreds of concubines live in the palace. On the first Friday of every month, the hundred oldest concubines are sent away, and another hundred young ones arrive crossing the strait in a barge. Their great Prophet Mohammed allows for the abuse of women even in Paradise. The Turks believe that there they will spend their time with amorous virgins, the men never exceeding the age of thirty, and the virgins fifteen, and they shall have their virginities renewed as fast as lost.

The Turkish women, like our noble women, live subdued lives

and, like in Venice, I rarely see them about the city. The women are dressed in black, a colour that the Turks detest. They say that those who wear it will never enter Paradise. Is this how the men make sure that their wives and concubines will not interfere with them while they shamelessly enjoy the virgins in Paradise?

The riders who will take the despatch bags to the post boat in Cattaro are leaving in a moment, and my letter must go with them. I long for the time when I can put this miserable life behind me, and dedicate my days and nights to our love instead. What is the point of constantly risking life at sea, or my neck in Constantinople at the mercy of some Turk's scimitar? Trading and sailing the seas was never for me.

Your Tommaso

NEWS OF TOMMASO
THE VENETIAN SECRET, 1620

23

Tomorrow at Dawn

Lupi feels the guard's hand on his shoulder, pushing him into the cell. The door is bolted from the outside. He is alone. Tomorrow at dawn. They had pronounced the sentence in the Hall of the Ten, his former friends and patrons, people with whom he had discussed his holy and religious work.

"You have been the owner of the bodies and souls of these poor women." Merely a few words to destroy him.

After the interrogations and months spent in the Pozzi, entombed in the clammy cell underneath the Ducal Palace, he had never doubted that he would draw his last breath between the columns in the piazzetta. But still, when Francesca Grimani's brother had spoken the words, it had been difficult to fathom their meaning. Not that he was afraid to meet his death and settle his accounts with God. No, that was not it.

It was rather the painful sensation of regret, the feeling of never getting his own back that had whispered through his veins. As Battista Grimani spoke, he had raised his eyes towards heaven, looking at the ceiling with Paolo Veronese's paintings, and that soft face had been looking down at him.

She was the last person he had expected to see. Marietta Morosini. How could Veronese possibly have painted her? Years before she was born? A cruel angel in disguise. There were no limits to female cunning and malice. Most women tell lies or deceive men. Being a father confessor, he knew. The Morosini girl had been his thorn in the flesh, and now satisfaction was beyond him. For ever, and ever.

He had felt in a trance when the guard pulled at his arm, shoving him towards a door hidden in the panelling of the Ten's hall, pushing him down the staircase, laughing, whispering in his ear, "now you have got it coming to you, priest," and he was back in the foul smell of the prison.

* * *

Tonight the tide is out. Only a trickle of water has found its way in underneath the low door. The last chimes of the Marangona sound the hour of midnight.

"Guard!" Lupi shouts at the top of his voice. "Bring me a pen and some paper! A taper too!" He listens for the approaching steps of the guard. On this his last night, they can't refuse his wishes. But all he can hear are the rats scratching and the sound of waves breaking against the bulwark of the Riva. It is the Sirocco blowing and, before long, it will whip the lagoon into frenzy. He must stand on the plank not to be immersed in water.

There is still time to write his confession. If only the guard would bring him the writing materials. He wants to unburden himself and be absolved when standing before God. Suddenly, there is an uproar, and the noise of clanking doors echoes in the corridors. The clamour of voices dies down abruptly, and he hears someone crying in the cell beside him.

TOMORROW AT DAWN
THE VENETIAN SECRET, 1620

"Guard!" Lupi calls out at the sound of a key turning.

"I heard you the first time, priest! What do you want with pen and paper? To confess your sins? We don't have enough ink or paper in store to cover them all! Your sands are running out faster than you can sprinkle them on your writings. Ha-ha-ha! I will be back," the guard grunts full of scorn, "as quick as my legs will carry me. Can't keep a Signore waiting, can we?"

Lupi can still hear the guard's laughter ringing in his ears when the hatch slams shut in his face. He wraps the heavy cloak closer around him. He imagines how the foul smell and the humidity enter his body to dissolve his bones. But it will be the executioner's axe that takes care of his bones in the morning, he thinks, and severs his head from his body. With little slow movements his probing fingertips feel the broad neck and carefully caress all the strong and sinewy muscles just beneath the skin.

The guard opens the door ajar.

"There you are, priest. From your humble servant! Ha – ha." He hands Lupi the writing materials with a smirk before banging the door shut behind him.

"It's closing time!" the guard's shout echoes in the corridors and penetrates the cell doors.

Lupi pulls the ramshackle plank underneath the barred window facing the lagoon. The casement will be his writing desk tonight.

The Riva is deserted. Between the thick iron bars, he watches the grey clouds hurrying past hunted by the strong wind. The moon sprinkles them with a touch of silver as they pass, as if she wanted them to make a halt, strewing salt on their tails. Much like showering a beautiful woman with flattering words to make

TOMORROW AT DAWN
THE VENETIAN SECRET, 1620

her stay, he thinks.

For one brief moment, the enormity of the waves frightens him. They seem to bare their teeth at him, hoping to crush his soul between their savage jaws. He dips the quill in the ink and begins writing:

I know that deep in their hearts, most men envy me the harvest I reaped in the convent, no matter what they might say to the contrary, the hypocrites. The nuns were my vice. They were mostly easy prey and during the two years I was their Confessor, only a few caused me any troubles. The high wall shielded me from exposure to the world and the nuns kept silent.

I knew all their secrets. They were my children. All I had to do was to delight in the pleasures of the table, and savour the white, unblemished virgins laid out before me. Not many have relished as great a number of unsullied maidens as I have - apart from the Sultan in his Seraglio, perhaps. It was as easy as blowing dust off a butterfly's wing. Chance and the moment rule all.

Not even were I to perish in the flames of hell would I regret what I did. Should the Redeemer in his unfathomable wisdom decide to chastise me and deliver me there, my only sorrow would be if, when her time came, Marietta Morosini didn't keep me company in purgatory, for it was she who turned the tide against me.

But I will find a path to salvation yet. We are all subject to frailty; I saw and knew of serious faults committed by others and it seemed to me that mine were inferior. God will forgive me for exorcising His consecrated offerings, humbled as I was by their beauty, taming their vanity. They are nothing but temptresses, possessed by the devil. I was spurred on by spiritual and not worldly motives, whereas the ungodly Morosini-strumpet will find no mercy and be eternally damned on the Day of Judgement.

I restored the nuns to the world of the living for brief spells of time, when their bodies sang out to me like heavenly hymns, like the solitary tunes of the nightingale confined in its cage calling for a mate. In those fleeting moments, they forgot their boredom and being buried alive, despite all their awkward pretensions and protestations.

To say I am a criminal, to call it profanation and violation, even spiritual adultery, and to accuse me of turning the convent into a whorehouse, is taking it too far. We carry Original Sin in our hearts, and with St. Augustine I say 'O happy fault to merit such a Redeemer! O felix culpa!'

But then, religion rests on the rules of paradox. It is simple: you win by losing.

The Morosini slut merely spoiled what little appetite I had out of spite and envy. I never desired her, and for that she couldn't forgive me. I have watched her blasphemous behaviour in the parlatorio with young Tommaso Contarini, blinded by passion, lusting for him, leaning up against the grates in her low cut dress, the red silk making her white skin glow, a string of small pearls showing off the pretty neck. I noticed her legs were adorned in fishnet stockings when she coquettishly lifted the skirts of her dress to sit by the grates. A scandalous sight. Her corn coloured hair braided with golden fillets and never covered by a veil.

And all this for a mere boy, a tamed monkey, a puppet, dancing whenever she pulls the strings.

True, he is a nobleman, and I a citizen, but still he is nothing to me. He has none of my learning of Greek and Latin, nor of philosophy.

TOMORROW AT DAWN
THE VENETIAN SECRET, 1620

Theology is the king of the sciences, and I am grateful that my father forced priesthood upon me. All the Contarini puppet can do is to captain a galley at his father's command.

That nobility is determined by moral quality rather than lineage is a lie. The way the noblemen of Venice flaunt their flowing togas, pretending to be as wise as the ancient Roman senators, is a disgrace to God.

But I am satisfied that she will never taste that delicate dark youth. He is promised to someone else. And she? She is not promised to any one because her soul is steeped in the filth of sin. In his anger God has twisted her tongue and turned His face from her.

I can only quote Ecclesiastics: 'The hopes of fools are vain and false: and dreams lift up fools. He who looks to dreams is like him that catches at a shadow, and chases the wind.'

Cordelia Tron, Sister Pellegrina, was a challenge from God. I had pondered on her plump body in the chapel for some time. I knew in my heart that it was God who wanted me to chastise her, and He who directed my attention towards her. Sister Pellegrina answered me flippantly, her gold earrings dangling when shaking her head in denial of something. But she was still tempting me with her beguiling spiteful looks, her silk dress adorned by a silver brooch showing a satyr, only to make me aware of her breasts, the fat pearls round her neck, and her hair always arranged in small soft curls at the temples. High and mighty she thought herself, a daughter of the prominent Trons. She would always try to appear as someone special in front of the others. I had to discipline her and teach her, allowing her a glimpse of my innermost sacred state of mind to help her on her way to God.

I had prepared my speech carefully when she came to the

TOMORROW AT DAWN
THE VENETIAN SECRET, 1620

confessional, as I always did when God desired me to take notice of a young choir nun. One day, when she knelt in front of me on the bench, and I placed my hands on her small rounded breasts to try the strength of her faith, she drew back from my touch. I greatly praised her firmness of spirit, and told her that God had asked me to test her in this way.

One sin she hadn't confessed to me. She was ill at ease when I told her how I had caught her in the act, a few days before, less constant in her faith than today, kissing the blond carpenter behind the new henhouse. Wearing a nun's habit doesn't mean that you don't boil at pressure. The spirit might be willing, but the flesh is weak. She blushed at my words, but remained silent. For once, I wasn't in for one of her impertinent remarks.

"I ought to denounce you to your superiors," I told her, "but I have decided to make an exception, and discipline you myself."

I never forgave her the slighting look when I asked her to meet me at the water entrance the following day at None.

Not a few of the choir nuns had confessed to the sin of listening to Sister Pellegrina's whisperings. She was tormenting me, spreading the rumour that I was bragging about my manhood when I was impotent. Now was the time to set her right.

"What are the tools of Good Works according to the Rule?"

"Not to say what is idle or causes laughter," she murmured in a trembling voice, fearing no doubt that I knew of her vile whisperings.

I carry the keys to the gates and the boathouse, and decided to take the gondola for my outing with Sister Pellegrina. She was waiting when I opened the gate, dressed modestly in her white nun's habit for once, looking demure and taciturn. I took the picnic basket I

TOMORROW AT DAWN
THE VENETIAN SECRET, 1620

had told her to pack, and helped her into the gondola. I took her
to a small uninhabited island, as I wanted to make certain no one
disturbed us.

There I taught her right from wrong. The wine and food were
excellent but she never touched it. She was my silent penitent, a
novice of only seventeen, sitting like an innocent white dove among
the wild flowers in the grass, her pretty hands folded. Strengthened
by the holy wine, I took her into my arms, and pulled her down
beside me.

"Priests don't do these things," she hissed like a cat, but I quickly
eased her mind telling her that this was no sin.

"This is our sanctified bed. We are both married to the church,
and therefore our spiritual marriage can be carnally consummated
without sin."

I lifted her skirts, and at the sight of her white plump thighs, I
blessed her and called her 'my prayer,' 'my altar.' I carefully
removed her undergarments, and my hand crept upwards, slowly,
gently touching her soft skin. There was not a single hair on her
body, as little as you would find on a piece of white marble. Sister
Pellegrina never uttered a sound, but lay quite still.

Before we got into the gondola, I asked Sister Pellegrina to confess
her sins, and absolved her.

When Sister Pellegrina gave birth to a boy nine months later,
Sister Teresa, Paulina Morosini, committed a crime so grave that
my own errors dwindle into insignificance beside hers. She played
the midwife to Sister Pellegrina on that night. Only a single taper
was alight in the cell, and shadows were dancing on the walls. The
girl was writhing in pain, crying out for the Madonna. Sly looks

TOMORROW AT DAWN
THE VENETIAN SECRET, 1620

and dangling earrings were a long way off. Sister Teresa muffled her screams with a knot of cloth between her teeth, and I had to press the girl down in the bed to keep her still. The moment the baby drew its first breath, Sister Teresa grabbed the navel cord, coiled it round its small white neck, and in a moment the baby was lying still in her arms. Sister Pellegrina cried out, a hideous cry that seemed to make even the shadows cringe.

This was not the first time a baby born in the convent suffered such a fate. Sister Teresa closed the baby's eyes, made the sign of the cross, wrapped the tiny limp body in a sheet, and we left the weeping Sister Pellegrina alone. In the cemetery, we went to the corner where the white roses climb the wall, and I dug a grave among the others. Here the old nun lay down the white bundle. I read over the child's grave before leaving, and I remember she asked me if by any chance I had noticed that the baby resembled me? I merely turned my back on her and walked away.

I never reported Sister Teresa's deed to her superiors because I know God will punish her eventually; she is a woman working hand in glove with the infernal enemy. Life is paradoxical, indeed. Some murderers end up between the columns in the piazzetta, others in the convents.

I carefully picked seven of the youngest and most vain novices. I summoned them for confession on the day of my 54th anniversary. One after the other, they entered the small confessional at the back of the chapel and knelt on the bench in front of my chair. I told them that the time had come to rid them of the devil, obsessed as they were with finery, only desiring to seduce every male who set foot in the parlatorio or the convent.

TOMORROW AT DAWN
THE VENETIAN SECRET, 1620

I told them to wait for me in the orchard behind the shed where the apples are stored the next day after Prime. I impressed upon them that the devil would rule and God would forsake them in all eternity if they disobeyed a priest, and that God had bestowed celestial visions on me. I had decided to chastise them using the birch on their bare buttocks should I meet with any resistance.

I did nothing but follow God's word. I made them sign a written vow saying that they promised never again to reveal their inner state without my permission, and with instructions to kiss the ground twenty-five times each day and lick thirty crosses on it. I repeated that on professing they had vowed obedience to their superior, and that signing my vow would simplify their way to God. I told them that we were now one in desire and love.

It was a heavenly sight that morning in May, watching their pale naked bodies in the sun like a row of white alabaster columns. They pleaded with me when I ordered them to undress in the orchard, and strip themselves of their vanities to be cleansed in the eyes of God. Their tears never moved me, and I never listened to their promises of abandoning their ornaments. I told them that my only alternative was to denounce them to the Holy Office. The two youngest novices even fell to their knees in front of me. I bid them stand in line with the others, atone their sins, and be silent before God. It was like a vision of a procession of pure angels parading in front of me.

I always preferred women to have small delicate breasts, to be slender, but still curved, and a little plump around the hips. To end up in the embrace of a woman only to discover that her body failed

TOMORROW AT DAWN
THE VENETIAN SECRET, 1620

to attract me, is something I have always tried to avoid.

It was my chance to study them and decide at my leisure who to enjoy in the confessional.

As a boy, I once dissected a butterfly out of curiosity, and I found that it has a long-chambered heart that runs the length of its body on the upper side. Looking at the maidens standing in line, my eyes were cutting into their souls, as my scalpel had once cut into the butterfly's heart, and all their sins and shameless desires were laid bare to me.

"I can see into your souls with the help of your guardian angels," I told them, "I behold things you have never spoken of to anybody nor written on paper. Don't forget I am a doctor of souls" They trembled at my words, because they knew they could hide nothing from me.

I made a mental note of the dark mysterious Sister Innocentia with the shy expression in her almond shaped eyes, and the untamed redhead, Sister Fede, never subject to obedience. The others were either too fat or too gaunt, but these two had nipples like rosebuds, and their buttocks were small and firm, like the ancient marble statues of Venus.

I was never disappointed in my choice. Both Sisters held an attraction of their own. I enjoyed the nuns on the chest in the confessional, on the table, lying across the small black chair, or beneath the Cross. When they were scared at the sight of blood on the floor afterwards, I comforted them. I told them it was Christ's wounds bleeding to atone their sins, His blood dripping onto the tiles. I gave them each a sugared almond to consume as a confirmation of our spiritual marriage.

They confessed their sin to me afterwards, vowing not to be led

astray by vanity again. But I knew in my heart that their repentance
was not genuine. How to absolve them?
Francesca Grimani was my associate from the start. She revered me
for my sermons and my learning. She consulted me in all matters.
Once or twice every week, she joined me in my rooms for supper
and shared the pheasants or partridges the lay nuns had prepared
for me. Often she smuggled a jar of the nuns' excellent wine from
the cellar, the same, Francesca told me, that Doge Antonio Priuli
enjoyed at Easter.
Such a vain and silly woman, her hair dusted with gold and thick
layers of rouge plastered onto her fat cheeks, smelling worse than
a church rat.
One evening after we had eaten well, shared a jar of wine, and
enjoyed some of the sweets I always keep in my room, she asked me
to exorcise her. The demon, Asmodeus, the devil of lust, had begun
touching her body every night at Matins, she said. He evoked cold
chills and certain feelings. Hands and a mouth were touching her
breast, and she felt it in her 'hidden parts'.
On the shelves in my chamber, I kept a considerable selection of
restoratives and aphrodisiacs to strengthen me for my duties in
the convent. I carefully picked a restorative for Francesca, telling
her that it was really all she needed to cleanse her soul and to rid
herself of the demon. It was a near escape, for I could never have
touched that woman, let alone put my hand on her head to bless
her. All the tiers of fat were disgusting to me. She found it difficult
to hide her disappointment, but she managed to appear grateful.
My accomplishments in the convent would have been a great deal
more complicated without her.
Through the years, I bought my supply of herbs at a great cost

from the wise woman Lucretia Columbin at the Arsenal. I have lost count of how many ducats I have poured into that woman's pockets. But it has been worth every soldi. Lucretia is nothing but a divine genius when it comes to mixing medicines of all sorts, and for any purpose, using recipes going back hundreds of years. The Holy Office might be interested in trying out one or two of her potions and decide whether or not it would be worthwhile looking into her practice.

I have sometimes wondered myself if Lucretia were in fact a sorceress.

Pietro Mudazzo was my faithful go-between and my hired bravo, as expensive as Lucretia, and as efficient. I have heard it said that he is now with the Uskoks at Segna, earning his way up in the world as their spy, quite out of reach of the powerful Ten and the most Serene Republic.

I paid him handsomely for dealing with the Da Mula girl. I felt certain that she would blacken my name eventually, and people might not understand my spiritual aspirations.

I always thought that she was meant for the convent, and it came as a surprise to me when she was chosen to be a bride, rather than her beautiful Sister. She was my favourite, easy to teach and so pliable. How could she possibly explain to Giovanni Loredan, on the morning of her wedding night, why there was not even the slightest trace of blood on the silk sheets? Nothing like the spots of blood on Sister Celestia's bed when I joined her in a spiritual marriage.

I always felt that God wanted me to be close to Sister Celestia. An exemplary nun, with her coy smile, serene expression, and nervous timidity. Never wearing the seductive adornments with which they all embellish themselves, the vain platform shoes with silk strings, or wide sleeves of fine fabrics in all the colours of the rainbow. The cut of a sleeve means everything to them. Sister Celestia's tunic was always proper, high-necked with abundant veils to cover her breast and shoulders. I never saw her kissing and fondling the other nuns in the corridors, lifting skirts, hiding hands in undergarments, like most of them do, and never did she participate in their womanish wars and rivalry, which I know so well from the confessional.

I was pleased when the Inquisitor Paolo Erasmo recognized my superior learning, and wrote me a letter asking me to exorcise Sister Celestia as a consequence of her escape and her visions.

I went to her in her cell during summer. God had directed my attention to her body as a tool for salvation. I told her what an honour it is to give yourself to a holy priest. How she would then be excluded from every temptation to evil, and carried to God on the wings of her imagination.

Sister Celestia had visions of the lion of San Marco breathing down her neck, and of the devil in the shape of a frightened wolf, or a dwarf breathing fire. Sometimes she told me, while weeping, that she dreamt of young men with horses' legs and feet, inciting her to join their forbidden acts. She knew this to be a test by God, and that hell was her cell.

"No, my dear daughter," I told her, "it isn't true that hell is your cell; it isn't true that you are in the devil's hands; no, no, it isn't true that you are abandoned by God. I protect your liberty and will not let the devil get you." I confided in her that I too knew the devil's tricks.

She wriggled and coiled, bit my shoulders and tore savagely at my hair when I joined her to me in spiritual marriage on the narrow

TOMORROW AT DAWN
THE VENETIAN SECRET, 1620

bed. I knew then that the devil had really taken possession of her. I struggled with him on the bed many times during the summer, and it came as no surprise to me when Sister Celestia threw herself from the bell tower in anguish of the evil one. I mourned her, and asked God to forgive me for not having succeeded in exorcising the infernal enemy from his abode in Sister Celestia's body.

Morosini took her chance and sought revenge for all the times I had slighted her. It was she who sent the deceitful letters accusing me of Sister Celestia's death and other infamies, slandering me in the eyes of God, the Serene Prince, and the Patriarch. Mark my words, she is nothing but a lying whore, and, standing before God, the members of the Council of Ten will regret that they ever listened to her.

The last time I laid eyes on her was in the confessional on the day of my arrest. She walked into the room in her arrogant and supercilious manner, wearing a scandalous low-cut green silk dress. I remember the sun falling on her hair through the window; it glowed like an angel's halo.

"You have come to confess at last?" I asked her.

"I have indeed, father.' She said smiling. "I want to confess that I've sent three letters: one to His Serenity, the Doge Antonio Priuli; one to the Patriarch, Giovanni Tiepolo; and one to my father, unmasking your sins. I have reason to believe that you will be arrested and, I pray, be safely in a prison cell before the Marangona chimes tonight."

I never understood why the Ten or the Patriarch paid heed to her lying accusations.

"Do you call it charity to turn against a faithful servant of God and a superior?" I asked her disgusted with her lies and slander.

TOMORROW AT DAWN
THE VENETIAN SECRET, 1620

She just answered in her usual arrogant manner. "When I think of charity, a priest's robe comes to mind. It covers up the base consequences of his hypocrisies."
She even accused me of faking deafness to lure the nuns into my confessional office instead of using the confessional in the chapel.
"You pretend to be deaf in order for the nuns to shout, and then to be able to talk in private you say confessions must take place in here. You have most cruelly abused the secrecy of the confessional."
I will never forget the look of spite in her cat's eyes, hard and cold as crystal. I couldn't look that demon in the face. I made the sign of the cross as I watched her walk away into the cloisters.
I know now why she was nosing about in the crypt. The Morosini slut found the ...

* * *

The first chime of impending dawn: the Maleficio. Lupi stops writing. He becomes conscious that his leather shoes and thin stockings are soaked through, even though he is standing on the plank. He looks towards the lagoon, counting the bell strokes. The storm has died down, and left the Riva shrouded in a fine mist. The waves have become no more than mere ripples wrinkling their brow at him, slurping softly against the stones, like a dog drinking.

Looking through the window, he watches day dawning upon him, and in the horizon the sky is painted with stripes of rose-pink hues. He can't help but consider it prophetic of his blood, soon to incarnadine the stones between the columns. Sacrificed on the gallows like Christ on the Cross, both of them atoning for

TOMORROW AT DAWN
THE VENETIAN SECRET, 1620

the sins of others, and, like Christ, he would be tried in the third
hour, when the bell struck nine.

'As I went down the water side,
None but my foe to be my guide,
None but my foe...'
he sings quietly to himself, humming the words.

He watches the Riva, which is empty yet, apart from a few Greeks
and Dalmatians who arrive to unload sacks of spices onto the
quay. The faintest scent of ginger and cinnamon reaches him in
the cell, and he watches two galleys lulled gently by the breeze,
the sails hanging slack, flapping a little. The gondolas are rocking
majestically. A row of austere swans dressed in mourning,
hushed, attentive, abiding their time.
Then he hears voices and the sound of water splashing in the
corridor. The door is unbolted, and a key turns in the lock. It is
pushed open, ploughing through the water.
"Are you ready priest?"
Lupi turns his head, and nods towards the guards and the friar,
just as the Maleficio bell from the Campanile chimes again: a
signal of his execution. He leaves the quill beside the inkpot and
the densely written pages, takes a look at the last unfinished
sentence, silently cursing Marietta Morosini for escaping him
one more time. Now they might never know... He steps into the
corridor.

TOMORROW AT DAWN
THE VENETIAN SECRET, 1620

24.

An Execution

"Hurry up, Zusanna!" Manuela Morosini is impatient. She wraps the long black veil around her and listens to the maid's heels tapping against the tiles in the portego. There is Zusanna, out of breath from running, panting like a dog. Her red hair is a mess; Manuela looks critically at the maid's freckled face.

"You have kept me waiting," Manuela snaps. "Put on your veil, and don't forget to lock the door."

Zusanna curtsies nervously and fumbles with the key. They leave Ca' Morosini as the chimes of the Maleficio sound. The pearly light is exactly right for the priest's execution, Manuela thinks. It is becoming that he leaves the world at this pristine hour of morning, having violated sacred virgins. Surely God has chosen this time of day on purpose.

"Zusanna, come on!" Manuela considers her maid quite hopeless. If only she had sent her away with Beatrice after all.

If only they could have taken the gondola, everything wouldhave been so much easier. Why Fabrizio ordered it this morning she doesn't understand. Normally her husband walks to the Piazza. Does he suspect that she is going to the priest's execution? Is he trying to stop her?

She would have liked to have worn shoes with low heels. Not

the high platform shoes, knowing that she will be pushed about in the piazzetta. The crowds will be milling around the scaffold. Half of Venice will be there. But that's impossible, being a noblewoman and a Cornaro. The thought of another broken leg is terrible. Even worse is the thought of Marietta sitting at her bedside, reading aloud, looking sullen. No, she would never want that again.

The priest's undoing is Marietta's work. But for once her daughter has done some good. Giovanni Tiepolo had praised Marietta's stubborn determination.

The spice dealers are opening their shops for the day in Calle dello Specier. Manuela is sensitive to the scent of foreign spices blending in the air. It is a long time since she has walked the city on her own. Only rarely does she venture into the alleys.

All the city marvels at the priest's deeds. She simply must be there to witness his end. Orsolo Lupi, who has ridiculed the entire city and committed crimes right under the nose of the Ten: a true infamy to the Council, which boasts its intelligence of any malefactor within the Venetian dominions.

Passing Palazzo Bellavista in Campo San Maurizio, Manuela stops for a moment to gaze up at Veronese's frescoes, the putti and the allegorical figures, searching for her face.

"Wait, Zusanna." She leans heavily on the maid's shoulder. There she is. Rosalba's angelic face smiling mockingly down at her from the friezes. Manuela flinches at the thought of the scandal the girl brought upon the Morosinis. Rosalba's face might have been Marietta's. She is struck by the resemblance. To run away from San Zaccaria, like Rosalba, creating new scandals, would be just like her. It had been wise of her to get rid of Veronese's painting all those years ago. Marietta had been fascinated with it. Manuela is relieved that Tommaso Contarini is getting married, because that will be the end of their childish infatuation.

She clings to Zusanna's strong arm through Calle delle Ostreghe to Campo San Moise. In Calle dell'Ascensione she catches a glimpse of the monastery of the Knights Templar now turned into the Albergo della Luna, which Domenico frequents. She worries when he goes there. It has such a dubious reputation and a most shady clientele. The owner is a greedy and unsympathetic woman, skilled in the art of tricking her clients.

She misses Domenico. In a month, he will back from Constantinople on board Francesco's ship, luckily, and not La Contarina. She is aware how much the voyage with Tommaso Contarini has upset her son. She rereads Domenico's letter now and again, and never without a taste of worry. His moods seem to have increased. His mood swings like a pendulum, ecstatic one moment and melancholic the next. The condition is not unfamiliar to her; she has observed the like in some of her ancestors.

The Moors on top of the Clock Tower strike the hour as they enter the Piazza. The priest will be facing the Archangel Michael on the corner of the Ducal Palace. And the clock, she thinks, as if God was forcing him to know the time.

The Piazza is packed. Two arsenalotti push past her and Manuela nearly trips. Her heart pounds and she takes a firmer grip on Zusanna's shoulder. The girl looks scared, biting her lips. They stay close to the columns along the arches of the Procuratie Nuove. All his waking hours Fabrizio spends here, and she feels just slightly annoyed at the thought of bumping into her husband,

AN EXECUTION
THE VENETIAN SECRET, 1620

at this hour, on this occasion.

The scaffold looms in front of her. "Stop here, Zusanna." For an instant, she stands still, gazing at the platform raised between the two columns. Then she pushes Zusanna in front of her through the mob. She wants to be in the front row.

Standing beneath the scaffold, Manuela cranes her neck to look at the Lion of San Marco. It seems to follow the commotion, undaunted from the top of its column. They stand at the foot of the steps to the platform. On all sides of her, people are shouting, pushing, laughing, and whistling. Manuela abhors having to grapple with workers and artisans. It makes her dizzy standing so close to the mob. The rank smell of armpits, urine and foul breath shrouds her, suffocates her. This is like watching a play in a vast theatre, the curtain rising on the first act.

A hush: the crowd falls silent. Manuela turns her head and looks past the Ducal Palace down the Riva towards the Arsenal. The procession is crossing the Bridge of Sighs, slowly approaching the scaffold, chaperoned by the Maleficio chiming, booming, sounding the way.

She hears the town crier in front repeating 'Orsolo Lupi, anointed priest, violator of God's sacred virgins, to let his life on the scaffold.' The drummer's beats, harsh and sharp as the morning air, are imminent forebodings of death. The priest is tied to the tail of the horse, and hauled across the paving stones of the Riva.

Close to the column with the lion of Saint Mark, the priest cries out: "Hypocrites! All of you! May the flames of hell devour you!"

Before the priest can utter another word, the guards are all over

AN EXECUTION
THE VENETIAN SECRET, 1620

him, and she watches how they cut his tongue out in a quick pull. She has seen it before, at the only other execution she ever attended, years ago. She remembers the thief cursing the crowds on his way to the gallows.

The crowd cheers, the blood pours from Lupi's mouth and wrist, where his hand has been cut off, even though the goat's bladder is wrapped tightly around the stump. Manuela is familiar with the procedure of the terrible spectacle. Lupi would have been taken to Canal Grande from the prison, tied to a pole on the barge going to the church of San Croce. Sometimes the friars of San Fantin could be seen to follow the raft in their gondolas, eating and drinking on the way. At San Croce, a heavy iron chain would be placed around the priest's neck, the chain attached to the tail of the horse and, to the accompaniment of drumbeats, the priest would be dragged through the calle to San Zaccaria, the scene of the crime. In the campo of San Zaccaria, a barber would be commanded to indicate to the executioner the exact point to cut off the hand, wrap the bladder around the stump and, afterwards, the procession would continue to the piazzetta. Manuela shudders, visualizing the priest's sufferings, feeling sick, now regretting that she has been so bold as to come to the scaffold.

Three friars of San Fantin walk behind the drummer dressed in black and white robes; one carries the large black crucifix in front of him, one the scourge, and one the large candelabra. A crowd of nobles, citizens, friars and priests follow.

"An Ave Maria and a Pater Noster for this our brother." The friars' shouts are accompanied by the loud jingle of their iron scourges.

AN EXECUTION
THE VENETIAN SECRET, 1620

She is still more curious that frightened, and strains her neck to get a good view of Orsolo Lupi. She has never as much as seen a glimpse of the priest during her few visits to San Zaccaria. What does a demonic priest look like, she wonders, because surely, it must have been a demon which has so agitated his wretched body.

In front of the scaffold, the guards unchain him and tear his priest's robes apart. Manuela feels like drowning, swept off on the wave of the crowd's yells and applause. The excitement gets to her and all she can think about is getting a glimpse of his face. Zusanna whimpers beside her and covers her eyes with the veil. "Shush, this is God's will," she whispers impatiently to the maid. Foolish girl, Beatrice can have her.

She watches the San Fantin friars climb the steps to the scaffold. The priest walks right behind them. Suddenly, he hesitates, and stops in front of her. It must be some devilish cunning. Manuela is afraid. He turns his head towards her, and meets her eyes. His face is smeared with blood; the deep set eyes seem to stigmatize her, and, for an instant, her eyes are transfixed on his bull neck. She lifts her gaze to his mutilated face, takes in the hawk's nose, the fleshy bloody lips, and flinches at his look of contempt. For an instant, she has a sensation that she is an accomplice to his imminent death; she dreads his curses. Manuela makes the sign of the Cross as Lupi is pushed by the guard up the steps to the scaffold.

In her mind she chides Marietta. It is her daughter's fault that she had to suffer the priest's curses. She looks up, as he sets his foot on the first step, and watches him move upwards.

The executioner waits beside the block; the guards and friars are

AN EXECUTION
THE VENETIAN SECRET, 1620

right behind the priest. They bless the prisoner, and suddenly Lupi turns around to face the crowd, shaking his fist at them. The people are mesmerized, aghast and terrified.

The prisoner creates a sense of fear which spreads like wildfire, like a long winding fuse coiling in and out among the onlookers. The executioner grabs Lupi by the shoulder, pulls him around, and forces him down on his knees. The priest's head is on the block and, with deft movements, the hatchet is in place. The executioner lifts his cudgel. He gives the hatchet a forceful blow, but Lupi's head never moves. A thrill of terror runs through the crowd. Manuela closes her eyes and clutches so hard at Zusanna's arm that the girl lets out a cry of pain.

When she opens her eyes, the executioner hits the hatchet again and again, but still the head doesn't move, and jets of blood smear the friars' white and black cloaks. Perhaps, she thinks, the executioner only pretends to deal the final blow. It depends on the kind of crime committed, and the instructions from the Ten. How much more suffering is Lupi in for? How many blows will God sanction?

"For pity's sake! The poor creature!" One of the friars cries out, snatching the cudgel from the executioner, giving Lupi six more blows with the bludgeon. But nothing happens. One of the guards hands the executioner a knife. Lupi's throat is cut. Finally his head is separated from his body.

"Justice has been done! Justice has been done! Viva la Serenissima!"

The people shout, and applaud. Manuela clutches at Zusanna, not to lose her balance.

Lupi's body will be quartered and fastened upon the Gibbets in

AN EXECUTION
THE VENETIAN SECRET, 1620

the lagoon, as food for the birds. An eye for an eye, she thinks. One piece is hung between the two columns, one goes to the island of San Giorgio, one is placed towards Mestre and another towards Padua.

Manuela is terrified. This is not what she had bargained for; she never imagined anything as gruesome. God in his anger must have deemed decapitation too light a sentence. It must be divine intervention. God alone prolonged the priest's agonies.

The merchant beside her whispers that the Ten has ordered the hatchet to be blunt because the priest had cheated them right under their noses. The Ten wanted to show what happened to anyone violating the sacred purity of the republic.

When standing again in the doorway at Ca'Morosini, exhausted, Manuela notices a grey-haired man in a shabby cloak coming towards her. Puzzled, she turns to face him. Whatever does he want from her?

He is a Jew! The yellow badge on his breast shows a long way off. She doesn't have any business with the Jews, apart from Isacco Vita, their doctor, a man of long tried worth. But this man? She never saw him before.

The Jews are parasites, she thinks, apart from the doctors, of course. She watches the Jew moving across the campo like a big black crab. Usurers: wealthy and prosperous on behalf of others. Our city must seem like the promised land to them.

Zusanna's eyes are darting from the small Jew to Manuela.

"Don't stand there gaping," Manuela growls at her." There's work to be done in the kitchen." The girl drops a curtsey, cheeks flushed and tear stained. For a moment, she feels like crying herself.

AN EXECUTION
THE VENETIAN SECRET, 1620

"Allow me to introduce myself, I'm Abramo Errera, pawnbroker." The old man addresses her with a wry smile, revealing toothless gums. "Signora Morosini? Such beauty only befalls a few of the most prominent noblewomen in Venice," he lisps and bows his head to her.

Manuela can't help feeling flattered. "Yes, I am the mistress of this house. What do you want?"

"I have something you will find interesting." He looks at her with his watery grey eyes.

"And what might that be?"

"A ring, Signora."

"What ring?"

"A most rare and precious piece of jewellery: a signet ring with the Morosini coat of arms."

From a pocket, the Jew produces a small crimson bag, which he hands her. Manuela feels the soft velvet between her fingers and the Jew's probing eyes on her face. Could it be the signet ring she has been looking for so long?

Carefully she pulls at the silk ribbons. She gropes for the ring with her fingers, feeling its smooth metal and the hard little stones. Slowly she takes the ring from the bag, is it …Sweet Madonna! She recognises it from the row of old family portraits in the Sala and, of course, from the Chess Players. She has studied the ring on Rosalba's finger in that painting God knows how many times. It belongs to her by right; it is supposed to be passed from a Morosini bride to her daughter. Fabrizio had sworn that the ring was still in the house, that Rosalba had never brought any jewellery with her to San Zaccaria. His father had told him. Well, so much for Fabrizio's fancies.

AN EXECUTION
THE VENETIAN SECRET, 1620

She looks at the ring in awe, forgetful of the old Jew. She caresses the deep red rubies, the soft pearls, and little hard diamonds. The signet ring with the red and gold of the Morosini coat of arms set in such rare and priceless stones. When she feels the back of the ring, her fingers touch a tiny knob the size of a pin needle. She looks at it, and it seems like a snap you can open. She has once seen a signet ring with this kind of snap, and pressing it, the back of the ring would open, disclosing a minute secret chamber. She slips the ring on her finger. It fits her perfectly, as if it were made for her.

"How did you come by this ring?" Manuela has quite forgotten the priest and her exhaustion.

"A young girl sold it to me. She was a pretty little thing and, as the ring was obviously valuable, I gave her a good price for it."

"What did she look like?" Manuela is incredulous.

"I'm sorry, Signora," he gives her a cunning look, "but my memory for young faces was never very good. They all look much the same to me. I remember thinking at the time that she was a wealthy bride wearing a string of handsome pearls round her pretty neck."

What a sly old man. He's lying to her. That's obvious. Of course he remembers the girl.

"But her name: she must have told you her name?"

"Dandolo...I'm not quite sure, though." The Jew hesitates.

She doesn't get it. Could he be talking about Beatrice? But how would she have come by the ring?

With Andrea ill, her daughter is free to wander round the city with nobody to keep an eye on her. Manuela will make it her business to find out. She simply must have the ring.

AN EXECUTION
THE VENETIAN SECRET, 1620

"How much?"

"Three thousand ducats, Signora. This is a fair price for a family heirloom of such rarity."

She wants the ring, and the price is not far off the mark. But three-thousand ducats!

"I'll give you two and a half."

She can see he wavers, hesitates, considering her offer for a moment.

"No, Signora, the price is not negotiable."

Manuela isn't surprised. They are all of them usurers. She feels waves of nausea sweeping over her. Impossible to haggle now, she is far too weary. All she wants is to throw herself on her bed and sleep.

"Wait here." She sighs. "My maid will bring you the money."

Fortunately, she has ready money by her. She always has, as she never knows when Domenico might need it.

"A pleasure doing business with you, Signora." The Jew bows courteously.

She bends down to untie the clogs and throws them into a corner. Then she climbs the stairs to the piano nobile. How could the ring possibly have ended up in Beatrice's hands? That is if the girl the Jew mentioned was Beatrice?

AN EXECUTION
THE VENETIAN SECRET, 1620

25.

Husband and Wife

"*B*ut Fabrizio, I saw it with my own eyes! And you know I was ill for days afterwards."

Manuela watches her husband from her chair in the Camera d'Oro, the only room warm enough during winter. She looks away from him at the harpsichord and spinet. They look desolate up against the wall, she thinks. It is such a long time since they have had a musical evening.

Fabrizio has moved close to the fireplace. He is wrapped up in his fur coat, and only his face is visible. He has a tired expression, and his countenance looks ashen. He hasn't been too well recently, he told her, when she came into the Camera d'Oro for her basket of thread and yarn. But she suspects that he is merely feeling sorry for himself. No one forces him to work long hours.

Through the window, she notices the snowflakes against the dusk. The finely carved figures and the foliage of the fireplace shine in the light from the late afternoon sun. This winter is as cold as last year.

That the lagoon is frozen over once again is incredible.

"Even though the priest's execution took place two months ago, I can't get the spectacle out of my mind."

She feels bitter. She wants to tell him what she witnessed that day, get it off her chest. She has tried going to confession without having achieved much consolation. She had even knelt by the small grave in the chapel, confiding everything to her dear dead child, Francesco. And as always when she thinks of her dead son, her eyes fill with tears, and she feels a stab of injustice. Why should she be made to suffer so? How could she possibly have offended God? The thought of Marietta always complaining about the convent makes her furious. The girl doesn't know the trials to be undergone by marriage.

They had never talked about the execution. How could they when Fabrizio only came home to sleep? Usually he woke her up shutting the door to his own quarters late at night. Not that she cared about him being absent; he was enervating company anyway. Tedious to the point of desperation. Always had been, throughout the twenty five years she had had to put up with him. But he must listen to her all the same. How can he expect her not to talk about this? She still has nightmares about the torrents of blood gushing from the priest's neck.

Fabrizio lifts his head and looks at her. "You shouldn't have been in the piazzetta in the first place, Manuela," he says at last in a tired tone of voice.

Why must he always criticize her? She can't seem to do anything right. Only Marietta is above Fabrizio's criticism. She feels a restless anger itching in her veins.

"I always knew it would turn out a misalliance to marry you. How could it be otherwise? You have forgotten that my family is far superior to the Morosinis."

HUSBAND AND WIFE
THE VENETIAN SECRET, 1620

She is shouting, furious. She feels years of regret throbbing in her breast. She loathes it when he merely stares at her with that familiar weary look in his eyes.

"If only I had married someone of my own blood," she screams at him. "My father wanted me to marry a Cornaro, not an outsider. My mother's fault entirely. You never acknowledged the superiority of my blood. No Venetian family is as precious as the Cornaros. That's recognized by all nobles in Venice but you! " She has to stop to catch her breath.

Fabrizio remains quiet a moment before saying: "Manuela, please, we have been over this so many times. We are none of us perfect. Perfection is such a strange concept, don't you think, because it eliminates both the past and the future?"

What kind of an answer is that? She won't let him get away with that.

"And the ring, Fabrizio: all these years you have claimed that it never left the house. You know what I think? I think Rosalba stole it, brought it with her to San Zaccaria, and that somehow your meddlesome daughter, Marietta, has come across it in the convent. Most likely Marietta asked Beatrice to sell it!"

Fabrizio shakes his head. "Impossible," he says. "It might as well have been a servant who found it by accident and sold it."

"But the Jew said the girl's name was Dandolo! A strange coincidence, don't you think?" When he doesn't answer, she is blinded by a white fury. "I am convinced that Marietta is up to something."

She rises from the chair and walks across the room, stopping in front of her husband. She yells into his agonized face. "I think your miserable daughter is planning to run away from

HUSBAND AND WIFE
THE VENETIAN SECRET, 1620

the convent! That's why she sends her sister to the Jews to pawn things for her. And if she does run away, the family honour will be stained to a degree quite unimaginable; it will be the Rosalba-affair all over again. Marietta will deal a last staggering blow to the Morosinis!"

She stops again to breathe. She feels her cheeks are flushed and sees from the way he looks at her that he has decided it is one of her tantrums, as he mockingly calls her outbursts of despair. But no, she isn't through with him.

"If Marietta runs away," Manuela hisses, "it will be your fault for being so soft and indulgent with her, encouraging her every whim, covering up for her, averting your eyes to her temperament."

"Manuela, Marietta will never run away from San Zaccaria. Where would she go? How would she live? Who would take her in? Now you must see reason, Manuela, and calm down. Marietta and Beatrice have nothing to do with the ring."

Fabrizio leans back in his chair, breathing heavily. "I am not feeling well today, Manuela, so please don't go on."

But she can't stop. "Francesco's death was your fault too. Not to send for the doctor when I told you to," she yells.

That morning in May, all those years ago, when her beloved child had suddenly gone limp in her arms and Fabrizio had wasted precious time trying to persuade her that it was probably nothing, that the boy would be fine in a moment.

She pauses, looking at her husband's white face, while thoughts of regret are coiling in her mind.

Why should her beautiful baby die and Marietta live? Her darling second born son: only two years old. All happiness had gone from

HUSBAND AND WIFE
THE VENETIAN SECRET, 1620

her life then, and it had felt as if she had lost a part of herself. To this moment she can feel the pain of throwing her body against the wall, till blood trickled to the floor, in her desire to sense a different kind of hurt. Ever since, her days and nights have become dreadful beyond description. Her sorrow has poisoned everything.

She had placed the Rose of Jericho under her pillow to give birth as easily as the plant blooms. The midwife had stuffed pulverized snake skins into the mattress. She had been so afraid. She had lost count of how many cousins had died birthing. She had written her will well before the due date. And then Francesco's birth had turned out to be so surprisingly easy.

She had almost died giving birth to Marietta. Three days of being in labour, and her eldest daughter was hauled out with tongs. Marietta: always a painful disappointment. The screaming baby had been swaddled in the same linen as Francesco before the midwife had handed the infant to her, while she was still crying from pain.

Somehow, she had expected to look into the face of her lost son. She remembers the strong feeling of resentment seeing Marietta's face. She had declined to hold her and returned her to the midwife. She had turned towards the wall and cried.

Marietta never possessed Francesco's tenderness. He had been a child of perfection with his corn coloured hair and eyes like bluebells. His small voice had been as gentle as the colour of dawn. Anyway, what is a daughter compared to a son? Nothing. Absolutely nothing.

Once, when Marietta had come into her bedchamber to read to

her, she had suffered the illusion, for one brief moment, that it was Francesco. It was the same face, with the little heart shaped mouth, the frank blue eyes and blond curls. For the space of one Ave Maria, she had believed that Marietta was her lovely boy come back, only grown into an attractive young man. She had pulled the bed curtains with a feeling of numbing despair, and, in the gloom of her alcove, she had once again turned her head against the wall and wept.

She is just about to blow a new blast of words into Fabrizio's face, accusing him of not caring for her, not listening to her nightmares, that she is alone with no one to talk to when Domenico is not there, when Fabrizio falls out of the chair hitting his head on the terrazzo floor.

Is this pretence? Manuela is uncertain, hesitant. She kneels down beside him, looking into his pallid face. She carefully turns him onto his back. Is he unconscious? She puts her ear to his chest. His breathing is hardly audible, very weak, and saliva trails from the corner of the mouth. She sits still beside him, waiting for him to open his eyes. But Fabrizio doesn't move an inch, nor does he open his eyes. He lies quite still on the cold black and white marble squares in his sable fur coat.

What if he should die? The thought pricks her like a needle. How much easier life would be for her and Domenico.

She gets up and opens the door to the freezing portego, calling for Zusanna. The girl is on her knees polishing the terrazzo floor.

"Run as fast as you can and fetch Isacco Vita. The Procurator has been taken ill!" she cries at the top of her voice. "Bring the new servant boy with you to the Ghetto. Don't return without the doctor! Hurry up, girl!" She hurls the words at the maid. They seem to hit Zusanna like a shower of pebbles because, for once, the girl is swift. She picks up her skirts and runs down the portego towards the stairs.

In a moment, Manuela stands in the large kitchen next to the Camera d'Oro. "Take the Procurator to his bedchamber. He has fallen suddenly ill." She shouts at the two Moorish slaves to make haste, undress her husband and put him to bed. "Go to the well in the courtyard for a pitcher of fresh water!" She orders them. "If the water is frozen, thaw some ice, and bring a bundle of sticks to light the fire. I will keep vigil."

HUSBAND AND WIFE
THE VENETIAN SECRET, 1620

26.

Setting Traps

"Are you quite certain?" Manuela starts. She is half asleep in the small gilded armchair beside Fabrizio's bed. Domenico back? At the maid's words she is wide awake.

"Yes, Signora. A flotilla of merchant galleys. My brother told me." She stares sceptically at Zusanna's flushed face. The girl's voice is hardly audible. "They are anchored beyond the Arsenal, Signora. The ice stopped them."

"Which galleys are they?"

"The Morosina and the Contarina, Signora. My brother at the Arsenal saw their standards flying when the Marangona sounded this morning. He came straight away to tell me. The other two are the Gritta' and Moceniga, Signora."

She can't help disliking Zusanna. The maid is a perpetual reminder of that dreadful day in the piazzetta, the priest's screams and the torrents of blood.

"Bring me my breakfast."

Domenico! She is desperate to see him, impatient to tell him of the ring and what it hides.

That the voyage has been a strain is obvious from his letter. If only Fabrizio hadn't sent him away. Of course, Domenico would be unruly, being so young. The Senate never would have touched him, a nobleman like themselves.

She studies her husband, who is breathing heavily beneath the crimson canopy. Manuela finds it hard to believe that he is bereft of his former eloquence, dumb, paralyzed and only able to move his left hand. She watches his sleeping face on the pillow, his arms motionless against the sheets. He looks careworn, older than his sixtyfive years. But then, the daylight is cruel and harsh. The dark hair and beard enhance his pallor even in spite of the warm red of the canopy. Actually, his face is as white as the hand-embroidered pillowcase. The family coat of arms on the white damask coverlet she had monogrammed as a gift for him years ago. His curved lips are a curious deep red, as if every drop of blood has been summoned to give him the strength to utter just one single word.

The painting above the bed enthrals her today as always. The Madonna's expression looking at the child enthrals her in particular. Paolo Veronese's Madonna always reminds her of the birth of Marietta. She remembers when Fabrizio bought the Veronese and the Botticelli years ago from the Medici at Bacchereto. He insisted that the painting of the Madonna be hung over his bed, because Saint Barbara reminded him of Marietta. She stares at the reflected light flickering across the Madonna's face and prays that her husband's sufferings won't be prolonged for months. Her eyes come to rest on the casket filled with documents. Does Fabrizio keep his will there? Or perhaps in one of the secret, locked drawers in his old walnut desk? His will might be tucked away in the office in the Procuratie Nuovo, behind the strong iron doors, where the sacks of ducats are kept in deposit.

The brass basin has not been emptied, and the servant has left the shaving knife adrift in the dirty water. The razor case is open on the small table beside it, and Fabrizio's ivory comb and ear cleaners lie on the white cloth. What slops the servants are! She has to keep an eye on everything to make the house run at all.

It doesn't bother her to sit by the bed when he is asleep. His smiles to the servants are sad; he is constantly clasping their hands with the hand that's still intact. But he never smiles at *her*.

She avoids the reproachful and scared look in his eyes when he is awake. Most likely he blames himself for all the times he has chided her in the past, seeing how she faithfully she watches over him now.

It is she who has to remind the servants to empty the bedpans, collect the ashes, keep the fire going and change the sheets. Sometimes the stench of urine is unbearable. This morning the linen has been changed, and the scent of quince apples emanating from the sheets pleasantly perfume the room.

Isacco Vita and his assistant have done what they can. They bled Fabrizio, but to no avail. When she asked them about his prospects, if his disease would be slow or speedy, they had been evasive. His prospects were dismal, they had admitted finally. Sometimes you saw an improvement in cases like Fabrizio's, Isacco Vita had added, and then the patient could linger on for months. All they could do was to bleed him, and give him the drugs. They had impressed on her that Fabrizio must be offered something to eat and drink at all times.

She keeps the recipe for the medicines in her Book of Secrets. Every day she has to apply to his side a hot concoction, made

SETTING TRAPS
THE VENETIAN SECRET, 1620

from the wool that lies around the testicles of the ram, with honey added, and, in order to keep the bowels regular, his navel must be smeared with an ointment made from boiled sage ground up with pork fat, twice a day. But Fabrizio's case is grave, and most likely no recipe in the Book of Secrets will help him.

She knows, however, that their Jewish doctor is among the most distinguished in Venice. If he can't help her husband, Fabrizio's life is in God's hands. Vita has written major works on medicine, even dedicated some of them to the Doge and holds doctorates in medicine and philosophy. What more can possibly be done for her husband?

Francesco and Domenico will arrive any time now. She wants to change her dress before receiving them, and Zusanna must do her hair up. She catches a sight of her face in the big gold framed mirror. Her hair is thick and curly, not so blond this winter, but still fair, and her skin smooth. When she puts on her foundation cream, her face will look handsomely pale, and a touch of the blusher will add just the right amount of glow to her cheeks.

What a blow it will be to Francesco. All his life he has doted on Fabrizio, admired the elder brother, and counted on him to solve any problem in their family partnership. Now Domenico must take over Fabrizio's responsibilities. Perhaps for good. And when Fabrizio dies, she will have her dowry back, which means that she will own a large proportion of the estates and valuables. That is something Fabrizio's four brothers won't like. But they will just have to get used to it,she thinks.

A soft knock, and Zusanna enters, balancing the silver tray with fruit, spiced wine and bread. When she sets it down on the trestle table, she spills the wine on the azure tablecloth, and the red

SETTING TRAPS
THE VENETIAN SECRET, 1620

drops penetrate the cloth. Like the priest's blood against the blue sky in the piazzetta. The sight makes Manuela feel sick.

"What a fool you are! Take the tablecloth to the laundry, and bring the bed warmer for the Signore." She glances curiously at the letter lying beside the fruit. She takes it, turning it over in her hand. She frowns to see the all too familiar seal before breaking it open.

The Abbess writes that Marietta has been weeping for days, neglecting her duties, lying on her bed most of the time, or she has been at the grates to talk to Beatrice, in the company of the twins and Maria Columbin. She wants Signora Morosini to know that her eldest daughter has entreated her closest councillors to be allowed to go home to attend to her father in his illness.

Of course, Francesca Grimani writes, it is impossible for them to grant permission for anything of the kind. She would have to petition the Patriarch and the Pope, and they would be sure to decline such a request, anyway. To leave the convent on any pretext whatsoever is out of the question, as everybody well knows. Marietta is now a bride of Christ, and, as such, she has vowed to renounce her family. She is not supposed to nourish strong secular ties with her relatives. Manuela understands from the letter that the Abbess has been unable to impress that much on Marietta.

The twins, Francesca Grimani says, are upset by Marietta's grief. It is ruinous to their fragile constitution. Beatrice has been to the parlatorio every day the past week, holding her sisters' hand. It is most harmful to life in the convent, as it causes gossip and slander. The choir nuns quarrel over the case, because they all have their different opinions.

SETTING TRAPS
THE VENETIAN SECRET, 1620

Would Manuela kindly write to Marietta not to go to such extremes as she does at present, and beg her to attend to religious life?

Manuela tears the letter up, throwing the pieces into the flames. Francesca Grimani ought to know better than to write her letters about Marietta. Why should her daughter listen to her in this situation, when she never did in the past?

Bianca Loredan and Sofia Conaro always said how brave she was to stand Marietta at all. They had been loyal friends through the years when she despaired of her daughter. They had even tried to reason with Marietta on a few occasions, and, of course, they had only met with her stubborn silence. What is the point of writing? She won't have anything to do with Marietta ever again.

She becomes aware of her husband's eyes resting on her face. Suddenly she is afraid that he reads her mind. He has never allowed her to forget that Marietta is the apple of his eye. She has heard it said that people hovering between life and death have the ability to look into people's souls, and that scares her.

She takes the goblet of water, and, lifting his head with one hand, she presses the glass against his lips with the other. Water dribbles down the corners of his mouth and soaks the pillowcase. She turns the empty glass goblet over in her hand. It was made on the occation of their marriage. They both drank out of it on their wedding night. Their portraits as bride and groom are delicately painted on the Murano glass.

She puts the glass down and calls out to the maid to relieve her. She turns the hourglass on the table by the bed. At last. It is with a strong feeling of relief that she closes the door to the sickroom behind her. She shivers in the cold portego and quickly crosses

SETTING TRAPS
THE VENETIAN SECRET, 1620

the hall to her bedroom. What dress to wear? The orange brocade dress will make her look radiant in the

cold winter's light, and her velvet mantel lined with ermine will keep her warm.

As Manuela opens the door to her bedchamber, a thought suddenly strikes her like lightening.

Tommaso! He will be in Venice too! She had forgotten all about him. Might he he at the convent already? Plotting with Marietta?

On the night before setting out for Constantinople, she knows that he had rushed to the parlatorio. Livia Loredan had come straight away to tell her. Her friend had seen Tommaso and Marietta whispering at the grates and Tommaso give Marietta a ring. One of the choir nuns had seen it later sparkling on her daughter's finger.

Surely as God is in His Heaven, the two of them are up to something. They were always plotting and scheming when children. So why not now? She remembers how they used to steal away from the schoolroom to play hide and seek, noisy ball games, or race up and down the stairs, screaming and laughing. She had been furious when they climbed the wooden horses in the Sala pretending to be wild warriors, when they imitated birds for hours or barked at the dogs. She had often found them in a niche hiding behind a tapestry, playing at chess or backgammon. To send Tommaso home and forbid him to return had been impossible due to their business relations with the Contarinis.

Tommaso Contarini, such a dreamer, never letting go of a chance to discard reality for the sense of adventure and play. Where do such dreams come from? She had watched through the door to the Camera d'Oro how he conspired with Marietta, drawing charts and galleys all over the terrazzo floor with chalk, inventing future voyages for the two of them. She had been fuming with anger and had tried talking to Fabrizio, impressing on him that girls should not be allowed to talk to boys, as the strongest emotional bonds are formed with one's first companions. Fabrizio had merely closed his eyes to their foolery as usual. When he came across them in the house, she had seen him stop to listen to them play the spinet and the lute, or singing in their warbling voices. Hugging and kissing Marietta whenever there had been an opportunity. No wonder Marietta had grown up spoiled as well as spiteful.

She had often wondered what happened at the time Marietta came home from the convent. How many times had she stolen away for secret meetings with Tommaso? She had questioned the servants, who had sworn that the main doors to the campo and the water entrance were always locked at night. There was no other access to the outside. She had tried keeping awake at night, listening if Marietta left the room above her alcove and tiptoed down the staircase in the cupboard adjacent to her bed.

Suddenly, she understands. Tommaso and Marietta are going to elope! The Morosini signet ring could be evidence of just that. The thought has been lurking at the back of her mind, like a thief abiding his time in the dark. The words of the astrologer she had sent for to cast Marietta's chart when she was born have never stopped making her uneasy. "When your daughter reaches the age of twenty, I lose sight of her destiny," he had said. "The stars are silent."

Did it mean that Marietta would die, she had often speculated.

SETTING TRAPS
THE VENETIAN SECRET, 1620

She will write to the Abbess. She closes the door to her bedroom and crosses the floor in a few steps, removing the table carpet from one of the storage chests in front of her alcove. She takes out the orange dress and cloak and changes quickly. In spite of the flames in the fireplace, the room is freezing, and she wraps the ermine around her. She finds paper and the inkstand in the chest of drawers. She sits down at her toilette rushing aside the pots and jars of ointments and lotions, knocking over the rouge powder and a bottle of perfume, and a heavy fragrance of jasmine instantly sweeps through the room which makes her feel faint.

She dips the quill in the golden ink, and as she writes, she looks up from the letter from time to time. Finally, she adds, if Francesca Grimani, knowing the story of the ring, will be so kind as to show the Morosini seal with which her letter is stamped.

She takes the candle and holds the stick of lacquer into the flame. She watches how it slowly melts, the heavy red drops merging, suffusing into a small spot the size of a ducat. She presses the ring into the red substance, leaving the Morosini coat of arms. When her daughter sees it she will no doubt recognise it. The size of the signet is unusual.

"Take this letter to San Zaccaria, and send Zusanna in here at once," she shouts opening the door, handing the letter to a timid servant girl, slamming the door to her bedroom.

SETTING TRAPS
THE VENETIAN SECRET, 1620

27.

The Ring

The bright winter sun sends its rays in through the windows at the far end of the Sala. Manuela goes to stand by a window, looking through the fine glass, watching out for Domenico and Francesco.

Suddenly she feels happy. The sunshine makes the Sala sparkle; the big mirrors in their golden frames catch the rays and play with light and shadow. Like the chiaroscuro in the family portraits on the walls. In the sharp blaze, the big white butterfly in one of the tapestries seems to come alive amidst the foliage and flowers of the garden scenes, ready to take off on delicate wings. The sun reflects in the metal of the swords and lances, trophies taken from the Turks through generations of Morosinis.

She sees them now in the campo. Domenico is nothing but skin and bones. She is alarmed by his sallow looking face. His clothes are too big for him, and his body seems like a peg piled with garments. He is in low spirits. His scowling look is a bad sign.

"Welcome home!" Manuela shouts as Francesco and Domenico come up the stairs. She shivers at the gusts of iciness and flakes of snow in their wake.

She throws her arms around her son, completely forgetting Francesco, tall and gaunt, standing beside Domenico. A chill emanates from her son's cloak, and she feels the cold of his cheeks against her lips. Domenico gives her an empty stare and presents her with one of the small disappointed smiles she knows only too well. He is depressed. She turns towards her brother-in-law and notices that he has been crying.

"Manuela! I was told the sad tidings only this morning," Francesco says weeping. "My brothers came on board the Morosina to tell us."

"The doctors are not very optimistic, I'm most sorry to say." She observes how Domenico pricks up his ears when she mentions the bleak prospects. He becomes attentive, as if waking from a stupor.

They walk across the Sala, and Manuela opens the door to Fabrizio's bedroom. When Francesco goes to sit by the bed, she notices how gently he takes Fabrizio's hand. He is weeping again. Domenico just glances at his father's bed and follows her out the room into the Camera d'Oro.

"I can see the voyage has been terrible for you, my poor darling," Manuela says, carefully caressing his hair, but Domenico pulls away from her. "I have missed you, Domenico. The house has been empty without you. Tell me about the voyage." She tries to smile into his sullen face and moves closer towards him on the divan in front of the blazing fire.

Domenico pours himself a glass of spiced wine from the pitcher and swallows it in one gulp.

"I hated every moment of that bloody voyage. First, being ordered about by Tommaso and then by Uncle Francesco in Constantinople. Charts and navigation don't mean a thing to me, mother. I detest ships, and I never intended to become a merchant. Ha! Father just tried to get rid of me. I'm sure he hoped I would perish at sea. Or get killed by a pirate or a Turk's scimitar."

She watches him drain another glass of wine, drying his mouth with the back of his hand. His black straight hair has grown long and hangs loose. When he bows his head, strands of hair fall into his eyes and cover his face.

"I think we should buy more land instead of sailing the seas. I want a Palladian villa on the Brenta, horses and fields. To come back to Venice, to the snow and ice, is awful. The sun must have grown old," he adds in an angry tone. "Every canal is turned to ice, and the Riva is covered in snow. We had to anchor far beyond the Arsenal. The lagoon is frozen all the way to the main land from the Fondamenta Nuove. The frost ruins the Carnival once more."

"And Tommaso?"

"He was constantly telling me off, and Maria Columbin's brother and that friend of hers, Arrigo, took every opportunity to snigger at me. Trying to stop their sniggers was like trying to stop the birds flying through the air with one's bare hands. Not that I didn't put them in their places, though.

Uskok pirates attacked us on the way out. The devils boarded the galley and their war cry ' Iesu! Iesu!' tore tore the ship asunder, like the trumpets outside the walls of Jericho. I rushed below deck to get more ammunition. When I came back, their leader had been killed, and the pirates were fleeing. Tommaso and Arrigo shouted cowardice in my face, and I shot Arrigo in his hand, just to teach him a lesson. Tommaso threw me into a cell and then took to his cabin for the remainder of the voyage. He had been hit in the shoulder, and, of course, he made the most of it. I must say I hoped it was the last I ever saw of him." He pauses to pour another glass of wine.

"But the devil looks after his own. Tommaso pulled through. Thank God for Francesco. If it hadn't been for him, Tommaso would have left me to rot in the ship's cell for months while in Constantinople. Never could stand Tommaso, the way he always considers himself aloof."

"But Constantinople, Domenico, tell me about the city. I've heard say that it is as magnificent as Venice." Manuela feels the need to change the subject seeing how annoyed her son gets.

"Remember mother, the city is crammed with brutal Turks. They are all slaves to the Sultan, and to keep his secrets their tongues are cut out. The Infidel pierce their skin with knives, arrows and maces to show their devotion to Mohammed. I couldn't wait to go home. Can't we talk of something else? I am not in the mood to talk about the voyage or Tommaso."

Manuela takes the signet ring off her finger and hands it to Domenico. "It is the Morosini ring I've been looking for."

He takes it, surprised at its magnificence: the glistering diamonds and rubies, the little pearls, the filigree work. He turns the ring over and over in his hand while listening to her story.

"Keep an eye on Beatrice's face when I show her the ring. She can't put on an act, never could." She is content that his mood has changed, that the ring has caught his attention.

"I bought it from a Jew who had it from a girl, a young bride, by the name of Dandolo. Strange, don't you think?" She cocks her head and watches him. "Look at the back of the ring, Domenico," she goes on. He turns the ring between his fingers again. "Don't you see!" Manuela shows him the delicate mechanism." It opens, like a medallion . Careful! Don't spill anything!" She has been so cautious with the contents.

"What is it?" Domenico dips his little finger into the white powder and is just about to taste it, when she grabs hold of his hand.

"Don't Domenico!"

He is so surprised that he is close to dropping the ring.

"It's poison! I know because I tried to give a tiny portion of it to one of the cats. It died on th spot."

He closes the ring, smiling, immersed in thoughts.

"Why would the Morosini ring contain such potent poison? Or any poison for that matter?" He asks her after a few moments.

"I haven't got the slightest idea, Domenico."

"There is no future for father, you know," Domenico says, smiling grimly at her.

THE RING
THE VENETIAN SECRET, 1620

28.
Alone in the Dark

Everything is ready. Time to go.

I look at my two sisters in the glow from the candle. Light and shadow play on their sleeping faces. It scares me. Is it a sign that life and death are fighting for their souls? They lie peacefully entwined in each other's arms, and, for a moment, I stand still watching them. I listen to their even breathing. The hushed velvety sound is soothing. I hate to think how much they will suffer when they wake up and find that Giulia and I are no longer there.

Going away is like dreaming. What does it mean to be free? I never really knew the meaning of the word, I suppose. Only writing my manuscripts gave me the sense of freedom of mind, even if my body was enclosed. Will we understand freedom in Bacchereto? Or will we suffer a different kind of captivity?

I fear leaving father, weak and vulnerable, in the hands of mother and Domenico. The thought brings with it sadness like a cold river.

Quickly, I rummage in one of the chests for my ink and pen. I take a sheet of paper and start writing: Dear Beatrice, don't worry. We'll be safe on the Lido. Your loving sister, Marietta. I fold it, and put it in the pocket of my mantle. If Domenico or my mother see us tonight in Ca'Morosini, I pray that my letter will serve its purpose and that they pick up the false scent upon finding it.

"Giulia," I whisper, and turn towards her, "Are you ready?"

She nods, hugging her two dolls. She looks at me unblinking. She is such a serious child. I wonder if Giulia has understood at all what we are about to do.

"I don't like to wear a mask, Marietta. The Sisters won't allow it. If they see it, they will punish me. Do I really have to?"

"Yes, Giulia," I whisper, "Don't worry, the Sisters can't see you. Tommaso and I wear masks too. Nobody in the streets must recognize our faces. "

Not to upset her more than is necessary, I have told her only that we are leaving tonight across the ice, that Tommaso is waiting for us.

"I'm tired, Marietta. Can't we ask Tommaso to meet us tomorrow instead?"

"But, Giulia, Tommaso is already there. The horses too. I can almost hear them stamping their hooves in the cold, impatient to take us to Bacchereto, can't you?" She doesn't say a word, just looks at me distractedly.

"My dolls will miss the twins," she says with that peculiar, sad expression on her face, which always makes me wonder if she is a child at all but rather some wise ancient soul in disguise. As she stands there in front of me, her small frail body wrapped in the black fur coat, her face pale and large scared eyes peering at me from behind the hood, I worry if she has the strength to go through with this.

ALONE IN THE DARK
THE VENETIAN SECRET, 1620

"Can't we take Fini?" Giulia whispers, and pats the dog's head.

"No, Giulia. Fini is far too old for such a long journey. He must stay with the twins. We will find a dog like Fini at Bacchereto."

"We can't, Marietta. There are no dogs like him."

"You must put your dolls in the bag when we are in the passage, Giulia," I go on quickly. "They won't be safe otherwise," I look at the frail china figures, but she just shakes her head firmly at me, and I know I have to leave it at that.

I feel the weight of the ducats and the soft hide of the goatskin pouch against my breast. Rosalba's jewels have fetched a good price with the Jew. I don't care if my mother has got hold of the Morosini ring. She can't stop me from going. Francesca Grimani knows something too; why else would she have shown me the seal on my mother's letter while scrutinizing my face?

"The boots, Giulia!" I suddenly notice that she is wearing her shoes with the thin leather soles. "You can't walk on the ice like that. Your feet will freeze." I become aware of the tenseness in my voice. My body is strained to the point of bursting.

"But Marietta, my boots are so stiff," she moans.

I realize I haven't been able to make Giulia understand the meaning of walking for three miles on ice to the main land. She doesn't even remember what the Lagoon looks like when it is not frozen. It doesn't make sense to her to walk on water. And a mile, what is a mile?

I stoop to change her shoes quickly. She doesn't object when I help her putting on the boots, she just stands there, quite motionless, hugging the small figures.

"Come on, Giulia, it's time to leave." Slowly, reluctantly, the child steps into the loggia. I take one of the oil lamps, light it, and

ALONE IN THE DARK
THE VENETIAN SECRET, 1620

quietly close the door to the cell behind us. I look at the church copula rising above us. Tonight it seems threatening, dark and sinister. The belfry towering beside the church makes me think of Chiara.

The bells are quiet, not claiming us yet. I pray they will remain silent until morning, for then they will surely chime our escape all over Venice, like a fist pounding a table.

It must be close to midnight. The cloisters are deserted. No one is out in the cold, and I pray that the chapel is empty too, as there are no Hours to sing until the morning.

I hold Giulia by the hand and feel her soft leather glove against mine. As if by magic, my agitation vanishes, and I am suddenly calm and composed. I walk briskly down the stairs, Giulia trailing behind me.

"Hurry up, Giulia," I whisper, and pull at her hand. We go through the cloisters towards the chapel, pausing in the shadows along the wall underneath the whitewashed vaults, listening into the dark. A vague noise reaches me from further down the cloister. It is freezing and the stars are out. They reflect in the mirrors of ice in the open courtyard.

"Look, Giulia, the stars light us on our way," I say, hoping to cheer her up. I have noticed the frightened look in her face.

"Yes, Marietta, I know," she answers distractedly. "Are these frozen puddles the same as the ice on the Lagoon?"

"They are, Giulia." I bend down and whisper in her ear. "Keep your voice down. Someone could hear us."

"What are the stars made of, Marietta?" She asks in a low voice.

"They are made of Juno's milk. One day, when the goddess was

ALONE IN THE DARK
THE VENETIAN SECRET, 1620

nursing Hercules, her milk sprayed across the sky and created the Milky Way"

"Can stars die too?"

"The stars are eternal. They hold sway over our lives. The Holy Virgin is the star of the sea, Giulia, and guides us tonight."

I become aware of soft footfalls in the snow and think I glimpse a silhouette. Someone must be hiding behind one of the white marble columns. A strange flapping of wings above my head makes me start, as a pigeon darts past me. My heart pounds at the eerie sound. I pull at Giulia's hand to go on, as she stands still gazing at the sky.

We reach the door in the terracotta brick wall. I push it open, fearing that the sound from the squeaking hinges which breaks the snowy silence will alarm somebody nearby. We step into the small crescent-shaped yard taking us to the chapel. I pray that we are unnoticed. The silhouette in the cloisters was most likely no more than a figment of fear.

Once inside the church, only the shadows from the tapers move. It is empty, and I scold myself for being so tense and apprehensive. I look around the chapel again, no one there. I drag Giulia towards the small steep staircase to the crypt, when suddenly she tears herself loose.

"I am afraid to go down there, Marietta," she cries. "The ghosts will kick us." Her small face is distorted with fear. "Adriana told me," she weeps, and in between sobs she whispers, "One night the ghosts of the doges came out of their graves. They kicked the priest because he said that ghosts don't exist. I won't go down there. The ghosts will grab us with invisible hands."

My agitation returns and, for a moment, I panic. I never realised

ALONE IN THE DARK
THE VENETIAN SECRET, 1620

what it meant bringing a child. I'm afraid to force her in case she starts screaming, and I am at a loss. Then I remember my dream, and I pull Giulia down beside me on the steps to the crypt. I have to take the chance of losing precious time.

"Listen, Giulia," I say speaking fast. "I dreamt of the crypt last night, and perhaps it is as beautiful tonight as it was in my dream, the ghosts at peace."

She stops crying and watches me questioningly, apparently paying attention to what I say.

"I dreamt that I came into the crypt one night and the floor was covered with white roses, the air filled with their fragrance. White butterflies with golden crosses on their wings were flying to and fro, and an angel descended in a mantle of shining gold with a golden censer. The room filled with smoke of incense, and the angel said to me, 'this is the place I have chosen for you,' pointing to the entrance of the passage we must go through. Then she rolled a golden apple towards me, and her whisper echoed, ' take it with you…with you… with you… It is the apple of love.'…of love…' You see, Giulia, the angels watch over us in the crypt, and no ghosts dare disturb them."

 She looks at me incredulously, bewildered. "Do you mean the angel on the altar?"

I hesitate. "Yes, Giulia, the beautiful angel with the soft smile. She will look after us, and nothing can harm us."

Giulia doesn't speak. Then she rises from the step, carefully holding on to the two dolls and walks down the stairs without another word. I follow her into the crypt. It is quiet. The silence is intimidating. Giulia stops in front of the white stone angel, and makes the sign of the cross.

ALONE IN THE DARK
THE VENETIAN SECRET, 1620

"Please, sweet angel, keep the ghosts away." She looks at me, and I see tears in her eyes.

"Where are we going, Marietta? There is no door," she says.

I place the lamp beside me on the floor, and kneel down. "Look, Giulia," I say, pushing at the circular ornament in the stone altar.

Slowly it gives way to the pressure from my hands. I take the lamp and set it down on the uppermost step beside the bag with our few belongings. A rancid smell from the passage penetrates my nostrils, and I am on the point of vomiting, when Giulia cries out.

"No! Marietta, I won't go into the dark. I'm afraid." She turns around and runs towards the staircase to the chapel. I grab her cloak and hold on to her. One of the dolls falls to the tessellated floor with a piercing noise and splinters in a shower of white fragments. I catch the other doll just in time and hug Giulia, who weeps desperately. The Christ-doll, Giulia's object of adoration, which she has paid homage to every day of her life in the convent. I feel her pain within me, because I know the doll possesses a magic of its own. I think of the white plaster doll of the infant Christ, which Aunt Fantina gave to me when I was Giulia's age. I doted on that doll to save me from my mother's rage; it comforted me when I was locked up in the dark cupboard. It never left me. My aunt claimed that all its virtues and force would be transferred to me. 'If you treasure this sacred image of the infant Jesus and hold it, caress it like the Virgin Mary, Marietta, you will grow up to resemble Her,' she said when handing me the small doll.

"Hush, Giulia, we'll be through the passage soon. The angel looks

ALONE IN THE DARK
THE VENETIAN SECRET, 1620

after us, and the lamp lights us the way in the dark to Tommaso. Come, help me pick up the pieces, and I'll mend the doll for you in Baccchereto."

I let go of Giulia, and she helps me pick up the uneven pieces, which we put with her other doll into my shrine in the bag. Giulia is still crying when I take her hand and gently push her in front of me into the tunnel. I pull at the bronze knob, and the opening closes. We are alone in the darkness.

ALONE IN THE DARK
THE VENETIAN SECRET, 1620

29.

The Beginning of a Long Journey

This is the only way out, unless you climb the wall, which is quite impossible. No ladder is tall enough and to try to use ropes is equally hopeless. All entrances to the roof are thoroughly barred. Since Chiara's escape, the Signori di Notte have bolted the gates to the campo from the outside every night.

The Marangona tolls midnight from San Marco. The bells have always been with me from my first feeble breath. We have a bell for everything. Their tolls have ordered my days and nights and will surely determine my fate tonight.

The black velvet bag is heavy. I carry it across my shoulder, take the lamp in the other hand, and tell Giulia, who still weeps, to stay close.

"Hold on to my cloak, Giulia. Keep your eyes shut and imagine the stars watching over us."

There is a dead silence in the passage, but I still have the feeling of something ominous hidden in the dark. It scares me, because in the quiet everything takes on new meaning. I am afraid of the big rats, and I pray that the light from the lamp will keep them off.

A vague noise breaks the silence, and I pause to listen. Is it a rat scurrying across the tiles? I imagine I hear light footsteps, as in the cloisters, as if someone is close upon our heels. But no one, surely, knows of the passageway, only Rosalba. Could it be her spirit trying to warn me? Or the Doges' ghosts angry to be disturbed, now breathing down my neck? It is easy to imagine things; I am aware of that. I try to concentrate my thoughts on Rosalba. Thinking of her in the dark sets my mind at ease. She was brave to snap her fingers in the face of destiny. She knew as little of her fate then as I do of mine. The bag seems heavier with every step, and Giulia pulls at my cloak. It is as if she wills me in the opposite direction, back into the lion's mouth.

"Just a few more steps, Giulia," I turn my head and whisper to her. She looks at me without a word.

At the end of the tunnel, I glimpse the inside of the hollow Madonna statue in the faint light from my lamp. Built into the wall on the corner of the sottoportego and the Riva, it couldn't be more perfectly situated for rescuing the nuns' relics in case of an emergency. My nervousness has fled, and I try not to listen into the void behind me.

This is the moment I have dreamt of in my cell. I set the lamp and the bag down beside me, pull out our masks, the three cornered hat and the white lace hood. I secure the ribbons of Giulia's mask around the back of her head. She shivers in the cold, and her eyes have a dreamy look behind the slits of the mask, which tells me that she has retreated into her own world. I have seen that expression in her eyes so many times.

I press the hat on top of the white lace Bauta which covers my hair and shoulders. The white canvas mask leaves me with only

THE BEGINNING OF A LONG JOURNEY
THE VENETIAN SECRET, 1620

my eyes exposed. It is the perfect disguise: everyone in Venice wears a Bauta at Carnival time. It will make us look no different from so many others in the calle going to the masquerades. I see before me how the houses of the nobles will have lanterns hung outside the front doors decorated with garlands to announce the feasts to anyone wearing a mask.

I hesitate briefly, and then I push Giulia's small body before me into the statue. To actually enter the figure of the Madonna upsets me. I feel blasphemous, frivolous, as if I defamed the Virgin by penetrating her sacred body, and I dare not see through the hole in the statue's navel to look for Tommaso on the Riva.

What if the statue should suddenly crumble, and fall to pieces like the dolls? Giulia and I would be unveiled to the world, standing for all to see in a heap of dust and white marble fragments. We will be Tiepolo's prisoners, and he will have to decide what to do with us. Would he throw me into the Misericordia, the convent prison?

"Sweet Madonna, forgive me," I whisper and close my eyes to conjure up Her smiling face from the Bellini painting. "Please, Holy Virgin, please save us in spite of everything."

I open my eyes and stretch out my arm towards the small hatch carved into the lower side of the Madonna's cloak. I reach beyond Giulia and, using all my strength, I push at the slab of marble.

When the hinged door gives in and opens ajar, I stifle a scream. A gloved hand invades the opening, and I watch the fingers closing around the marble hatch, pushing it open, slowly... slowly.

I hold my breath. Discovered so soon! We *have* been pursued after all.

THE BEGINNING OF A LONG JOURNEY
THE VENETIAN SECRET, 1620

I stand still, mesmerised by the black leather glove. Then I notice the ring on the gloved finger in the light from my lamp. It carries the Contarini coat of arms. Giulia doesn't make a sound and stands as still as the statue.

"Wait! Someone is coming." I hear Tommaso's voice, and, suddenly, his masked face appears in the opening. My relief is immense. He is here! Sweet Madonna, thank you!

Giulia starts when he swiftly closes the hatch in her face. I listen to steps creaking in the snow, voices, then laughter, then silence. The abrupt spectacular quiet outside is menacing, and I concentrate on the darkness behind me. Are there footsteps sounding in the passage? But all I catch is the void, the emptiness of the tunnel we have left, and the feeling of foreboding, of something sinister following us, leaves me.

The marble slap opens wide. Giulia must be dazed, because she doesn't say a word when Tommaso carefully pulls her through the opening and onto the Riva. His head is hidden beneath a black lace Bauta and his face behind a mask, but Giulia doesn't seem to notice anything. He whispers to her, soothing her in his reassuring voice, and Giulia recognises him at once.

Tommaso takes the bag from my hand. As I squeeze through the opening, a small obscure and muffled cry in the dark passage alerts my attention, and, on impulse, I turn my head around trying to penetrate the blackness with my eyes. I discern nothing but emptiness. Tommaso reaches for my hand, and I am on the Riva. I close the marble slab, and, once again, the beautiful blue-eyed Madonna is at peace, unsullied and undisturbed. I take a step back to look at the statue. She seems to study me in the lamplight, the steadfast glass eyes hold me with a potent spell,

THE BEGINNING OF A LONG JOURNEY
THE VENETIAN SECRET, 1620

and I pray that I am forgiven for interfering with her serenity. Giulia doesn't speak. She merely holds firmly on to Tommaso's hand. I throw my arms around his neck, and the reassurance of his body like a bulwark against mine is comforting, securing me from my interior rivers of terror and imagination. I cling to him as I would to a piece of driftwood in a whirlpool. Feeling his arm around my body, I push the mask to the back of my head and bury my face in his shoulder. I breathe in the familiar smell of salt and tar, the smell of the sea which has always drawn me towards him. Tommaso puts his arm around my waist and gathers me to him.

"My father, Tommaso," I whisper. "I can't leave without saying goodbye to him one last time. It isn't far to Campo San Stefano and Ca'Morosini."

"Of course, we will go. Lorenzo di Medici waits for us until dawn," he whispers soothingly in my ear. "Arrigo took my few belongings to the main land to Lorenzo. Lorenzo remains in San Giuliano and leaves the horses in their harness ready to go. We can leave for Bacchereto at a moment's notice." When Tommaso speaks in his low constant voice, I feel reassured. He kisses me gently. It is an odd sensation, because his lips are so warm against my freezing cheeks.

"Come, Giulia. We must go. Or would you rather ride on my back?"

"Oh, yes, please, Tommaso." Giulia has come alive again, smiling at Tommaso. "I am so tired, and I miss my doll. Do you know it splintered, because the angel couldn't keep the ghosts away from us? Now my doll is in terrible pain." She has taken her mask off and looks at him with a melancholy expression on her face.

THE BEGINNING OF A LONG JOURNEY
THE VENETIAN SECRET, 1620

"But Giulia, it won't feel a thing. It is asleep." Tommaso lifts her onto his back, and her hands are around his neck.

"Put the mask back on, Giulia. It's important."

He carries the bag in one hand and has a firm grip on Giulia's long cloak with the other. I walk beside him with the lamp dangling from my hand. Our shadows dance in the light, and I imagine that we are accompanied by two shimmering guardian angels.

We must walk slowly not to slip in the snow. Fortune is on our side, because this part of the Riva is quite deserted. Looking towards the Piazza, lots of lights are moving, and, as we come closer, I hear the tones of faint music lingering in the cold air. I have to watch my step, and I hold on to Tommaso's arm. I look towards Giudecca. The moonlit lagoon is all ice, and, where the waves are wont to ripple, the surface glisters like marble, as if the foam-crested waves have been arrested by the hand of God and turned into a white blanket. A chilly wind blows, and when I look towards the two columns where Orsolo Lupi lost his life, I imagine the third with the crocodile on top, which lies scattered at the bottom of the lagoon, broken by the frost.

Will the silhouette of the crocodile emerge tonight? Will it break through the thick layer of stony ice and roar as they say it does? People say it happens every time a young girl disappears from the city.

It feels so unreal walking beside Tommaso and Giulia in the snow, away from San Zaccaria, away from Venice. It is like dreaming, like when we explored the White Land, the imaginary country of our childhood. But now, all of a sudden, I have become a real explorer, an explorer of my own life.

THE BEGINNING OF A LONG JOURNEY
THE VENETIAN SECRET, 1620

I haven't been in the city since I escaped at night from Ca' Morosini to be with Tommaso. I think of Chiara walking here on the Riva, as I do tonight, to find the mail boat, just a short while ago, alone and terrified. And I think of Lupi when we cross the Bridge of Sighs, on his way to the execution slab, and how the nuns at San Zaccaria had opened the gate ajar, peeping into the campo when the priest's right hand was cut off and hung around his neck, before the guards tied him to the horse's tail, dragging him off to the scaffold. I feel a heavy sadness within me for the cruelty of the world, for the evil and the suffering that we inflict upon ourselves and others.

A beautiful young woman all dressed in white catches my attention. She leans on the arm of a Harlequin, who passes us on the bridge. Her face is covered by a white mask. She reminds me of one of the fairies which sometimes appears in Venice at night. They say they are the spirits of the women who died giving birth. I don't know why, but she makes me think of Rosalba.

I can't remember that I have ever been the victim of my imagination, haunted by old wives' tales and superstition, as I am tonight. I try to think how to take leave of my father, and I fear that Domenico or Manuela, or both, will unmask me in my old home.

"Maria went to Ca'Morosini last night to unlock the secret door from the campo to the portego," I whisper to Tommaso. "You and Giulia can hide among the wine barrels and sacks of spices in the corner. Nobody will see you there. Giulia can sleep, even if it is just for a short while." I pause to breathe before I am able to go on. My heart is pounding, and I feel dizzy.

"Beatrice keeps vigil by my father's bed. My mother and Domenico will hopefully be asleep." The words stumble from my mouth, and my fingers squeeze Tommaso's arm. "Beatrice is waiting for us." I swallow a few times to control my breathing. "Maria said that if a lamps shines in my father's bedroom window, Beatrice is alone, and I can go straight up."

Behind me, I hear the snow creak. I spin around, but as far as my eye can reach in the lamplights from the Piazza, the Riva behind me is deserted.

THE BEGINNING OF A LONG JOURNEY
THE VENETIAN SECRET, 1620

30.
The Last Goodbye

"Tommaso look! The lamp!"

I crane my neck and look up at the window at the piano nobile. The light shines brightly from the lone lantern. I have worried that Beatrice might not be there, that my mother would keep vigil by my father's bed. I feel a tremendous relief at the sight of the light. Without saying another word, we hasten along the wall, past the gate, to the corner of the palazzo. We let ourselves into the portego by the secret door. Tommaso sets Giulia down behind the stacked barrels of wine. She is silent and immediately lies down on the sacks of spice. A few tapers still glow in the lanterns on the walls, and I leave the lamp with Tommaso. I push my mask to the back of my head, and my lips barely brush his cheek in a light kiss, before I am through the deserted portego towards the stairs to the Sala.

I always thought that I would never set foot in this house again. That I climb the steps now to see my sister and father is hard to believe. All is quiet, and inside the house it is as cold as outside. I know each step to my father's bedroom. I pray Domenico's dogs won't be there to alert the servants. I take care not to trip over one of Manuela's cats, which I know she allows in here. As I sneak down the empty Sala, I am terrified of meeting my brother. I can easily imagine Domenico storming towards me, grapping my arm, twisting it as he used to do, when we were children, shouting for the servants to run for the Signori di Notte. 'Take her to San Teodore, straight to the prison. Leave her in the hands of the jailor!' Domenico would shout as he dragged me down the stairs, and, most likely, he would sneer in my face when they took me away. 'My dear sister, escaping a convent calls for a severe punishment. You have grossly dishonoured our family.' I can almost hear the gale of his mad laughter.

And Tommaso and Giulia?

It strikes me that I don't know if Domenico is asleep in his rooms or out, perhaps about to come home. Will he suddenly stand on the threshold to our father's bedroom?
My ancient aunts and uncles are on the second and third floors. They won't hear a thing. But Domenico's and Manuela's rooms are close by my father's. I know I risk my life, and those of Tommaso and Giulia too. But I also know that I will never be at ease if I don't see my father before going away.
Carefully, I turn the door handle to his bedroom. I open the door just wide enough for me to slip through. The fire in the hearth is sizzling. The room is far too hot, almost stifling.
I am tempted to turn the big iron key in the lock from the inside, but for some reason I decide against it. Startled, Beatrice looks up from her embroidery as I close the door behind me. She sends me a swift, anxious smile when she recognises me in spie of my white Bauta and black mantle. The next moment, my sister's

THE LAST GOODBYE
THE VENETIAN SECRET, 1620

arms are around my neck, and I hug her frail body, not wanting to let go of her. I push the mask to the back of my head and look across her shoulder, towards the bed where my father lies propped up by pillows, breathing heavily underneath the canopy. His eyes are wide open. I pray that he knows me again. With the door shut behind me, it feels for a moment as if the world is contained in this room that embraces my father and my sister. The fire crackles peacefully, and the flames shroud the room in a warm glow. Only the restless shadows from the candles on the walls are disturbing. I stand still for what seems an eternity, watching my father's pallid face, while clasping Beatrice's warm and comforting body in my arms. My beloved father, unable to speak, helpless, capable of moving only one hand.

It frightens me to see him thus, his vigorous and strong body lying still, and it grieves me to watch the scared expression in his eyes. I notice that the painting of Paolo Veronese's Holy Family is balancing at the foot of the bed, leaning against one of the walnut pillars, where he can study it at his leisure. It affects me to see it standing there, because he told me once that Saint Barbara resembles me. I feel the strong bond between us and, even though he failed me and forced the veil upon me, I forgive him.

He smiles sadly at me. His face still looks handsome in repose. I let go of Beatrice and walk over to the bed. I sit down beside him and take his hand in mine, kissing his brow. The first thought to enter my mind is, absurdly, that he'll never be a Doge now.

I try to imagine what the world looks like to him from where he is, now that he is ill, perhaps even dying. He inhabits such a different world from mine, and yet, I think, the danger we both face, of losing our lives too soon, unites us, and maybe now our

THE LAST GOODBYE
THE VENETIAN SECRET, 1620

perspectives are not that different after all. I feel closer to him than I have ever done before. I suddenly remember when I was six or seven years old, that I took his place at the dinner table, just for the fun of it. It struck me how completely different the room looked from that angle, that the room looked new to me, and I wondered if my father's world was entirely dissimilar to my own, even when we gazed upon the same things. Later, when I asked him about it, he explained to me that any object will look different depending on one's position.

He claps my hand lightly and smiles at me again, as if he is content that I have left San Zaccaria in spite of the dishonour to the family. Beatrice has told him I would come, that I will be going away with Tommaso and Giulia tonight.

"Don't worry about me, father," I say as calmly as I can. "Hell can't be worse than the hell I've left. The convent never made me happy, you know it didn't. I'm not afraid to leave Venice."

"Domenico is out, Marietta," Beatrice whispers, drawing her chair close to the bedside. "I was afraid that he would stay at home with the dogs, because he always leaves the house much earlier in the evening. But he came in here, no more than an hour ago, curious to know why I was watching over father, as I have kept vigil only on Tuesdays and Fridays the past weeks. I told him that Andrea was better today and that mother needed to sleep." She stops with a strained look on her face before continuing.

"He merely gave me one of his looks and left. Most often, he stays out all night. I know mother is asleep. I glanced into her room when I put the lamp in the window." I listen to the agitation in Beatrice's voice, and the tense look in her face mirrors my own

THE LAST GOODBYE
THE VENETIAN SECRET, 1620

inner turmoil.

"I had fantasies about Domenico stopping me when I crept through the Sala," I whisper and take her hand. "I left a note on the floor in the portego to put him on the wrong scent, should he pursue us."

"Oh, Marietta, I will miss you every day. If I could choose, I would happily go back to the convent, to my friends and the twins. It is the only life I really know. I am not fit to live on the other side of the wall. Ever since my marriage I've been unhappy. The world doesn't agree with me; nothing is as I imagined when I was dancing in the Sala. I long for the tranquillity. And what will happen to the twins when none of us are there?"

"Perhaps you'll go back one day, Beatrice." I try to sound convincing.

"But the convent dowry and the fees? You know I have no means," she mutters.

"Rosalba's Priuli-ring will help you. You can sell it to the Jew for a good price, or send it back to Antonio Priuli and ask for his help." I squeeze her small cold hand and turn towards my father. He lets go of me and slowly raises his hand from the bedcover to point to the heavy walnut desk.

"What is it, father?" I watch his strained tired face. He points to one of the small drawers, but there is no key.

"Where is the key?" With an effort he raises his hand again and points to Veronese's painting. I get up from the bed to search the painting, back and front. I look inquiringly at my father. He gestures with his hand towards the frame, and my fingers travel across the wood, exploring the carvings and the small chubby cherub on top.

THE LAST GOODBYE
THE VENETIAN SECRET, 1620

When I touch the cherub, my father seems excited. I take a closer look. I see that the cherub's head can be opened. I tilt it carefully and find a key is inside the small hollow angel. I remove the key and step over to the desk. When I turn the key in the lock, the drawer opens. Inside is a brown suede pouch the size of a breviary. I look at my father and he smiles nervously, his hand impatiently indicating that he wants me to take the purse. It is heavy and, when I open it, full of ducats.

My mother is in the doorway. Her long hair is untied and floating torrents of tentacles shade the faded nightingales on her dressing gown. She stares at me with irrepressible fury. I just gaze back at her, too shocked to say a word, and my feet appear to be glued to the floor. My father's hand tapping the coverlet sounds like the flutter of small bird's wing. Beatrice's muffled scream wakes me from my stupor.

"What are you doing here?" my mother's shrill voice floods the room. On impulse, I dart towards the door, clutching the purse in my hand in a desperate hope of pushing past her. I feel her hands against my chest, stopping me, forcing me back into the room. I trip over the old oriental carpet and cling to a bed pillar with my empty hand still facing my mother.

"Have you given her money, Fabrizio?" she shouts. "You give everything to that girl. There will be nothing left for me! You are not going anywhere, Marietta." My mother looks at me again, her eyes hostile, as she hurls the words at me. She reaches for the purse, closing her strong fingers around it, trying to wring it from my hand.

"I knew you would be here, the moment I saw the lantern in the window. But The Blessed Virgin has turned her face from you,"

THE LAST GOODBYE
THE VENETIAN SECRET, 1620

she hisses at me as she grapples to get hold of the purse.

Her words cut deeper than years of her railings of contempt and resentment against me. What makes her hate me so?

Out of the corner of my eye, I see Beatrice standing motionless in a corner, crying, and I hold on to the purse with both hands. "Let go of me mother! " I scream in her face. Desperation makes me kick her shins as hard as I can. She trips, I feel her letting go, and she reaches for the small ivory table by my father's bed. When she takes hold of it, the table reels, and the hourglass is swept to the floor, exploding in cascades of sand and fragments of glass. She knocks the table over, and I hear the dull sound of her head against the stone floor.

My father's breathibg is troubled. I turn towards him, and his eyes are transfixed on the scattered pieces of the hourglass. Quickly, I glance at my mother. She is on her feet, a small stream of blood trickling from her nose. It runs across her lips and down her chin, and, like someone in a trance, she lifts a hand and touches the wound on her temple, smearing blood over her face. In a glimpse, I remember Chiara's dead face on the spikes. In a frenzy, my mother throws herself at me, but I am faster than she is.

"You will never get away, Marietta! Not you, nor your precious Tommaso! You have always been the thorn in my side, just like your father!" My mother's rambling, hysterical voice reaches me when I stand in the doorway. Her words sting my chest, and I feel a profound, sad pain. I grab the handle, and open the door. I don't have time for a last look at my sister and father, before Beatrice is at the door, slamming it in my face. I hear the key turn in the lock, and my mother shouting behind it.

"Run, Marietta, run!" my sister's cries penetrate through the door,

THE LAST GOODBYE
THE VENETIAN SECRET, 1620

"The key is in the fire! Run for your li..." I hear the sound of my mother's hand smacking against my sister's face. On impulse, I pause, holding on to the purse, but then I run through the large Sala and down the stairs.

THE LAST GOODBYE
THE VENETIAN SECRET, 1620

31.

Escape

"Tommaso!" I cry, "My mother knows." I throw myself down beside him, hidden from view behind the barrels.

"Where is she?" he whispers, alarmed.

"Beatrice locked her in and threw the key into the fire." I say quickly, breathless from running.

"Take the bag, Marietta. I'll carry Giulia."

As he speaks, the hinges of the gate creak, and, peeping through the chinks between the barrels, I can just make out Domenico's silhouette, half lost in the dimness, and his two enormous black dogs, Uno and Due, following him closely like evil memories. I know how dangerous the dogs are, the cavacani. Beatrice told me, not so long ago, how Domenico trains them for the carnival bullfights. The dogs will know how to attack and go for their victims. I pray it won't be us. I have seen how these fierce dogs lacerate a bull's ears.

The jewels in their broad collars gleam like countless vigilant eyes in the candle light. My brother kicks the gate shut behind him. I can hear the dull thump of his heavy boots as he takes a few steps into the portego. Then he stands still, listening into the silence. I take Tommaso's hand and pray that Giulia doesn't wake up. One of the dogs begins to growl faintly, and, with its nose to the ground, it sniffs in between the sacks of grain left by the entrance. I pray the Madonna is still watching over us, when I hear his voice.

"Uno! Due! Here!" They obey immediately and follow him towards the stairs. I watch him stop, stooping down to pick up the crumbled sheet of paper I dropped on the floor.

"Sit!" The sharp command cuts through me, and I shiver. He steps over to the small, lighted shrine with the blue Madonna to read my note. I beg that he takes my bait. One of the dogs pricks up its ears and looks our way for just an instant. Then it growls menacingly again. Domenico hesitates. He looks into the semi-darkness and turns his head this way and that for what seems an eternity.

"Stay!" and slowly, very slowly, he ascends the steps, stopping, turning his head from time to time to look back across his shoulder. The dogs remain at the bottom of the staircase. We watch him disappear towards the Sala, my bait in hand.

In a little while, he will stand in front of the door to my father's bedroom, turn the handle and find the door locked. At that moment, my mother will shout and hammer her fists hard against the unyielding wood, urging Domenico to pursue us. In less than a second, he'll be back down here with the dogs.

We have to get out. We have to be swifter than the dogs. Tommaso grasps the sleeping Giulia as if she was a bundle of clothes. I take the bag and cram the goatskin purse into it.

"Go!" Tommaso whispers and we are at the secret doorway and tear it open. Tommaso and Giulia are through, and, when I slam the door behind me, the dogs bark loudly, scratching furiously at the wood as we hurry from the house into the campo.

ESCAPE
THE VENETIAN SECRET, 1620

"Maschera, I greet you!" a man says brusquely when I bump into him. His eyes stare at me briefly from behind his crow-like mask with the tremendous beak.

"Careful, Marietta," Tommaso whispers when the man is past, "people will take notice."

I cling to his arm, trying to control my excitement. Elation flows in my veins as well as the acute sense of sorrow. I glance at Giulia, relieved that she is still asleep in her brother's arms, her masked head resting on his shoulder. Flaming torches along the walls of every house show the nobles in colourful costumes as they dance or promenade up and down the paved walkways in front of a gazing crowd. The campo is clear of snow, and the crimson banners with the golden lions wave in the light wind.

"Uno! Due! Quick!" Domenico's yell splits the air between the houses when he cuts through the crowds, followed by the barking dogs, in the direction of San Maurizio. I gaze uneasily at the two savage dogs knocking over three wild men in animal fur, the garlands of green leaves wound around their heads torn off and the leaves blown across the stone tiles. Frightened, people jump aside as the great jet-black hounds cleave their way in between groups of masked people, like two sharp stilettos.

"Domenico took my bait, Tommaso," I triumph, certain that my brother is on his way towards the piazza and the Lido.

Tommaso smiles quickly at me and pulls gently at my hand in the direction of Calle dei Frati. We walk towards the narrow street trying to bridle the urge to run. The cold sharp wind in my face is reviving, like a gust of hope blown our way. Our Lady is helping us, in spite of everything. Perhaps She forgives me for what I never was and never could be: a true Bride of Christ.

ESCAPE
THE VENETIAN SECRET, 1620

Suddenly my sense of being followed returns, but when I turn to look, all I see is the small figure of a Pantalone with the long pointed beard and a black merchant's robe walking some way behind us.

A group of Mattaccini catches up with us in Calle di Cortesia: masked boys in gaudy trousers with coloured feathers in their hair who hurl their eggs at us. An egg hits me on the cheek, and a cry escapes me as I feel the ink soak my Bauta. The wet sticky sensation on my cheek conjures up my mother's face, stunned, smeared with blood. I can feel the strong force of her resentment against me once again, hear the sound of her skirts and swift steps in the corridors of Ca' Morosini. The boys run past us laughing and hollering, and Giulia is wide awake.

"Where are my dolls, Tommaso?" she asks, lifting her head a little from his shoulder.

"They are safe in the bag."

"I want to walk beside them, please Tommaso."

He puts her down, and she holds tightly on to the bag, walking beside me. It slows us down, and it seems like ages before we reach Campo San Luca towards the Rialto. I turn my head, and again I notice the Pantalone sliding out from the darkness among the people in the calle. But, I impress on myself, the streets are full of Pantalones, the most popular costume apart from the Bauta. It is a coincidence. As a child, I used to fear the masks. I believed that they were dead souls who had returned from the underworld and not people at all.

The wind has slackened and it hardly snows now. The moon is out lighting the streets, helping us to find our way in the dark. We pass the large Fondaco dei Tedeschi, and Tiziano's lifelike frescoed figures glare at us with suspicion. What if they came alive, a shadowy army, and brought us back with them to set in the walls of the warehouse forever and ever?

We are in the Salizzada di San Giovanni Chrisostomo when I look across my shoulder again. The Pantalone is nowhere in sight. A shrieking humpback Pulcinella runs towards us, and Giulia hides her head in my mantle. He resembles a large white bird in the black mask with the long nose. He frightens me with his white clothes which look like a corpse's shroud.

As we move into Cannaregio, the number of people in the streets thins out. We turn a corner and walk towards the Fondamenta Nuove through the Salizzada Casciano and past the church. I have never been to this part of the city. I only really know the area around Ca'Morosini, a little of Canal Grande and the Rialto, the Piazza and the Riva, of course. But apart from the nightly trips with Tommaso to Murano years ago, my knowledge of the city is scant. But Tommaso knows his way through every narrow and crooked alley, all of them sparsely lined with ramshackle houses covered by the snow. I never knew that Venetians lived in houses as squalid as these.

Calle del Fumo is empty. At the end of the alley, the white frozen sea spreads out before us. We walk onto the Fondamenta Nuove, Giulia still with her hand clutching the bag. On the ice, dots of scattered little lights from lanterns signal to us that others try their luck tonight across the lagoon. Surely carnival guests from Mestre and Campalto, who, like us, take the chance and walk on the ice across the two miles that divide the city from the mainland.

ESCAPE

THE VENETIAN SECRET, 1620

"Look, Marietta, Casino degli Spiriti. Tomorrow would have been too late. I had a difficult time keeping up the pretence that I was going through with my parents' decision." Tommaso points to the left, to his family's large villa built for literary soirées and festivities. Light teems from its windows, and silhouettes move behind the windows. I know what he means and why the house is busy at this late hour. They are preparing for Tommaso's grand betrothal tomorrow to Livia Loredan. All the most distinguished noble families will be there.

"Let's go to the end of the Fondamenta. Don't worry, Marietta. In an hour or two we are safe with Lorenzo."

It is still snowing, and the gentle wind blows the snowflakes into my face. I am cold, and, even if I don't care to admit it, I'm afraid to step onto the ice. No more than a few days ago, two men perished in the water because they strayed from the beaten track on the ice while walking to the mainland. The ice is thin in many places and full of holes, they say.

Tommaso picks up the bag, and I take Giulia's hand in mine.

"I want to walk on the ice, Marietta," Giulia says seriously, looking up at us. "I want to tell my dolls that I walked on water."

32.

A Travelling Companion

At precisely that moment, a hand grabs me from behind. I feel strong fingers pressing against my lips, and no more than a smothered scream escapes me. For an instant I feel as if I lose consciousness and that the Fondamenta dissolves beneath my feet.

"Marietta! Don't be afraid. It is me, Cordelia!" I recognise the voice. Cordelia?

Giulia cries. Tommaso tears the Pantalone mask from Cordelia's face, and I stare at the pale pretty face behind the mask. It is her! Tommaso is as shocked as I.

"Hush, Giulia," he takes the child in his arms, and pushes the cat mask from her face, drying her tears away with his sleeve.

"Don't you see? It is Cordelia." Giulia studies the nun's face before smiling vaguely.

"Did you come because you were sad?" Giulia says between tears, looking at Cordelia.

Her question makes sense. She has seen Cordelia crying in the cloisters lately. I know the reason for her tears. The fiery, scornful, laughing Cordelia quenched by Orsolo Lupi. I have heard her mumbling to herself in chapel about her dead baby.

"Yes, Giulia, I felt sad, just like you." Cordelia says quietly. Then she turns to us. "Please take me with you. I won't be in your way, I promise."

"Of course, you'll come with us. You didn't think that we would abandon you to your fate, did you?" Tommaso's answer is unhesitating. I love the sincerity of his smile when he smiles at Cordelia. He has the ability to choose the right word and to guide with a simple gesture. I was always conscious of the movements of his body, trying to decipher its singular language. He sets Giulia down beside the bag.

"I am glad you found the courage to go away, Cordelia. It was sad to leave you." I embrace her, still feeling confused, because she is there with us in the snow, on the Fondamenta. "But you nearly scared me to death. For a moment, I thought we were done for."

"I'm sorry, Marietta. I was frightened you would cry out when you saw me. Somebody might have heard."

"How did you guess we were going away?"

"I've kept an eye on you for some time. I knew you would never stay. Your father being ill, I thought it couldn't be long before you left. I had packed a few things, and when I came back from the cemetery tonight, and into the cloisters, I saw you and Giulia. I had already picked up my costume in the theatre chest in the attic. I put it on, grabbed my belongings, and followed you. How clever of you Marietta to find the passageway in the crypt!" She looks small and forlorn, standing there in her merchant's costume. I'm happy she is with us and not in the convent.

"We must go." Tommaso takes the bag and starts towards the Sacca della Misericordia, Giulia by his side. I take Cordelia's hand and we walk close behind them. I look towards the quiet inlet of San Michele, across at the smoking chimneys of the Murano glass-works, to the mainland on the left. I know it is the last I'll ever see of Venice.

We pass the huge Ca'Dona delle Rose and come to the end of the Fondamenta right across from Casa degli Spiriti. The water is almost level with the bulwark, and we step onto the frozen sea. The sensation of ice underneath me is unnerving. My feet are freezing even in spite of the fur I tucked into them, so we tread carefully. At this end of the Fondamenta, there is no track in the snow.

The Fondamenta is empty. We are alone on the ice at this end. Only further away, towards the mainland, do we see tiny blinking lights from lanterns. The creaking ice sounds like someone grinding his teeth in a rage.

Now the Casino degli Spiriti looms in front of us, and we pass underneath the windows. When I look up, people are still moving about in the Sala. Quickly we turn the corner of the large house, keeping close to the façade. Suddenly, the balcony doors are thrown open, banging violently against the walls.

"He is not in the Bovolo house! The servants have looked for him all over!" A man's deep voice, which at first I don't recognise, is shouting angrily.

"But didn't you send someone to the Contarina to look there?" The woman has a polished breezy voice, which sounds like some harbinger delivering solemn dispatches.

Tommaso turns his head and looks at me. His parents know.

"My parents! Hurry up," he whispers to Cordelia, taking Giulia into his arms. The snow is almost up to our knees, and, with the

A TRAVELLING COMPANION
THE VENETIAN SECRET, 1620

sound of angry voices trailing behind us, we struggle through the drifts. The people scattered on the ice are some way off, and we have still not reached the beaten track to the mainland. I squeeze Cordelia's hand, and she smiles at me, a tired melancholic smile.

We are silent, our senses engaged in the escape.

At last we are safely less than half a mile from the coast of Campalto. We are the only ones left on the ice. My feet are stiff in the leather boots and walking hurts. I see lights in a few houses, and Tommaso points to the hostelry of The Black Swan where Lorenzo di Medici is waiting.

"Look Marietta!" Tommaso points to the coastline. "On my voyages, I always thought that an unknown coast was an enigma. 'Come and find me out,' it seemed to whisper. Like when we were children, spellbound by the blank spaces on the maps in the Camera d'Oro." He squeezes my arm tenderly.

"Put me down, Tommaso, I want to walk on the water." Giulia sounds determined, and Tommaso sets her down gently.

All of a sudden, she tears herself loose from his hand, and runs into the virginal snow outside the track.

"Look, my doll!" Her shrill voice brandishes the word in the air.

"Giulia, come back!" The three of us shout in one voice, but she doesn't seem to hear. Someone has placed a shrine with the figure of the Madonna, and three or four crimson lamps burn beside it. Our Lady enthroned in great glory to watch over people walking on the ice.

Tommaso is behind her in a few steps. Just as he reaches out for the child, she falls. The ice groans, cracks, and she is gone in a matter of seconds. Tommaso is flat on the ice, pushing forward on his stomach towards the hole. His arms disappear in the dark water. Seconds slip by. Then he has got her. He pulls Giulia carefully out of the water, dragging the small body towards him onto the ice.

Cordelia is weeping, I am paralyzed. Tommaso stands beside us with Giulia in his arms. She doesn't move   We remove her black cloak and tear the white habit to pieces to get it off fast. I take my mantle and wrap it around her. While Tommaso holds her, Cordelia and I rub her arms and legs, trying to force the blood to circulate in the small body. I look at her pale face with the closed eyes and listen intently. She is alive, but her breathing is faint.

Even without my mantle, I don't feel the cold. Cordelia opens up her cloak, and throws it over my shoulder. We walk beside each other, covered by the thick cloth, too stunned to talk. Tommaso walks in front, carrying Giulia. We hurry, taking long strides. The Black Swan is close to the coast, and I can distinguish a silhouette standing with his back to the inn. Pray, let it be Lorenzo waiting for us.

I hold the lamp level with Giulia's face. She seems to be asleep, her skin translucent, pale with light blue shadows.

"Make a sign to Lorenzo with the lamp, Marietta," Tommaso says, "Move it slowly back and forth a few times. He will know the signal and have the horses ready."

I do as he tells me, moving the lantern slowly from side to side, and watches the black silhouette disappears into the building. Ashore, I stand still for a moment praising the solid ground beneath my feet. There, the Black Swan right in front of us. I hear horses stamping their hooves and the rattling of a coach

A TRAVELLING COMPANION
THE VENETIAN SECRET, 1620

across the stones in the yard behind the house. A black carriage drawn by four horses turns the corner of the hostelry and comes to a halt beside us. The Medici coat of arms is wrought in gold on the door.

"Steady!" The coachman has trouble keeping the black horses still. Their nostrils are blowing and their breath turns into a white mist. A young man opens the door to the carriage and stands in front of us.

"Lorenzo! God be praised." Tommaso smiles at his friend and disappears inside the coach with Giulia. Lorenzo hands Cordelia her bag when she is inside, and mine to Tommaso. I take Lorenzo's outstretched hand, and stepping into the carriage, I turn for a second to look at him. The moonlight is on his face, and, when I look into his countenance, it is like looking into a mirror. He returns my smile and looks as surprised as I feel.

I sit down beside Tommaso in the soft velvet seat. I swiftly remove the rest of Giulia's wet clothes. I take her woollen undergarment from the bag, and Cordelia and I dress her carefully. We wrap Giulia in a big fur skin; she is asleep, still breathing faintly. We lay her across our legs, her head on a cushion. I suddenly realize how tired I am, and I rest my head against Tommaso's shoulder. Lorenzo steps inside the coach and, slamming the door behind him, asks if we are ready to go. When Tommaso nods, he knocks hard at the window twice and falls into the seat beside Cordelia. I hear the coachman shouting at the horses. The carriage is moving, and we are off at a breakneck pace.

A TRAVELLING COMPANION
THE VENETIAN SECRET, 1620

Bacchereto, 1621

33.

Villa Banci

I can feel our child growing in me. My few dresses have become too tight, and I have had to borrow one of Rosalba's, which she must have worn when pregnant. Her dresses are still in the chests in our bedchamber – as if Rosalba were yet alive and had just left the house to go on a short trip. They are all the colours of the rainbow. The one I wear is a warm canary yellow. The silk rustles and is soft to the skin. Like all Rosalba's dresses, it carries a slight scent of lily of the valley.

As so often before, my mind wanders off to my father. He seems to be close to me, as if he was present among the flowers and the foliage. I can't believe he has been dead for two months. Lorenzo brought me the sad news upon receiving a letter from Venice. I miss my beloved father beyond words. I tend to be always thinking about him when I sit here, imagining how pleased he would have been to see me with Tommaso: free, beloved, and with child.

I have been in the garden for hours, impatient for Lorenzo and Tommaso to return. The bells have just sounded midday, and the heat is beginning to bother me, though if it is only May. It is a dry dusty kind of heat, so very different from that of Venice. Lorenzo's old dog lies at my feet. It follows me everywhere, and I get the impression that it worries about me.

Giulia is asleep beside me, where I sit in the shade of the mimosa and wisteria, the delicate fragrance all around me. A chorus of birds chirping from every tree breaks the silence. The bees flock around the fountain dipping their wings in the water, barely touching the surface. A blue and white butterfly keeps me company. It has settled on the arm of my chair and seems to contemplate the tranquillity of the soft curves of the hills. The water murmuring in the fountain and the quiet rustling of olive leaves in the breeze make me drowsy.

I gaze into the valley below, beyond the wine and olive fields to Bacchereto, and all the way to the towers of Florence. I look towards Toia, watching out for the two horses, and I wonder why Tommaso and Lorenzo have not come back yet. They left hours ago for Cantina di Toia. Tommaso had been so curious to see the house where Leonardo da Vinci grew up with his grandmother.

I can see the high stone walls of da Vinci's house no more than a mile away. His house is part of the estate, but empty since the end of the harvest in November. The tenants moved out a while ago, Lorenzo told us, and he asked us if we would like to live there. As his guests, of course, he added.

Just before they set out, Tommaso whispered that he didn't want me to give birth in Rosalba's bed. I dread it too. How could I give birth in the bed where Rosalba died bringing Lorenzo's father into the world?

Lorenzo has given us Rosalba's house in the garden at Villa Banci, as it is the most airy and spacious. Full of light too. I love to gaze at the hills covered by the large fig trees when I'm at the desk in our bedroom. The view from the first floor is unparalleled. Sitting there, I often think how strange it is that Rosalba and I should share the same house, the same dresses and escape from the same convent. Our fates seem entwined, two images that overlap, like the bedspread Rosalba has embroidered, which is still on the bed. The different threads, meaningless on their own, coming together, form the winding, flame-like arabesques. I am terrified that I will die too, leaving my baby and my husband behind, like Rosalba did. Is that what the astrologer meant when he told my mother he lost track of my destiny at twenty-one?

I feel sick again. I've felt like this for more than three months now, nearly all the time we have been here. Cordelia tells me that she suffered too.

We cannot wait much longer to decide if we should leave or stay. People gossip. Standing at the altar in Villa Banci's small chapel, when the priest pronounced us man and wife, I heard the two witnesses in the front row whispering about us, and my sense of not belonging became even more acute. We are still outsiders, Tommaso and I, but, this time, exploring the blank spaces on the maps in the Camera d'Oro is no game.

Lorenzo's aging servant, Luca, does everything he can to make us feel at home, and I am grateful to him. He has even mended Giulia's doll. I noticed it lying abandoned in a corner this morning. "Don't forget your doll," I said to her. Her answer upset me. "I don't want it, Marietta, it lured me into the cold water." I worry about her a lot. She lives in her own world most of the time and becomes more withdrawn every day.

Our child is due in six months' time, counted by the phases of the moon. In Leonardo da Vinci's house, we could enjoy privacy and, perhaps, peace of mind. We wouldn't have to worry about money for a while. All the same, I fear it isn't safe to stay in the village. The servants are far too curious about us, as are the townspeople. The maids' inquisitive looks are only too obvious when Cordelia answers 'Ave' every time someone knocks at her door. She says she can't help it because she has lived in the convent most of her life. When the bells ring, she falls to her knees or makes the sign of the cross. Yesterday, when the maid asked her if we were ready for lunch, Cordelia answered "Yes, dear Sister." I told her to be more careful because I noticed that the maid was tittering as she ran from the room. I am afraid of Cordelia's absentmindedness. I see her bow to strangers too, and, when I ask her not to, she says she does it involuntarily. One day her behaviour will give us away.

I have come to appreciate our daily routines. I have noticed how much they have come to mean to us, in order to create a new life out of nothing, and not just cling to the memory of a city we can no longer inhabit. Small details seem to make up our world, and I find new meaning in these. Rising every day at dawn, writing for an hour or two, reading, walking in the gardens or in the village with Cordelia and Giulia, lessons with Giulia, and being with Tommaso and Lorenzo. Every night it seems nothing less than a miracle to lie beside Tommaso, luxuriating in his caresses. To be in the company of someone I love, and who honestly returns my love, has made me fall in love with life itself. I marvel at my joy in him.

Yesterday Lorenzo received a letter from his Florentine envoy confirming my worst fears. We have been sentenced to perpetual banishment from all the dominions of La Serenissima, and Domenico has even put a price on my head. A thousand ducats to the person who brings me back to face the Inquisition. It seems that the Inquisitor, Paolo Erasmo, has been instrumental in these proceedings and strongly supported our banishment.

The envoy is unaware that we stay at Villa Banci, Lorenzo says, but the old coachman might have put two and two together by now. Rumours travel fast between Venice and Florence. But he is an old and trusted servant, who has been in the service of the Medici all his life. I pray that no one in the village will learn of Domenico's prize. Lorenzo says not to worry, that we are safe at Bacchereto. "Nobody will dare touch you as long as you are under the Medici's protection. Prize or no prize."

It makes me uncomfortable meeting people we do not know. I don't like it when the Medici hunting parties crowd the house. We keep to our own quarters then, frightened to run into anyone in the corridors of the main house. It is very unlike me to hide from people. Tommaso, who is used to being a free spirit, sailing the seas, captain of the Contarina, never confined like me, acts like a caged lion on these occasions, pacing the floor at night. I have woken up during the night several times and seen him like this. I realise how much it torments him to have dishonoured his family, even if he doesn't talk about it. Our identities are caught up with the past whether we like it or not.

He says he wants us to go to Amalfi, that he has trading connections there that might prove useful. I know he hopes to be able to earn our living using his experience as a merchant. I don't mind going to Amalfi, if only we are together and safe. I know so little of the world; I want to learn and experience new shores too. I have my own hopes too. Lorenzo said he would find a publisher for my writings of convent life in one of the printing houses in Florence.

I strain my eyes and look across the fields again: still no sign of Lorenzo and Tommaso.

VILLA BANCI
THE VENETIAN SECRET, 1620

The Twins, 1620, San Zaccaria, Venice

34.

A Letter From Venice

"*C*an I sit beside you, Marietta?" Cordelia's voice comes out of nowhere. It disturbs the blue and white butterfly, which decides to fly away. I hadn't even notice that she stood beside me.

"Cordelia! Yes, of course you can." She sits down in one of the white marble chairs.

"I can't seem to get used to being around other people, Marietta."

"Neither can I, Cordelia. They make me so terribly apprehensive."

"Yesterday, when we passed by the marketplace and I watched people, I was certain that the paintings from San Zaccaria had come alive and walked about the village."

"What do you mean by 'come alive'"?

"All the women looked like the Virgin with babies in their arms; Saint Peter, as he looks in Bellini's altarpiece, was selling fish, and a Judas smiled cunningly at an old fat monk. At the vegetable stall, I noticed a huge bearded Goliath leaning against a tree. His face resembled the severed head in the painting on the organ shutters in the church."

"We have lived in the convent a long time, Cordelia. That's what makes real people seem unreal. After all, we mainly know people from the outside world from paintings, as mere illusions. Did you forget that painters use people from the streets for their models?"

I watch Cordelia's sad face. She looks wistfully at me, and I know she thinks of her baby. I curse Lupi under my breath. Will she ever change back into the flippant, laughing Cordelia with the pretty smile?

Lorenzo is attentive and gentle towards Cordelia. I don't know if he is actually fond of her, or if is the fact that she used to be a nun that fascinates him. Last night at dinner, he told us that he had heard a nun singing in the choir in the village church, behind drawn curtains. He had fallen in love with her beautiful voice on the spot, and ever since tried to imagine her lovely face.

The Patriarch Priuli once said that nuns' singing corrupts them body and soul. But it appears to corrupt the audience rather than the nuns.

I have been contemplating paintings again recently. In fact, I have tried to recall any painting I have ever seen of the Madonna and Child. How else can I imagine becoming a mother? I have decided that Bellini's painting in the church of San Zaccaria is different from the others. I often looked at it from the nuns' choir, after Tiepolo told me to. It is the sweetest of them all, showing the fullness and perfection of motherhood; the Madonna cradling the baby's foot gently, leaning her head lovingly towards the child. Nothing like the stern face of my mother in the portrait with me as an infant at Ca'Morosini. Or Paolo Veronese's Holy Family in Francesco della Vigna. Negroponte's Madonna on the opposite wall, seems so detached, not touching the infant on her knee. Most often, mother and son look sorrowful, I find, and in some paintings the anguished child seems frightened of an eerie outside force, clinging to its mother. I can't believe motherhood is anything like that. I want to be like Bellini's Madonna, loving and caring.

I want to nurse my child too. I would never have a wetnurse. I have noticed a painting in the salotto showing the Madonna suckling Christ. I never saw a painting like that before. Not at Ca'Morosini, nor at the convent.

I have placed the Rose of Jericho by my bedside to have an easy delivery and the pulverized snakeskins Maria gave me under my pillow. I pray my delivery will be as tranquil as Tintoretto's Birth of John the Babtist in the church of San Zaccaria, with the mother serenely in bed and the newborn baby in the arms of two women admiring the infant. The scene is peaceful, even in spite of the descending angels and the agitation and turbulence they bring along.

'Maritar o monacar,' has finally become a meaningless question. I'll keep my daughters close, like a ship hugs the wind, and teach them the love of books and music.

In the distance, I see them drawing nearer. Tommaso on the black mare and Lorenzo on the light-bay stallion. They are cantering across the fields. I hear the gravel crackle under their hooves. I turn my head. Tommaso and Lorenzo are already in the courtyard. The horses are excited, dancing and tossing their heads. Lorenzo takes a letter from the saddlebag. I watch him turn it over in his hand and open it. He quickly folds it up and lets go of his horse. His thick fair hair is wet with sweat, and he tears at the buttons to loosen his shirt. He has a resolute way of doing things, as someone who is used to be in charge. The groom gets a firm hold of the reins and leads the restless horses off to the stables.

A LETTER FROM VENICE
THE VENETIAN SECRET, 1620

Tommaso looks so different in Lorenzo's riding clothes. The noble merchant has completely vanished in the green breeches, high boots of Spanish leather, doeskin jerkin and the purple velvet cap adorned with jewels. Tommaso has become fond of hunting, and most days I watch him ride out with Lorenzo's huntsmen and falconers into the valley and the woods, bringing back wild boars, hares and pheasants.

"The da Vinci house will be fine, Marietta," Tommaso says, still breathless from the ride, bending down to kiss my cheek. "When the baby is strong enough, we will go to Amalfi," he whispers in my ear.

"Marietta," Lorenzo says, smiling at me, "I have a letter for you. It bears my name. That's why I broke the seal, but, seeing the feminine handwriting, I realised at once it was meant for you."

I look at the letter in my hand and recognise the slanting handwriting.

"It's from Beatrice, Tommaso!"

I feel agitated and anxious at the same time. I look up at Tommaso and meet his eyes. I see distress painted in his face. I take his hand, and we rush to a bench at the far corner of the garden beneath the honeysuckle. I unfold the letter, and we hold it between us. Sitting close we begin reading:

Venice 22nd May 1621
Dearest Marietta,
I hardly know where to begin. So much has happened these past few months. One catastrophe has followed in the wake of another.

A LETTER FROM VENICE
THE VENETIAN SECRET, 1620

But the most important thing is that the four of you are safe.

My life is completely changed. I am back at San Zaccaria, dear sister. I am a novice and with the twins!

I know you wonder how this is possible.

Andrea died from his wound almost three months ago, and the Doge has paid my dowry to the convent. But first I'll tell you about the twins, knowing how much you crave for news of them.

No need to worry, Marietta. They are fine. Like me, they are convinced that Our Lady will help you all to find a new and happy life. Maria has looked well after them till I got back. She saw them through the first lonely nights after you left. Always remember, Marietta, that the twins are happy with their lives here.

Maria has left us now. She is going to marry Arrigo and live with Biancafiore in a small house next to Lucretia. She misses you; it is like having lost a dear sister, she says. She will write to you.

You know how ill Andrea was, ever since he suffered the wound inflicted by the glass stem. It never healed, and in the end he died from internal bleeding. That's what the doctors said. I would be a hypocrite to say I was sorry to lose him. I was terribly frightened of what was going to happen to me, because I had to vacate the house in two months. The Dandolo family decided I was better off at home.

As much as I hated staying at Ca'Dandolo, I feared the prospect of going back to live at Ca'Morosini. My only comfort at the time was that I would be able to look after father. After Andrea's death, I would be left with virtually no means at all. With no children, my dowry would be returned to our family.

At home, I discovered that mother and Domenico couldn't wait to lay their hands on the family fortune. All they thought of was

A LETTER FROM VENICE
THE VENETIAN SECRET, 1620

father's death. Domenico had spent vast sums on a fraud called Mammon Bragadin. He had been cheating all of Venice for some time, claiming to possess 'il spirito d'oro', the spirit of gold, saying he could turn dust into gold.

I heard mother complain to Domenico several times of how exhausted she was from keeping vigil, that it ruined her health and her looks. 'What is the point of keeping him alive?' she would say. 'He'll die soon, anyway. Isn't Fabrizio better off in heaven?'

If it was a matter of such a short time, I don't understand why they didn't leave father in the hands of God. Instead, they took his life into their own hands, and decided to kill him.

One day, when I offered father a glass of water, mother came into the bedroom. 'Put the glass down,' she said, 'your father isn't in need of drink or food. Nor medicine.' 'Why?' I asked her and I felt father squeeze my hand, not wanting to let go of me. 'Your father is dying,' she said. 'We shouldn't prolong his sufferings.' I summoned all my courage, and asked if she considered dying of thirst and hunger less painful.

'You don't understand these matters, Beatrice. I've sent for the priest.'

When the priest arrived, father let go of my hand and tried waving him away. But in vain. Everybody ignored him. Under the bed I noticed a knotted cord and a wax figure stuck with pins, and I knew for certain that mother and Domenico had asked a witch for help with their foul plans.

When our doctor came the next day, I heard mother say, 'Bleed my husband once more, Doctor. Don't you think it might improve his condition?' Thereupon she handed him a small purse. Father died that same night. I sat with him, holding his hand when he drew

A LETTER FROM VENICE
THE VENETIAN SECRET, 1620

his last breath.

His body was taken to San Francesco della Vigna the following night. In the morning, his body was carried through the city to the Piazza. It was raised three times as they always do with procurators. The bells of San Marco tolled the last farewell to our dear father, two strokes at a time. The Doge was present at the funeral, and Giovanni Tiepolo performed the service over the body.

When the Doge was leaving, I went up to him and slipped my letter with the Priuli-ring into his hand. I trembled that he would not take it, as it was given to him in such a secret manner. He just smiled at me and put it in his pocket. In the letter, I had begged him to help me to return to San Zaccaria. How could I live in a house with murderers?

Of course, mother and Domenico ignored father's will. As it turned out, he had given Ca'Morosini as security for mother's dowry, and she and Domenico were free to do what they wanted.

Mother came into possession of nearly everything because her dowry had been so large. She let Domenico spend as much as he wanted.

He had paid Mammon Bragadin enormous amounts of money to own 'il spirito d'oro'. The money he had borrowed from the Jews and he was forced to repay the loans. The family fortune is no more, Marietta! Perhaps mother and Domenico can't even afford to keep the house.

As a consequence, dear sister, there is no price on your head. Domenico retracted his promise publicly weeks ago. 'Why waste as much as a ducat on my miserable sister?' I heard him say to mother. This is an immense relief as all the treasure hunters are no longer on the rampage, and you and Tommaso will be left alone.

A LETTER FROM VENICE
THE VENETIAN SECRET, 1620

The convent magistrates are still on the lookout for you, though. And so are Tommaso's parents. They also worry about Giulia a lot, Adriana tells me.

As you can imagine, everybody in the convent whispers in the corridors about your flight. Livia Loredan is furious and gives me slighting looks whenever I see her. Agnese wrings her hands and blames herself for telling you Rosalba's story. The Abbess has had to retire due to the great scandal, not only because of your escape, but also because of Orsolo Lupi. I won't be sorry to see old Francesca leaving the post.

Aunt Paulina had hoped to become the new Abbess. But as God willed it, she suffered a stroke in the refectory and hasn't recovered the use of her limbs.

Without Antonio Priuli's help, I would never have been allowed back. He pays my annual fees, the twins' too. He has made a will stating that his estate pays our expenses until our dying days,

He wrote me a letter thanking me for returning the ring to him, saying that it was a memory dear to him. 'A long time ago I gave it to someone I loved as much as my own life.' He didn't mention Rosalba's name, but I feel certain it can only have been her that he meant.

I pray for your unborn child, and I beg you to write to me whenever possible. I am aware that the danger of sending letters is great, but we must not allow ourselves to be scared. We will remain close even if we are apart. The Madonna will shield us, Marietta. Always. And who knows if we will meet again one day?

Rosalba has helped us all. I thank her in the early dawn when I

A LETTER FROM VENICE
THE VENETIAN SECRET, 1620

wake up, and I pray for her soul. Without her courage, what would have become of us?

Your loving sister, Beatrice

A LETTER FROM VENICE
THE VENETIAN SECRET, 1620

35.

Rosalba's Secret

"This must be Rosalba's," Lorenzo says as he hands me a small leather-bound book. "I was looking for our ancestor's *On the Well-Ordered Republic*, and I found this on the shelf among Rosalba's books. It was pushed in behind the others."

I turn the volume over in my hand. It has a golden lock and brass ornaments in each corner in the shape of exotic birds, which shimmer in the late afternoon sun. There are faint traces of pigment on the binding, vermillion and yellow stains travel over the back.

"I never opened it," Lorenzo says. "The key is missing, but Tommaso will help you." He smiles at Tommaso and pours wine from a blue glass jug into the goblet. "Don't forget to tell me my grandmother's secrets."

"Thank you, Lorenzo. I won't forget."

I caress the soft binding of the diary and notice the Medicean symbol of a cluster of diamond rings in the centre, encircled by two golden lines.

What secrets has Rosalba confided to its pages?

Tommaso takes his pointed hunting knife and picks the lock. He hands me the small volume with one of his generous smiles, and kisses me on the nape of my neck. I take the diary to our rooms.

ROSALBA'S SECRET
THE VENETIAN SECRET, 1620

It is dusk now, and I have to light the oil lamp on the small table beside the bed.

I lie down and rest my head against the pillows. I pull Rosalba's bedspread with the dancing flames across my legs. I open the diary on the first page. This is not Rosalba's! Why didn't I guess straight away? The vermillion and yellow stains on the cover ought to have alerted me. This belongs to Veronese! His name is on the inside cover in bold handwriting. How did it end up here?

I am excited and disappointed at the same time. I turn the pages over slowly and read the last three entries:

Venice 2nd May 1569

	Lire
Drawing paper, pigments, nails	5
To a woman for undressing	4

Villa Banci 4th May 1569
I have been riding all day and night to get here in time. Antonio Priuli's letter arrived by messenger two days ago urging me to go. I left at once in spite of Elena's protests.
My beautiful Rosalba is dying having born a son. Our son?

Villa Banci 5th May 1569
I am sitting by Rosalba's bedside looking at her lovely face. I have made a promise to her. I must write down her instructions for a painting. The Chessplayers, she calls it. It is heartrending

to see her so appallingly weak. She can only raise her voice to a whisper.

The Chessplayers must be the painting of an enigma, but understandable, she whispers. It must show the entrance to the secret passage in the crypt at San Zaccaria. It should be a help to any Morosini girl forced to take the veil in the future. The motif must attract the attention of a young girl. And most important, I must present the painting to her father.

I put the diary on the table beside me and gaze at the flaming pattern in red and orange, that Rosalba has embroidered on the bedspread. Suddenly I discover that letters are dancing between the winding flames, like arabesques. The letters make sense: *'Veronese is the father'* it says simply.

* * *

"Tell us of Rosalba. We don't know what happened to her. After all, we owe her everything." Tommaso asks Lorenzo when we are seated at the dinner table.

"I don't know a lot." Lorenzo says. "My grandfather, the Grand Duke Cosimo, didn't seem to enjoy life, apart from women and, of course, hunting, his prime passion. That was how he met Rosalba. He preferred to come here to hunt; he never went to the bigger Medici villas. Cosimo was a friend of Antonio Priuli and he knew Paolo Veronese too, whom he had commissioned to do some frescoes in the Palazzo Pitti. When the two of them asked Cosimo for help, he arranged for Rosalba to hide at Villa Banci. She became his mistress, and he fell deeply in love with her. All Veronese's paintings bear witness to her loveliness. He signed the villa over to her as a present. When she was dying in childbed, he fulfilled her last wish: to see Veronese one last time. The painter was sent for, and he made it just in time. Rosalba died the following day.

"What happened to your father when Rosalba died?" I ask Lorenzo.

"My father, Pierfrancesco, grew up here. A wetnurse cared for him, and Cosimo appointed a guardian. Rosalba left the villa to my father; she made the will a few months before the baby was due, judging from the date. My father was born prematurely – two months, I think. But he was a strong healthy baby, according to his old wetnurse. She said to me, when I was older, that my father wasn't born prematurely at all, that he had been too big for that, implying God knows what, but, you see, she never liked Rosalba.

My father lived here all his life. He was killed by an accidental shot while hunting roebuck nine years ago. My mother, a Venetian like Rosalba, died four years later from a nasty fall from her favourite horse, and I turned out to be the sole heir to Villa Banci. My father's half-brother, Francesco, became the new Grand Duke when Cosimo died. He wanted the villa back. But we made an agreement that as long as the Medici were allowed to go hunting here, I could keep the house. He fell in love with a Venetian noblewoman, just like Cosimo and my father, Bianca Capello, who always boasted about the perfection of Venice. The Florentines disliked her. They both died here on the same day in October 1587."

"Tommaso says that you might go to Amalfi" Lorenzo continues

ROSALBA'S SECRET
THE VENETIAN SECRET, 1620

suddenly looking serious. "I have relatives who own a trading house at Amalfi and a small villa which they never use. I'll write to them saying that a merchant family, good friends of mine, come to live in Amalfi and want to let the villa…if you would like me to, that is."

"Oh, please do, Lorenzo, I say, grateful that he cares so much for us as to make this proposition.

"Yes," Tommaso says, looking relieved. "Amalfi is not a bad idea at all."

We eat in silence for a while. I don't feel like eating the roasted pheasant on my plate, and I bite into a slice of bread instead. The plates are decorated with a dark blue glaze, painted over in white and blue with hunters chasing roebucks. The roebucks look frightened and the hunters appear aggressive. I have no appetite, and I return my small silver knife and fork to the slim case attached to my belt. The dining room is pleasantly cool, and the nausea leaves me at last. I have felt sick all day, unable to keep any food down at all.

It is comforting sitting at the large oaken table with Tommaso, looking at Cordelia and Lorenzo. At the door, the lifelike torch bearers carved in the shape of blackamoors stand guard in their liveries, holding the flaming torches in ebony hands. They are Venetian Nubian slaves, and a gift from Cosimo to Rosalba. Looking at them, I miss Beatrice and the twins. Will I ever see them again? And Maria? What of her?

The glow from the torches and silver candelabra seems to force the darkness outside to retreat, like a hostile army retracting its troops. Our future seems hidden in the dark. I can't see it. Where to look for it? Will Amalfi be safe? In my mind's eye, when I look towards the horizon, it is shrouded in mists, a ghost of the morning. It doesn't scare me. I just gaze at it, my eyes trying to penetrate the haze.

The End

Marietta Morosini, 1621, Villa Banci, Bacchereto

AUTHOR'S NOTE

One day, standing in Campo San Zaccaria admiring Maoro Condussi's handsome church façade, I happened to overhear two Venetian women talking about the former cemetery of the nuns of San Zaccaria. Apparently, the grounds were now turned into a building-site.

"They found the bones of more than two hundred new born babies in the nuns' cemetery during excavations," one woman said with a shudder. "Imagine the goings-on!"

"Most noble nuns lived tragic lives," the other woman said sadly, looking towards the beautiful ancient pillars where the entrance to the cemetery used to be. "Priests and monks took advantage of the poor things and abused them no end. It happened in every Venetian convent."

This conversation set my imagination going, and I had to express in words the sorrow and compassion I felt for the young women shut away by the Republic of Venice in the former prestigious convent. Three years of thorough research started, in which I delved into the archives and libraries of Venice to learn as much as possible about life in the Venetian convents until they were closed down by Napoleon to rid himself of powerful Venetian institutions once and for all.

I had the good fortune to live in Venice, and I speak Italian, two prerogatives without which I could never have written this novel. I treasure, like most people who have been to Venice, a deep love and fascination for the city and its beauty, and with the stimuli of the old faded documents in the State Archives, Biblioteca Museo Correr and the Biblioteca Querini Stampalia, the canals and palaces, I found it easy to take off on the wings of imagination and plunge headlong into seventeen century Venice. Yet another animating factor when writing a historical novel is all the dedicated people you meet, who go out of their way to help you, and who experience joy sharing their knowledge with you.

Fortunately, The Venetian Secret is related to my second historical novel, The Devil's Chord. It leaves me free to continue the story of Marietta and Tommaso and some of the other characters, even if the novel takes place during the time of Napoleon. The great pleasure of writing The Venetian Secret often meant that I forgot time and place completely. Sitting in the archives reading the ancient papers written by the notaries in the seventeenth century, actually holding the documents in my hands, was an awe-inspiring experience because isn't this the closest we can ever get to history? I read criminal cases affecting nuns, reports of Patriarchal Visitations, cases of escaping nuns and numerous other aspects concerning convent life at the time. A fascinating but sad picture emerged from the bundles of old documents, testifying that life in enclosure behind the convent walls was harsh and severe, not least because the majority of the women had no vocation at all. Most noble nuns had been forced to take the veil due to the high dowries a marriage called for, and thus the girls were sacrificed for the republic to subsist. The family fortune had to stay in as few hands as possible and, because Venice was governed by the nobility, the nobles needed the money to carry out their obligations. Substantial amounts of money were necessary to undertake the different public duties imposed upon any nobleman during the time of the republic.

Only one daughter got married: if you were noble and had more than one daughter, the rest were locked up in the convents for life, whether they liked it or not. Granted, the Venetian convents were not as inhuman, strict and merciless as convents in the rest of Europe and in other parts of Italy (see e.g. the case story of La Monaca di Monza, just to mention one true and terrible story of nuns being 'walled in' as a punishment for trying to escape) and the rest of Europe.

Descriptions of everyday life are hard to come by in historical sources because everyday life is taken for granted. Those who did write about contemporary society were not inclined to writing about things they considered trivial or obvious: how the nuns tied their boots, what kind of laces or ribbons were used, where the nuns kept their personal belongings, what type of undergarments they wore in winter, what they whispered about in the cloisters or how young children experienced life in the convents.Myriads of questions present themselves when undertaking to write a historical novel in which you desire a framework which is detailed and in correspondence with life at the time.

The case stories in the archives gave a very strong idea of everyday life in Venice and in the convents and I was lucky to come across Archangela Tarabotti's writings on convent life. She writes in great detail of every aspect of life in a Venetian convent. Archangela Tarabotti (1604 – 1652) is a contemporary of my fictitious nun, Marietta Morosini. She was forced by her family to take the veil when she was sixteen at the convent of St. Anna (now demolished). She detested convent life, directing all her bitterness at the fathers who forced their daughters into convents.

A highly intelligent and intellectual feminist writer, well read and with strong viewpoints, her writings seem unbelievably modern, quite out of tune with seventeenth century Venice: more like a Mary Wollstonecraft one century later, and sometimes even reminiscent of Virginia Woolf when she discusses the conditions of women. A century later, Tarabotti was considered to have been one of Italy's 'most learned women' (Discorsi accademici di vari autori viventi intorno agli studi delle donne, Padua: Accademia de' Ricovrati, 1729, p. 14) A few of her works have been translated into English but, unfortunately, most of her works are still only available in Italian. (Emilio Zanette, Suor Archangela, is an excellent biography in Italian.) She wrote e.g. Tirannia Paterna (Paternal Tyranny) which was published shortly before her death, and then immediately attacked. 'Pimps and procures' she calls the fathers who sacrifice their children for their own gain. Men, who for reasons of state, bury their daughters alive, and she attacks the government's selfish and unjust treatment of women, which the Patriarch Giovanni Tiepolo of the novel realises all too well. Archangela speaks for those women with no real vocation, and for them she pleads alternatives. In another work, Inferno Monacale (Monastic Hell) (ed. F.Medioli, Turin, 1990), she also shows her anguish and anger of contemporary views of women, e.g. writing against the charge that women had no souls! In this work, Tarabotti describes the clothing ceremony the novices went through when they took the veil. It is a scary and heartbreaking

account, and I have based Marietta's experience on Tarabotti's description.

In the Venice of Marietta there were about 50 convents, and sixty percent of the noblewomen were locked up in these religious hideaways. There are still convents in Venice today which are enclosed, and if you go to talk to the nuns you will never get so much as a glimpse of them, restricted to communicating through a small brass grate in the door. But the essential difference from the time of Marietta is that today no one is forced to live in enclosure against their will.

Marietta's convent, San Zaccaria, is now the headquarters of the Carabinieri. Whether there was a hollow white marble Madonna facing the Riva dei Sciavoni is uncertain, whereas the white stone angel on the altar in the crypt underneath the church of San Zaccaria is still there today. In the church the grilles have gone, covered by large paintings. A painting of the nuns by Antonio Zonca (1652-1723) shows the Doge visiting the convent at Easter. If you are lucky, or unlucky as the case may be, to enter the headquarters of the Carabinieri, you might have the opportunity to view the two cloisters by Mauro Condussi and Antonio di Marco Gambello and the beautiful raised loggia behind the church.

The Venice into which I have placed Marietta is fact. To imagine her life, I had to go back into the city as it was, to a Venice actually not that different from today. Most parts of Venice stand as they have done for centuries, and it seems as if the city has lent itself to the present and allowed modern life to unfold in the past.

But when we come to the sounds and smells they are of quite another kind.

What did Venice sound like 400 years ago? First of all, the bells governed and dominated life in the city. Every Venetian knew the sound and significance of the various bells. If a nun escaped her convent, all the bells of Venice would sound. What cacophonies! The Marangona in San Marco chimed to open the sitting of the Great Council and to mark the beginning and end of the working day. There were other bells of San Marco: the aptly named Trottoria, so-called because when the nobles heard it they rushed to the Ducal Palace pacing their horses to trot; the Nona, which rang to mark midday; the Mezza Terza that chimed the meetings of the Senate; and the Malaficio, which rang when executions were to take place at the Piazetta – the same bell which accompanies Orsolo Lupi to his death.

Venice was also a city full of music; you would hear music on every corner and on every bridge. The Venetians sang as they walked the streets and rowed the gondolas; an entire city set to music applauded by the lapping waves in the canals.
But there was silence too. Imagine Venice without the noise of the motorboats and Vaporetti. If you take a walk late at night in certain areas of the city you will experience the same quiet as Marietta did: the water whispering in the canals; the sound of footsteps echoing; and, perhaps, the ore of a gondola touching the surface of the water. Imagine walking at night with no street lightning, in complete and utter darkness, unless you happened to come upon a link boy who could light your way with his small lantern for a few coins.
Contrary to my historical settings, most of my characters are children of my imagination. But some are based on contemporary

characters, although I have spun a tale around them and allowed my imagination free rein. The Patriarch Giovanni Tiepolo was a very compassionate man when it came to the nuns of Venice. He was the Patriarch of Venice from 1619 -1631, and has left behind several religious treatises and sermons. Antonio Priuli was Doge (born 1548) from 1618 -1623, much loved and respected by the Venetian people. He was a seaman and a soldier, very religious, and married with fourteen children. The father confessor is based on an actual priest whose execution took place in November 1561. He was not the father confessor of the convent of San Zaccaria, but of the Convertite nuns on the Giudecca, a convent for repentant prostitutes. The priest's name was Giovanni Pietro Lion, and his confession is among the old documents at the Biblioteca Museo Correr. The papal nuncio to Venice, Ippolito Capilupi, wrote letters to Rome describing the priest's atrocities and the actual execution. ('Di Ippolito Capilupi e del suo tempo', Archivo Storico Lombardo 20, G.B. Intra, 1893, pp.75 - 142)

Paolo Veronese, or Paolo Caliari, 1528 – 1588 knew how to use colour in such a way that it became the actual subject of his paintings. The painter very often used religious stories as an excuse to abound in colour and show the sumptuous feasts in the Venetian palaces. He created realistic representations of social life among the nobility, dominated by the refined elegance of dress, celebrating the wealth and power of Venice in the 16th century. In 1573 he was called before the Inquisition of Venice to justify the presentation of the Last Supper for the refectory of the monastery of Santi Giovanni e Paolo. Paolo Veronese was at some point of his life imprisoned by the Venetian state in the monastery of San Sebastiano for one year due to a crime committed. Giuseppe Tassini mentions this incident in his book about the history of Venice (Curiosita veneziane, Filippi, Venice, 1990). We don't know the nature of the crime, but couldn't it very well have been his amorous affair with Rosalba?

The painting I call The Chessplayers is not a painting by Veronese, but a painting of my imagination.

But it is true that the face of the same blonde girl reappears in numerous of his paintings. Take a good look at his paintings, and see for yourself. There is the beautiful young Venetian woman with the delicate face and an intent thoughtful expression, sometimes depicted as Venus, and sometimes as an allegorical figure. In all the books I read on Veronese, Mary McCarthy is the only one who has mentioned the fact. "Whenever this young girl appears, with her simple hair-dress, and her slender circleted neck, there is visible a struggle for meaning." (Venice Observed, Penguin, 2006, p.263)

Chiara's story is inspired by the real case of a nun trying to escape from the convent of San Sepolcho in 1618 to a pious monastery near Padua. (Arcivo di Stato di Venezia, Providitori sopra monastery, Busta 265)

The Poison Cupboard in the room of the Council of Ten is another historical fact. Horatio Brown gives a detailed description of its contents, the letters from poisoners, and assassins offering their services to the state of Venice. The letter Pietro Mudazzo writes to the Ten is based on one of the tenders for murder Horatio Brown reproduces in his works on the history of Venice.

Several studies have been indispensable in the writing of this novel, and the Venice I describe is deeply rooted in research. But being a writer of fiction, and not a historian, mistakes might crop up in spite of this research. In the case of The Venetian Secret, I have relied heavily on Venice, *A Documentary History, 1450 – 1630*, edited by David Chambers and Brian Pullan, Blackwell, 1993. This anthology consists of the voices of those who observed life in the city in past centuries, lived in it, and shaped its history.

The difficulty of writing a historical novel is to keep the balance right, and not turn your story into a dusty old history book full of flat characters with no life of their own. You must strive within the historical framework to create rounded characters with whom the modern reader can identify; "We read to know we're not alone" is a beautiful quote by CS Lewis. All errors, inaccuracies, improbable fiction etc. are my own.

Brutality, war, terror, torture, and religious hypocrisy are not limited to any historical period. All these concepts thrive in our so-called modern world. But, honestly, what is so modern about it? If technology as we know it was eliminated from the face of the earth, wouldn't we turn out to be much like the characters in The Venetian Secret, for better or for worse? We are reminded daily that women are still abused and oppressed, and forced marriages are not a thing of the past. Terrible things still go on in convents, even if it is hard to believe. I came across a piece of news long after having written my story of Chiara's death: "Nun dies after Convent Exorcism, Romanian, 23, Was Gagged, Tied to Cross, and Left There For 3 Days"(Tanacu, Romania, June 24, 2005, CBS News). It seems reality always surpasses the imagination.

Greed and money are still the driving forces of life, just as they were four hundred years ago in the Venice of Marietta and Rosalba. Money is still our second blood.

We never change, do we?

TO BE PUBLISHED

The Devil's Chord, a historical novel by Giulia Morosini set in the time of the fall of the Venetian Republic. A continuation of the story about the Morosinis.

When I Was Still King, a historical novel by Giulia Morosini about Napoleon's son set in Vienna and Venice. A continuation of the story about the Morosinis.

Map of Constantinople